ELLE HARTFORD

Labyrinth of Crime

The Alchemical Tales #9

To that little version of me, reading and rereading Greek myths each night. Psyche and Eros may not show up in this book, but the echoes of their story certainly do.

Contents

Welcome

Long, long ago, a coven of witches created a world just beyond ours—a realm of fairy tales.
In Beyond, humans rub shoulders with mythical creatures, and magic mixes with science.

There are only three rules:

Happily

accept that we share the same home

Ever

remember that what you take, you must also give

After

struggle will always lead to new beginnings

So, if you are ready . . . you are welcome here.

* * *

Helenia & its Harbor

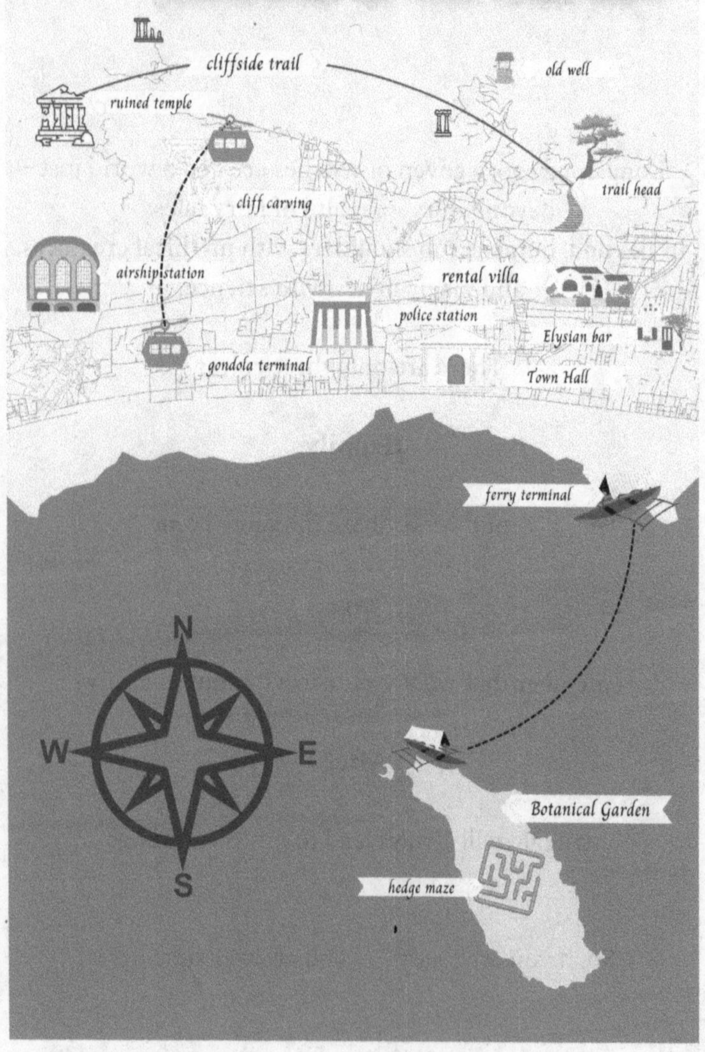

Cast of Characters

Top fifteen, in alphabetical order

Eurydice of Korinth: artist in residence at the Botanical Garden and painter at Town Hall; nickname Eurie

Gloria: owner of Hair & Beauty by Gloria in Belville, Red's friend and neighbor

Herakles, Officer: young officer on Helenia's police force; nickname Herc

Hestia: secretary at Town Hall, very involved in policy and the Botanical Garden

Idunn Skaald: lives and works at the Botanical Garden along with her mother, Edda; nickname Ida

Luca: bookseller and scholar, now engaged to Red; back in Belville

Pandora: pen name of a curious reporter chasing down mysteries at Town Hall; full name Tilia Pepper

Pluto: rumored to be a powerful dealer in illicit magical

artifacts; full name Marcus Antoine Pluto

Quinn: local consulting detective and collaborator with the Botanical Garden; full name Quinn Doyle

Raffael L'Etrange: musician who named his band Orpheus; dating Eurydice

Red: alchemist and child of Seers, full name Cinnabar Sunset

Rhea Minotaur: a local legend who built her bakery from scratch

Sakura: shadow witch and owner of Pomegranate Cafe in Belville; nickname Saki

Thorn, Officer: half-orc policewoman in charge of keeping law in Belville; first name Mina

William: canine familiar, capable of protection magic and plenty of sass

1

A Promising Start

We were lost two minutes after the magitech balloon set us down in Helenia. Which was impressive, given that the arrivals hall had been specifically designed to funnel us—and dozens of other passengers—directly to the front doors and the bright, balmy isle beyond. I caught whiffs of sea salt and scrubby pine every time the glass doors opened, and the patterns of sunlight over travelers' hats and the white station walls were tantalizing. But I had no idea if I had come to the right set of doors, and more importantly, my companions had scattered on the breeze.

Pulling to one side of the wide hallway, I steadied myself against the wall and rose on my tiptoes to scan the crowd. Paradoxically, it was the smallest of my companions that I located first. Sakura was further along than I was, nearer to the exit, but she'd stopped—the crowd was parting around her. Though Saki barely topped five feet tall and normally would have been impossible to find amongst the disembarking passengers, black sparkles of magic holding her pink luggage in the air above her head gave her away. She seemed to be facing two taller people, whose faces I could see: they were clearly having some animated conversation. I could also just barely see that the two strangers were wearing matching visors embroidered with a teacup design. That solved the first mystery: Sakura had wandered off and made new friends. No doubt they were discussing scintillating details of the café-running business.

The second mystery was slightly more perplexing. Looking back the way I'd come, I caught sight of my next companion across the hall and so far back that the crowd was thinning around her. The plume of red feathers rising up from her head made her easy to locate; I honestly wasn't sure how I'd lost her in the first place until I saw what she was doing. Gloria, my sarcastic, irascible loner of a neighbor, was leaning to one side and walking in tiny, slow steps. With one hand she'd hoisted her duffel bag onto her shoulder, and with the other hand, she was supporting a child by the elbow. The child's other arm was held by an older adult, perhaps a grandparent, who appeared to be talking Gloria's ear off as they went along. Judging by the awkward sticks held in the grandparent's free hand, it seemed that the child had planned to walk using crutches—until those crutches failed, maybe broken by heavier luggage during the flight. Gloria was doing her good deed for the trip, it seemed. When she caught me looking at them, she made a face, rolling her dark eyes upward. I tilted my head in a *want me to come back there?* gesture, and she shook her head. They'd catch up soon enough.

And that gave me time for a third and particularly *thorny* mystery. Our final companion, Officer Wilhelmina Thorn—or perhaps just *Thorn*, now that we were on vacation?—had vanished into the crowd, which should have been nearly impossible. Not only was she half orc, with mossy green skin, long black hair, and a broad stature that made her head and shoulders taller than an average human, she was habitually *loud*. In fact she was usually the one cutting a path through crowds—a helpful trait when you're a police officer investigating something (or bringing it to an abrupt halt). She'd been right behind me as we walked down the gangplank. Now, it was only because most people had left that I finally saw her. There was a line of dark windows set into the wall across from me, each bearing a sign along the lines of *lost luggage, taxi inquiries,* or more generally, *tourism.* Thorn was systematically going up to each one. By focusing on her and listening closely through the din of voices, I could barely distinguish what she was saying: "Don't any of you have anything to *eat?*"

I chuckled to myself. I'd warned her to bring snacks along, and had she listened? Of course not. My brief feeling of superiority reminded me of the two companions I'd left at home—Luca, my fiancé, and most especially William, a magical familiar who would have thoroughly enjoyed this moment. Actually, William would never have let us all get separated in the first place if he had come along. But Sakura had been quite firm when she'd proposed this little trip. It was supposed to be a girls-only adventure, a chance to have fun before I got lost in wedding planning, a chance to relax without any mishaps or crime raising its ugly head.

Off to a promising start, I thought wryly to myself as Gloria came nearer, and Thorn's inquiries across the hall grew louder. *But at least nothing has actually gone wrong. Yet!*

* * *

For all I had my wits about me, I was the last of my friends to actually make it outside.

The trouble was customs. Once I'd waited for Gloria and rounded up Thorn, we all trooped toward Sakura and freedom—only to meet our last hurdle. Just before the doors there were half a dozen desks and a maze of stanchions set up to block traffic. Behind those desks were uniformed officials who asked my friends questions like, "occupation?" and "reason for visit?" before waving them through. But then they got to *me*.

"Occupation," the dwarven officer said.

He was staring right at me. I felt like saying, *isn't it obvious?* Even though I was on vacation, I still had my alchemist's goggles on my forehead and fingerless gloves on my hands. Old habits die hard—or not at all.

"Alchemist," I answered, taking the high road, "and merchant. I run a potions shop."

I thought this was fairly innocuous, but apparently the customs officer did not agree. He stared at me again, like he was seeing me for the first time.

"Name?" he asked, squinting at the canvas bag on my shoulder.

"Cinnabar Sunset." I fought the urge to look behind me for whatever he was staring at. "You can call me Red."

"Why?" His attention returned to my face. His skin was deep and ruddy, his eyes light blue and *far* more suspicious than I'd been led to believe that most of the people of Helenia might be.

"Um . . . it's just my nickname?" I flailed a bit for an answer, thinking that he couldn't possibly be interested in the story of how my future-seeing mothers had decided I would benefit from a daily reminder of the *Little Red Riding Hood* tropes. "Also, cinnabar is red, generally. If that helps?"

"What materials are you bringing in?" The officer asked.

Apparently, my useless fact of the day had *not* helped. "None?"

He didn't look convinced. I knew I didn't sound convincing, but the encounter was too strange for confidence. I added, "I'm here with my friends for a vacation. I didn't plan on doing any business in Helenia. Except the usual tourist business, I suppose."

The official leaned over his desk. "Such as?"

"Um . . . *such as* buying souvenirs? Paying for boat rides? Getting massages?"

Okay, I'm not actually that good at taking vacations. I did say this had been Sakura's idea, didn't I? And where was she in my moment of need? I looked around to see the grandparent and child waving at another customs officer as they moved toward the doors. My friends were standing in a clump outside, enjoying the sunshine. I was the only one who hadn't made it out.

"No organic materials?" my officer asked pointedly, staring at my bag again.

I bit my cheek and counted to five to keep from informing him that technically, most of what he and I were wearing was *organic*. Cotton, linen, leather, where did he think these materials came from?

Instead I put on a smile that would have made Saki proud. "Do you mean botanical?"

The officer nodded begrudgingly.

"I was careful not to bring any unprocessed plant materials, including seeds and fruits," I went on breezily. "I'm well aware that as an island nation, Helenia has to be careful about what pests or diseases reach their shores from foreign climates."

"That too," he admitted sourly.

I probably could have breezed right past him, but I paused at that. "What do you mean, 'that too'?"

"There's a tax on them."

"Pardon me, but there's not," I said firmly. "Not on anything *I* might have brought with me purely for personal use." I might not have prepared for whatever relaxing activities Saki had planned, but I *had* looked up local rules and regulations. I'd spent long enough as a traveling alchemist before settling down in Belville to know that a traveler's best friend is information.

At this point we'd attracted the attention of the other officials. One of them walked over to the desk in time to hear my polite protest. With an air of authority and a particularly drab brown uniform, they stood over my interrogator.

"You're correct, of course," they told me. "We're so sorry about that. Of course you're free to go on. There's just a little confusion about tariffs that *might be* put in place," they added, with a severe look at the officer below them.

The officer had the grace to look abashed. "But . . ."

"Consider this practice," I told him, softening a little. It probably *was* tough to keep up with trade and political decisions, on top of dealing with weary travelers all day. "No harm done. I have to say, though, I hadn't heard about any potential tariffs?"

"It's all still being decided," the manager informed me. A scarf decorated with antique patterns covered their name badge. "Nothing you'll have to worry about on your vacation, I'm sure. Aren't you with the group outside?"

"I am, thank you." I understood that I'd been dismissed. Dismissed from customs—like I'd *wanted* to stay there!

Well, I was a little curious about the mix up. And it was hard not to take a professional interest in tariffs on "organic" "botanicals" . . .

I kept my head down and my increasingly nerdy thoughts to myself until I'd managed to join my friends. It was the air that hit me first. From the high-ceilinged, cool interior of the station, moving into oppressive sunshine was a shock. The sun beat down, of course, but it also reflected off the plaster walls behind me and the white stone terrace beneath my feet. It was like being hit with a heat spell from all angles. Fortunately, the sensation wasn't scorchingly hot—just surprisingly warm.

Next, of course, I heard Thorn talking.

"I've solved a number of tricky cases, myself," she was saying. As my eyes adjusted to the light and I came closer to the wide planter where my friends stood, I saw that she'd made a friend. A gnome in a blue security vest was sitting on the stone wall holding back broad-leafed ferns, his mouth full of what looked like little bread sticks.

"Not like this one," he assured Thorn. Saki and Gloria were also listening in, with varying levels of interest. "You should've seen him at work!"

"Oh look, Red made it," Sakura interrupted, sounding rather relieved.

As Thorn turned to me I got a whiff of the snack her security guard friend had shared: fish. Small, fried fishes, apparently. "Have you ever heard of this Quinn person?"

"Have I ever?" I parroted, my mind still half on tariffs and taxes. "No, should I have?"

"He visited here not a moon ago," the gnome officer informed me. He held out a paper cup in his hand. "Fish straw?"

"No, thank you." I looked to Saki or Gloria for clarification.

"Good choice," was all Gloria said.

"He's some kind of great detective," said Thorn.

"The *greatest*," said her new friend. "A hero!"

"You're all done here, right, Red?" Sakura asked sweetly. "I think it's time for us to go."

Thorn looked hesitant. "Maybe we should hear more about—"

Gloria, the only one of us who could rival Thorn for size, grabbed the off-duty officer's shoulder with an audible sigh. "Maybe we shouldn't."

"Seconded," Sakura said. "Thank you for sharing a snack, but we really should get to our rental and put down our bags. We're just here for a fun trip. We promised Red a real vacation," she reminded us all as she began guiding us away. With the air of a parent telling children not to argue, she added, "Great or not, there will be no mysteries!"

2

Vestiges of Greatness

The rental villa Sakura had chosen was perfect. That said, nearly everything about Helenia seemed perfect. Both the island and its capitol city shared the same name, and both were popular tourist destinations. The mountainside around the city was known for ancient temples and a massive carving in the rocky cliff, perched high above the tiled roofs and narrow, winding streets. The mountain and town curved along a wide harbor, the sun glinting off gorgeous turquoise water. We got a good look at all three as we caught a ride on a local wagon with our luggage, crossing town and enjoying the balmy breeze.

Our ride dropped us off in a neighborhood high above the water, where each house—or *villa*—had a patio covered in vines and its own view of the harbor. The steepness of the mountain meant that neighbors were more likely to be on top or below one another, rather than side by side; each property seemed carved out of the cliffs. The road was narrow, too narrow for our wagon: we'd have to walk the rest of the way over its well-worn stones. After all our sitting and standing, though, I was eager to stretch my legs.

But perhaps not *as* eager as Sakura was for some proper food! As soon as the wagon let us off at the intersection, she made a beeline for some nearby food stalls. Enterprising souls had clearly realized that tourists renting villas might like to walk down the road and pick up provisions at their leisure. And since Saki had been the one to choose our home-away-from-home, it made sense she remembered the practicalities—like the empty kitchen we were about to find ourselves in. She bought a basketful of vegetables and cheese from one stand, and then waved me over to help her at the second one.

I could smell it even before I crossed the road to join her. The second stall was a bakery cart, laden with fresh bread and adorned with a large picture of a smiling woman with curling horns framing a poofy chef's hat.

"Welcome to Minotaur Bakeries," said the person behind the cart—the woman herself, in fact. She was clearly recognizable by those horns. "And welcome to Helenia! Is this your first time?"

"It's that clear, huh?" I smiled at her as Saki leaned in, examining loaves of country bread and stacks of muffins.

"Everyone gets that look after a long journey," the baker assured me, friendly. As she spoke, she toyed with a round pendant on a long chain. "But, honey, you have come to the right place! Are you here for the theater? Antiques?"

"Relaxation," Sakura answered firmly. "And food! That oatmeal loaf looks lovely. Can we get one of those—and one of the pancake mixes, too?"

"Not a problem, dear." The woman took a jar of flour from a pyramid display by her elbow and tucked it in a burlap bag, followed by the bread. "If you're looking for good food, try

Elysian Moments later. It's just down the road, and a very popular dinner spot—if I do say so myself."

"Do you own that, too?" I asked.

The baker tipped her head back, laughing. "Look at you! You're a sharp one. I like to have little ventures, side projects. They keep me busy."

"A bar named for the underworld would have to," Saki commented, searching through her purse for the proper change. "Can we get a bag of cookies, too?"

"Another sharp one, eh?" The woman smiled as she put two bags of cookies in the sack for us, winking at me. Her eyes were large, brown. The way they matched her horns made me wonder if she was oxkin, perhaps. Gloria was phoenixkin, and because of some magic in her blood had phoenixlike qualities, including her plume of feathers; and I knew that many kinds of -kin were possible. "You'll find Helenia is a place still steeped in the ancient lore," the baker went on. "Many of the ancient gods remain among us, they say. I've always had a soft spot for Hades, myself."

"And for good baking, if the smell is any indication," I said.

She laughed again. "You come back later and tell me if you think so after a slice of this bread. You can find these carts all over town!"

As Saki finished the transaction and led me back to our friends, she said, "See? Already off to a good start. Now that we're actually *here!*"

"We aren't there yet," Gloria reminded her as we joined them.

"At the rate they're going," Thorn declared, grinning, "we'll be locals before we even set down our bags."

* * *

We may have thought we were blending in with the locals—for perhaps a minute. That's how long it took for someone to ask me the purpose of our trip.

Elysian Moments *was* popular, and there seemed to be good reason for it. The whitewashed building was well kept and cozy, full of tables covered in eclectic crocheted tablecloths and scents of wild mint and honeysuckle. But we were only in it for a minute. A waiter whisked us from the front door to the back, which opened out onto a wide terrace. Fairy lights cast a warm glow as the sun set over the water in front of us. Every small table was crowded, but we were just in time to catch an empty corner at the bar that sprawled across one end of the patio.

I'd barely settled on a stool with Sakura to my left when the stranger on my right spoke up.

"What brings you here?" she asked cheerfully, as though I was no doubt a celebrity with important places to be.

"A very stubborn friend," I answered, matching her light-hearted tone. Sakura leaned past my shoulder to wave before picking up a menu.

"I have one of those too," my new companion said. While she was pale and flushed, with a purple summer dress on and gold hair escaping a topknot, the friend she indicated was darker, elvishly slender, and definitely more retiring. Her anxious brown eyes darted away from my glance. "This is her favorite bar!"

When this supposedly stubborn friend spoke, her musical accent gave her away as a local. "Ida, I just don't think—"

"It's fine," Ida assured her. "I'm sure it'll only be a little bit more." To me, she added, "We're waiting for a friend to join us."

"I hope we didn't take seats you were saving?" I asked politely.

"Oh, no, by all means, stay right there," she replied, green eyes sparkling. "You're just our *newest* friends, didn't you know? I'm Idunn, by the way, but call me Ida—everyone does. And that's Eurie."

I tried to smile at Eurie, but once again, she refused to look reassured by this friendly conversation. I gave up and focused on Ida, introducing myself and the rest of my friends.

Ida continued chatting with us as we ordered appetizer platters and drinks. Though she and Eurie ordered a second round for themselves, they declined our offer to share food. In fact, Eurie spent most of her time tugging at the springy curls in her shoulder-length brown hair.

If there was any lack in the conversation, though, Ida made up for it. "I'm new here too," she told us eventually, her third drink propped a little carelessly in one rounded hand. "That is, if you asked Eurie or anyone else, that's what they'd say! Unless your grandparents' parents were born here, then you're new, you know. That's how it is. My mom and I moved here years ago now, but we'll always be new."

"No matter how different small towns are, small town life is the same anywhere," Sakura quipped sympathetically. "Red and I are 'newcomers' in our town back home, so we understand, believe me."

"Nothing wrong with small towns," Thorn said around a mouthful of falafel.

"Is there anything you think we definitely *have* to see?" I asked Ida at the same time.

Her light eyebrows drew together as she thought. In the brief pause, I noticed her jewelry—earrings made of gold and delicately preserved violets, with a necklace pendant to match. "There's a hike along the foothills that has amazing views of the bay. It's not very hard," she added quickly, no doubt seeing Saki's disapproving look. "And there's the ruins, and the carving, everyone goes to see those. And they should, they're very impressive, but, you know—they're not—"

"Something *locals* would bother with," Gloria concluded for her, sounding rather smug.

Ida smiled. "It's true that people always forget to visit whatever's in their backyard. My mom and I say that all the time. She runs the botanical garden, by the way—my mom. You should definitely see that. You have to take a boat to get to it, but it's totally worth it."

"Are you just required to say so?" Saki teased over her wine glass.

"Maybe, but it *is* true," Ida said playfully before downing the rest of her cherry-colored drink. "Eurie and I both work there, don't we? Eurie's the resident artist. She puts on the *best* programs. And she makes jewelry too. She made my earrings, did you see them? Aren't they sweet?"

At Ida's insistence, Eurie leaned into the conversation—and at the compliment, it was as though someone had turned on a light inside her. Her face instantly opened, the worry lines smoothing out as she spoke earnestly. "People don't realize how plants affect everyday life."

"I do," I told her, smiling. "I'm an alchemist, I deal with them all the time."

"Aren't they amazing?" This time, Eurie needed no prompting. She even returned my smile. "I just love them. I always have. But I never had the green thumb Ida has, so I learned to paint them instead."

"I'm sure your art is incredible," I told her, and I meant it. Anyone so passionate about their subject was bound to create something lovely. Her passion reminded me of Luca with his books, and my heart shuddered, reminding me that *we are getting married.* Luca, in his effervescent way, also had the same passion about *me.* I'd always been the more reserved one of us two—probably from long years of scientific training, as much as from any personal inclination. But—seeing it in Eurie, seeing the way she blushed and beamed about her art, drew it out in me too.

"My friends and I came here because I'm getting married soon," I told Eurie and Ida impulsively.

It must have seemed awfully random to them, but Ida cheered and lifted her glass. "Good for you! The world needs more love. Let's get another round, and celebrate!"

3

Plans Interrupted

The next morning, I was the first of my friends to wake. To be fair, I had expected that outcome. Though Saki ran a café and catered to early-morning risers, when left to her own devices she slept in if she could. Gloria was not known to be a sociable morning person either, and Thorn had downed *quite* a few drinks last night at the bar. Still, when I came in from a morning run and found no one in evidence in the communal kitchen and living room, I was a little surprised.

I decided to take advantage of my good fortune, though. After a quick shower, I tossed on a short paisley sundress and grabbed a magicked mirror from my luggage before heading out onto our little veranda.

The hand mirror glowed blue as I held it up. It was William's magic, but I knew for a fact that William wouldn't be awake at this hour either. It was even earlier back home than it was here. Before I left on this trip, William had strengthened the charm on this communications device, making sure that it connected to its partner securely, allowing me to see and talk without fear of the signal being intercepted or lost. After a moment, the mirror's glass surface shimmered and revealed a wooden ceiling—a shelf full of books—and finally, bright green eyes shining out of a dark, familiar face.

"Red!"

"Luca," I returned, smiling. I hadn't been gone even a whole day—and I was very glad to be on vacation—but it was still a relief to see him. William hadn't wanted the mirror that connected with mine: in fact, he had insisted Luca should have it. *So that you two can do that silly lovebird thing you do*, he had said.

And we were definitely doing it. Separated by thousands of miles, we grinned at each other goofily. Again, my heart shuddered. "You'll never believe it," I told him. "Here we are on a once-in-a-lifetime trip, and everyone else is sleeping the morning away!"

"Frank has informed me that anything pre-breakfast doesn't count as 'morning,' it's 'dawn twilight,'" Luca returned with good humor, referencing his shop assistant—a wizened, three-legged mink who tended to dislike anything that wasn't books or Luca himself. "Not everyone is as energetic as you. You're lucky *I'm* up."

"It's later here," I reminded him in my own defense. "Also, you look suspiciously like you never went to sleep."

"I did," he protested mildly. But his bookstore was a few blocks from my apartment, which we now shared; he'd rented out his own rooms to some visiting scholars. As if fully aware where my thoughts were going, he glanced at the store behind him with affection. "I just had some work to do and I couldn't get back to sleep earlier, so I figured I might as well come over here and do it. Turns out, I kind of miss you."

"I miss you too," I admitted. "But this place is amazing. Look." I turned the mirror around so that he could see the view: the tiled patio, the low wall and trailing vines, and then the roofs of town sloping down to a turquoise sea. On the horizon, other islands were visible in the gentle, misty haze of morning.

Maybe it *was* a little early yet.

Luca whistled appreciatively. "We'll have to go back there sometime together, if you don't get tired of it."

"We'll definitely come back," I promised, smiling as I turned the mirror back to my face. "We've already seen a bit of the nightlife. Gloria insisted we go to this local bar we'd heard about, where we met two women who work at the local arboretum, which they say is really cool."

"I'm surprised you're not there already, knowing you," Luca commented.

I chuckled. "I know, I woke up a little bit antsy. I've already gone running."

"Is there something bothering you?" Luca knew me very well—in fact, he'd gone with me to visit my home island, a much more deserty place than this, where most of the locals were Seers. My mothers and extended family could practice divination to look into the future or learn about the world around them. I'd never had the skills they did, but I *did* sometimes get unexpected insights. Or see ghosts, or ghostly unicorns. Mostly, though, my inheritance amounted to very fleet feet and sparkly strands in my hair, with not a lot else to show for it.

I hadn't thought to check in with my intuition until Luca said something. Now that he had, I hesitated. "I don't see how it could be," I said. "I mean, this setting couldn't be more idyllic. What could be bothering me here?"

"Idyllic places can be dangerous, too." Luca leaned into his mirror, the dim light in the bookshop catching on the horn that rose up from his forehead and the mossy tattoos that covered his head. Marks that were usually covered up by some handy magic in his scholarly robe and hood. "Not that you're in any danger at all, I'd imagine. I hope. I'm positive," he said, sounding not quite convincing. I gave him a look. He laughed and added, "It's just, you know your track record with such things."

"*Our* record," I reminded him. "Any time I've run into a crime, you've been right there too."

"Fine, our track record," he agreed. "But—it might just be something small that's making you feel out of place. Maybe just all the travel. But whatever it is, you've taken Belville's police force with you, so you should be fine. And you know William and I would find a way to get there if we needed to."

"You don't need to," I assured him. Inwardly, I rebuked myself for making him worry. Just like Saki had made everyone promise to *rest* on this trip, we'd also profusely promised Luca and William that we'd stay out of trouble. *So much for that, already! But nothing has actually happened,* I told myself. Aloud, I added, "I'm sure it's nothing. I had a weird conversation at customs yesterday—that might be it. But like you said, Thorn would take care of anything."

A bump and some mild cursing resounded from the nearest bedroom window, indicating that one of my companions was up. I thought it sounded a lot like the officer in question, and smiled to myself at the coincidental timing.

"Her replacements were in yesterday," Luca said blithely, most likely unable to hear the ruckus behind me. "Asking for maps of town."

That distracted me. Lately whenever she had to leave town, Officer Thorn would get two enthusiastic young officers, centaurs, to cover for her. They'd trained with her for a while, and had taken over before. I laughed incredulously. "She didn't make them memorize the geography already?"

"That's what I asked them," Luca replied, grinning. "They were very embarrassed, but from what I could gather, Maggie has been testing them."

"Tell Maggie I say hello," Thorn said, stumbling out onto the veranda. Her hair was tousled and she was still wearing pajamas, but there was a steaming mug of coffee in her hands. *Priorities*, I thought, amused.

"Maggie's not on the call, it's Luca," I told her, holding up the mirror for her to see. Maggie was Thorn's girlfriend, and together they lived in snug rooms behind the police station, so I could well believe that Thorn had tasked her with keeping an eye on the replacements. "How'd you get coffee already?" I added.

"Hi, Luca," Thorn said, bravely concealing her disappointment. To me, she added, "Sakura's up. She's taken over the kitchen. Thought this was supposed to be a girls-only trip?"

"Luca isn't *here*," I pointed out wryly. "No one said I can't still talk to him."

"I didn't realize we'd done enough yet to warrant a report," Thorn commented.

I chuckled. "Maybe *you* haven't. But—"

"Ho!" cried a new voice from outside the veranda. "Who's making reports already?"

I sprang from my seat, taking the mirror with me. Thorn set her coffee on a nearby table and strode toward the noise.

A stranger in a straw hat poked his head around the edge of some vines—a stranger in a straw hat and a police uniform.

"Just friendly chatter," Thorn told him, with the ease of one professional to another. Though she was wearing purple silk, there was no mistaking her authority. "What's all this? We didn't think we had any close neighbors."

"I tried the front door, but someone just shouted to go away," said the officer. "So I came back here. This residence is rented to Cinnabar Sunset and party, that right?"

I gulped. From the mirror, Luca's voice reached my ear. "Red? Are you okay?"

Thorn set her hands on her hips. "How about you tell us what's going on."

"I was hoping you'd tell me," said the strange officer. "Two women went missing from the bar last night, and you were the last ones to see them."

* * *

"Let's start from the beginning," Thorn suggested, five minutes later.

We'd gathered in the living room. Saki was perched on the back of an armchair, apron still tied over her seafoam green nightgown. I had quickly hung up with Luca, and sat nervously next to Thorn on the sofa. Gloria was the only one of us who looked composed: she'd apparently been up for a little while, as her hair and makeup were already perfect, and she wore a black blouse and capris like we might go out sightseeing or shopping for antiques at any moment.

"I can do that," said the strange officer. As he faced us from his sofa, he almost looked nervous himself, as if he was being interviewed for a job. But unlike me, he seemed to thrive on the feeling. His knees were bouncing, his feet braced, with just the toes of his sandals planted on the ground. His blue uniform looked exactly like Officer Thorn's, except for those leather sandals and a rather ragged straw hat, which rested on the table between us. And like Officer Thorn, he was large—perhaps part giant, even. His skin was deeply tanned and his wavy hair was bleached blond by the sun. His light blue eyes shone as he leaned forward to speak. "I'm Officer Herakles. Call me Herc. I'm a junior officer down at the police station. They sent me up here this morning to see what you all had to say. You were at Elysian Moments last evening, from dinner time onwards, right? And you met two women there, Idunn Skaald and Eurydice of Korinth?"

"We got there just after sunset and sat at the bar," Thorn confirmed. The rest of us were only too glad for her to be spokesperson. "Ida introduced herself to Red, here, and kept up a conversation."

Though it hardly seemed possible, Herc leaned even farther forward. He wasn't taking notes. He seemed to be physically hanging on to Thorn's words. "Did they act off at all? Did they say anything?"

Thorn looked down at me, raising an eyebrow. I understood my cue. "They did mention they were waiting for someone, or some people, I think."

"We'd never met them before," Saki added. "So we wouldn't be able to tell if they were acting 'off.'"

"Who were they waiting for?" Herc asked me.

I thought about it, then shrugged. "I don't remember any name. Does anybody else?"

My friends shook their heads, and Thorn took over speaking

again. "We left at closing time to come back here. It was my understanding Ida and Eurie were heading home too."

Bold words for someone who walked out leaning on Gloria's shoulder, I thought, though I kept my face blank. Gloria was smirking.

"Maybe whoever was supposed to meet them was actually waiting outside?" Saki suggested. "There was quite a crowd as we left."

"There always is. That's the problem." Herc sat back, finally, and some sympathetic tension in my own back eased. Judging by his energy and lack of wrinkles, he was too young to worry about stiff joints just yet. His knees still jiggled.

"You'll find out when you take down our names and details," Thorn told him, with an almost professorial air, "but I'll tell you now, I'm a solo officer back home."

"Are you? Awesome!" Herc leaned over again.

"I am." If Thorn sounded slightly smug, I figured she could be forgiven. "And I know a tense investigation when I see one. Tracking down friends who have gone missing after a night out is a good cause, but there's something more here. What are you looking for? What's got you on edge?"

"Between you and me," Herc said, glancing around as though he might see eager faces pressed at the windows, "it's what we've already found that's *really* awful."

"But if you found them, why are you here looking for them?" Saki asked.

"No, no—we didn't find *them*," Herc replied. "We only found Eurie. On the cliffs beneath the bar—deceased. An injury to the head. But not on the side where she fell."

Saki gasped, and my hand flew to my mouth. I could see Eurie so clearly in my mind's eye, saying, *people don't realize . .*

. She'd seemed so lit up in that moment, talking about what she loved. Full of promise. How could someone with such purpose meet with such an abrupt end?

Even Gloria snapped to attention. Thorn nodded grimly, as if somehow she'd guessed as much.

"Chief says it could have been an accident," Officer Herakles continued. "But I saw the scene this morning, and I think it must be homicide."

4

The Disappeared

Herc remained looking at Thorn, like a puppy waiting for a good word. Like, I realized, a *trainee.*

And that was when I knew there was no way we could disentangle ourselves from this investigation.

Meanwhile, Saki and Gloria were clearly thinking it over in their own way.

"She hardly said a word all night," Saki recalled.

"Hiding something," Gloria suggested.

I didn't agree, necessarily, but they were gaining speed as they played off each other.

"How did the two get separated?" Saki added.

"Maybe they didn't," said Gloria. "Until Ida turned to crime."

"No theorizing," Thorn told them sternly. "We don't even have *half* the facts. Isn't that right, Herc?"

"Absolutely. We know pretty much nothing," he said, eagerly. "But—I can say—your friend there might not be so wrong . . ."

"Well, we can't help you," said the indicated "friend," Gloria. "We know even less than nothing."

"Are you interviewing everyone who was there last night?"

Saki asked, turning her attention to Herc as though Gloria hadn't said a word.

"Trying," he confessed, with what I had to admit was an endearing gesture of humility. "It was easiest to find you all, since the bartender knew your names and you're renting nearby. As for everyone else . . ."

I was watching Thorn. I saw what I expected. She frowned. "You're one of how many junior officers?"

"Four," said Herc, turning to her as though she'd asked just what he needed. "And the chief, and a couple trainees. But half of them are on the kidnapping task force, and one's on permanent assignment at Town Hall, and like I told you, Chief thinks the murder was just an accident. They didn't send anyone out for interviews but me, and, I do my best, but . . ."

"How long have you been out of school?" Thorn's voice had a familiar tone. She didn't mother her trainees—she was a little too gruff for that—but she still had definite "mother hen" tendencies.

"A year this summer," Herc said proudly. "And I solved my own case last spring."

"That's good," Thorn said, and he beamed. "But when it comes to a potential murder—"

"I'm sorry, back up," Gloria interrupted. "*Kidnapping task force?*"

"The town hall thing confused me, too," I admitted. "Do you really need a permanent officer there?"

"I was promised a fun and safe vacation," Gloria added, glaring over us at Saki.

"Yeah." Herc looked abashed. "It's perfectly safe! The tourists are fine! But . . . there've been some disappearances, just of locals I mean, and folks are pretty worked up about some new town laws."

"Do you think Ida's disappearance could be connected to the others?" Saki asked, interested.

"Even Eurie's death could be," Thorn answered, as though the case was already hers. "You have to keep an open mind."

"Oh, I do!" Had he been standing, Herc would have been bouncing on the balls of his feet. "Only, the other officers . . ."

I caught Saki's eye, then Gloria's. "Herc, would you mind giving us a moment? Maybe you could head into the kitchen and get yourself something to drink?"

"Don't touch my sun tea—leave it in the window to brew! And not the pancake batter either!" Saki added, as the junior officer amiably got up and went. The living room, kitchen, and dining nook of our little villa all blended into one open-air room full of cozy sofas and counter tops and as many windows as possible. A series of columns that loosely defined the "living room" partially blocked him from view once he got to Sakura's domain.

"He's doing well, but he shouldn't be out doing high-stakes interviews on his own," Thorn commented, keeping her voice low, especially for her. The four of us gathered on the sofa for a quick, sort-of private conference. "His method needs oversight. He shouldn't be leaving us alone, for justice's sake. Who knows what we could be planning?"

"I'm only interested in planning which sights to see," Gloria retorted. "We've told him what we know. Other than that, there's nothing we can do."

"Herc doesn't seem to think so," I pointed out, still eyeing Thorn. In the back of my mind, Eurie with her artistic passion still lingered.

"And it *is* awfully interesting," Saki said.

Thorn frowned at her. "It's somebody's death."

"I meant about the kidnappings," Saki protested. "But, yes, I see your point."

"Somebody we were just talking to last night," I added, now thinking of Eurie's anxious face. *Purpose and danger* can *coexist, I* reminded myself. *No matter what promises we make . . .*

"You've always been too soft," Gloria told me. "But I expected better of you two," she added to Saki and Thorn. "I can't believe you're considering getting involved!"

"Not involved," Thorn said. When the three of us looked at her incredulously, she added, "I'll just give him some advice, that's all. If he wants it. We can still go sightseeing or whatever it is you wanted to do."

Something clattered in the kitchen, and Saki said upright. "Herc! You can come back now!"

"Thanks, uh, sorry about that," said the officer, scooting back into the living room. Had the ceiling been any lower, he would have had to duck. As it was, he looked grateful to be on the sofa again. "So, what do you think? Do you think it was murder?"

"We don't know enough to say," Thorn reminded him. "And I'd be willing to bet you don't, either. But you've got good instincts. Keep going with it as far as you can. Have you got your notebook on you?"

Herc sat up and patted his massive chest pockets, searching for a moment before extracting a crinkled standard-issue journal and a pencil bitten down to a nub.

"I've never been much of a writer," he admitted, looking regretfully at the unsharpened lead point.

"Don't worry about it." Thorn took the pencil from him and used her pinky nail to chip it into shape—benefits, perhaps, of orc heritage! She then took his journal and flipped to a new page before writing down a few prompts. "The key is consistency," she told him. "Ask everybody you meet these questions. Don't let them wriggle out of it or ask *you* too many questions instead. You have a lot of energy. Think of it like putting that into harness, driving the investigation."

"'Driving the investigation,'" Herc echoed, taking the notebook back and giving Thorn a look of pure admiration and gratitude. He might not have noticed her pun, but I did. "I will. Thank you! And if I find anything I'll let you know!"

"There's really no need . . ." Gloria said, but gave it up. Herc was already halfway out the door.

* * *

Over Sakura's salted caramel pancakes, we did our best to make a normal, crime-free girls' trip plan for the day. Or at least what could pass for *normal* with such disparate participants. Gloria wanted to check out a few blocks of the market known for antiques shops; Saki agreed on going to the town center, but then Thorn accused her of going just so she could stake out the town hall and see why they needed a police guard; when pressed with coming up with her own plan, Thorn mostly wanted to go to a dinner theater that evening. When we pointed out that she probably wanted to go because the bartender last night had told her that the theater offered local wines, she shrugged it off.

"Who would have suspected Belville's upright officer of being such a party animal?" Gloria commented as she rose from the table, gathering up plates that had been all but licked clean. "I'm telling Maggie when we get back."

"She'll probably say we drive her to it," Saki said airily, while Thorn sputtered. "And in the meantime, I suspect Belville's upstanding alchemist just wants to go to the botanical garden?"

"Well, it *was* pretty high on my list," I admitted. I rose, too, joining Gloria at the sink. The kitchen was airy enough that it was easy to carry on the conversation over the counter top. "But with Eurie gone and Ida missing, I don't know. Tensions must be pretty high over there. Maybe it'd be best if we left them alone?"

"At last, a sensible approach," Gloria agreed firmly. "If you need to commune with nature or whatever, we could try the trail outside of town."

"That'd be a good way to get the lay of the land," Thorn said.

As she wandered over and grabbed a towel, I grinned at her, thinking, *she's probably just glad we've moved on from making fun of her!*

"Hold on." Saki, who had remained sitting and seemed perfectly content to let us take care of cleaning up—she *had* done all the cooking, after all—hopped up to lean over the kitchen counter. "When I went to close up after Herc, I noticed a paper on the front step—here it is," she said. I glanced over my shoulder from the sink to see her holding up a rolled sheaf of thin, pale yellow paper from among various mixing bowls and utensils left strewn about. Our villa had a lending shelf for books, all well-worn novels and travel guides, but what Saki pulled out was in fact a thin newspaper. As she unfurled it, headlines like *Changes to the Bonfire Schedule* and little boxes proclaiming *Best Price on Donkey Rides!* identified it as a local tourism paper.

"But we just almost decided what to do," Gloria protested,

her exasperation evident as she began stacking the dirty mixing bowls together. I could hear the noise, and the emotion, clearly though I'd turned back to face the dishes.

"I'm confirming it for you," Saki informed her. She rifled through the pages. "Here, the local weather predictions. I knew it'd be here somewhere. Looks like today is supposed to be the coolest day we're here, so maybe a hike isn't such a bad idea. If we must go on one, let's try not to give ourselves heat stroke, at least."

I chuckled over the running water. "Saki, are you sure you don't mind going?"

"If I really minded, I'd say." When I glanced back again, she winked at me. "Let's get it over with. Just give me a few minutes to get ready."

Despite any misgivings, both Saki and Thorn were ready in record time. Armed with a map and bags of sandwiches and drinks, the four of us set out.

From our little rental on the hill, we only had to walk up the road past other similar homes until we got to a crossroads— and a staircase. The stairs led up to a small bluff above town, where our trail began. I remembered Ida telling me it was the hardest part of the walk. Fortunately, Saki had an answer for that.

Though she was never afraid of expressing her opinion, Sakura wasn't actually one to complain without cause. She had a good reason for being a little less enthusiastic about stairs and hiking: from the knee down, both her legs were prosthetic. They served her very well, but she didn't have quite the same *feel* for the ground beneath her feet the way the rest of us did, and that made her more careful in unfamiliar territory. Faced with several stories of stairs, she pulled out her "secret" weapon: her own very powerful—and wholly unorthodox—magic.

While Gloria, Thorn, and I huffed and puffed our way up the mountainside, Saki floated along beside us, perched on a crackling black cloud of pure magical energy.

"Why do I feel like I would have to report you for doing that if we were back home?" Thorn asked, eyeing the convenience.

"There's nothing actually illegal about shadow magic, Officer," Saki said smartly. She'd never hidden the fact that she was a shadow witch, but it *was* on the vague outskirts of convention. Most magic users in Beyond were scholarly sorcerers or Witches, who went to official schools and got official posts in towns and cities, and obeyed a strict code amongst themselves. "Just because I chose not to be *official* about it and say a spell and wave some herbs around doesn't mean it's dangerous."

"And the fact that you draw power from emotions and fears . . . ?" I pointed out. I was doing my best to control my own fear by not looking behind us just yet.

"Oh, *that* part gets dangerous," Saki said with a wide grin. "Did you know some of my favorite shadow deities are supposed to live around here? Just like the baker was saying yesterday, Red. Old legends say people would bring offerings to the temples, most of which are ruins now, to keep the deities happy. The gods could create earthquakes if they were displeased—"

"No talk of earthquakes," Thorn interrupted. Though she was very fit, she wasn't quite the hiker Gloria was—or I was, for that matter. She looked to be wearing a bit thin at the seams the higher we climbed. Saki fell silent, though an amused smile danced across her face.

Once we got to the bluff, all was well. The view was fantastic. Below us, the town clung to the mountainside all the way down to the bay, which was marked by a brilliant white crescent of sand. Roads cut along the landscape like terraces, and tile roofs vied with each other for the best lookout position. Short, wizened trees dotted the vista as well, trees much like the one clinging to the bluff and providing us with some welcome shade. The sun sparkled off the water far below. Behind us, the mountain kept rising, receding back to gentle slopes covered in tangled brush and hardy herbs.

The trail we'd come to find was wide and welcoming, mostly level as it followed the curve above the town. For the first time since we'd talked to Herc, I felt like this day might turn out fun after all. Ida and Eurie faded from my mind, and I thought about what Luca would say if he was here. Something very scholarly about why the temple ruins were so high up, no doubt.

"Okay," Saki said, taking a swig from her glass bottle of iced tea as she considered the view. "This was a good idea after all."

It was hard for any of us to find anything negative to say as we set out along the trail. Here and there, wooden signs marked ancient springs or sites of ruins, mostly foundations and tumbled-down stone walls. The most intact ruins, the ones everyone came to see, were at the end of the trail: a temple whose marble columns rose two stories in the air above a wide, perfectly flat rectangular floor. The altar and any artwork were long gone, but the fallen rocks from the old roof and back walls created a maze-like playground for anyone who wanted to search for old carvings or hidden secrets.

We got to the ruined temple just in time for a picnic lunch, and took our time there, resting in the shade of old stone walls and exploring little alcoves which once had housed statues. By that time, other tourists and local hikers had joined us, but it was still a deeply moving and personal experience to visit such an old, quiet site. Even though I considered myself firmly on the side of science, as a student of alchemy, I could feel a sense of peace that pervaded that hillside.

A sense of peace . . . and something else. A sadness, maybe. Or maybe it was that I was thinking of Eurie and Ida again. Wildflowers of white and yellow grew all around the ruins, creeping and waving over the stones. It made me think of how fleeting life and love could be, which was hardly appropriate for a pre-wedding trip. I made sure to keep my momentary melancholy to myself.

We took our time walking back. Saki and Gloria were deep into a conversation about historical legacies and the way they interacted with the present when a little side-trail caught my eye. The wooden sign beside it said that it led to an old well. While Saki and Gloria sat on a nearby bench and continued talking, Thorn nodded and followed me down the path.

"We don't have to go very far if it turns out to be a long detour," I told her over my shoulder as we left the main trail behind. The sun overhead was hot, but a nice breeze wound its way through the scrubby trees. "I'm just curious about the well and if it still has any water. That kind of deep groundwater can be really powerful in potions and high in mineral content."

"No sampling," said Thorn. She knew me well.

I laughed. I *had* brought along a few alchemical things, but today my belt with its handy pouches and vials was just for holding touristy equipment like a water bottle, snacks, and sunscreen. "I just want to see it, that's all. If I want a souvenir, I'm sure we can find a potions shop downtown."

"It's a good thing the trails up here are popular," Thorn commented. The ground beneath our feet was well-worn and bare, but the foliage around us was growing thicker with every step, and the path itself wound through a series of tight turns. "I don't plan on becoming another disappearance for Herc to investigate."

"He'd be over the moon to come to your rescue," I said, still amused by how quickly Thorn had established herself in a mentor position.

"Jumping over the moon and wishing on stars is no way to do a rescue," Thorn replied. "That's what these young heroes never learn. I don't know what they're teaching them at the Guild these days. 'Course, there's nothing like experience to wisen you up."

"You're sounding very wise recently," I observed. "When I first met you, I don't think I could ever have imagined I'd be going on trips with you and seeing you teach local officers how to take notes, of all things."

"I've always been good with my notebook," Thorn protested. "You, on the other hand—"

"Me!" I interrupted with a laugh. "I don't see how *I* come into this—"

"—getting me into trouble—" she was saying behind me.

"Excuse me! You're the one who volunteers people—"

"—strange investigations and endless trails! Shouldn't we have gotten to the well yet?"

I gave up arguing and picked up the pace. "It should be right around—"

And then I ground to a halt. With no warning, Thorn ran into my back, knocking me forward. Fortunately, she also immediately reached out to grab my shoulder and stop my fall, asking, "Why'd you stop?"

Then she saw my reason. Standing next to the tumbled-down old stones of a forgotten well, practically within arm's reach, was Ida.

5

Dark Tales

"Ida? What are you doing?" I asked, once I regained my breath.

"I was waiting for you." She seemed to be wearing the same clothes we'd seen her in the night before. Her hair was messed up, and there were twigs and flowers caught in it. One of her shoes was missing.

"You were waiting for us?" Officer Thorn demanded over my shoulder.

"You knew we were going to come here?" I added, confused.

"I didn't *know* you were going to come here," Ida clarified, "but I came up here myself, just to think, and then I heard your voices on the trail and I knew you were taking the well trail, so, I waited."

My mind was reeling. I knew that Thorn, now in full Officer mode, would never approve, but I had to ask. "What happened to Eurie?"

"No idea," said Ida, but she looked guilty as could be.

Officer Thorn took over—even if we *were* on vacation. "When did you last see her?"

"Last night as we were leaving." Ida sat abruptly on the stones, her hands moving restlessly in her lap. "Somebody came up and wanted to talk to us."

"'Somebody'?" Officer Thorn pressed.

"I really shouldn't tell you. I just, I don't want to get you all involved. You've been really nice to me."

I glanced at Thorn, wondering what we should do. Who knew *what* we were getting into—like Ida said, it was definitely outside of our area of expertise. But Eurie needed someone to ask questions for her sake. Stuck in indecision, I decided to focus on practical matters. Ida was the one right in front of us, right now. "Are you alright?"

Ida seemed surprised at that. "Yes, I'm fine."

Thank goodness for that blessing, at least, I decided. "Did you know that people are looking for you?"

She glanced uneasily over her shoulder, as if she might see Herc leading a search team through the trees. Or someone else. It didn't seem to me that Herc might make a person look so threatened . . . unless, perhaps, they'd broken the law. "I had a feeling," Ida admitted finally. "But I . . . can't go back yet. It isn't safe."

Now even *I* was dying to ask the big question: *what is going on?* But I did my best to play it cool. "How did you wind up *here*?"

"I had to go *some*where," she said, eyes cast down. It was not an answer to my question, but it was obviously all she was going to say on the subject. For now.

"Why wait for us?" asked Officer Thorn. Clearly, she was less able to control her curiosity. A professional hazard, most likely.

At that, Ida looked up, hopeful and determined once more.

"When I heard you, I just thought, *I'm saved.* I have to try, I have to ask. Will you let me stay with you?"

I glanced at the officer beside me, then at Ida again. Neither one of us could just leave her out here. I still had my reservations, but if this was the next step to getting her to the local police station, and getting some answers about Eurie . . .

"Why don't you come with us for now, at least," I said, "and let's all get something to eat while we think things over."

* * *

We got back to our villa by dinner time, with Ida in tow. Nobody on the road seemed to have noticed her amongst us, a group of tourists. But nevertheless we had a problem: Thorn's dinner theater was starting soon, and—more worryingly—Ida flatly refused any notion of going to the police.

In fact, she seemed downright scared of them.

"Please," she repeated, standing with me in the living room, holding on to the back of a sofa as if it might keep her from getting swept away. "Just let me stay the night. One night. If things look different in the morning—or maybe—if I explain everything for you? Then you can tell me what you think I should do."

I watched her face as she spoke. The urgency in her voice was so different from when we had met her in the bar, but it seemed genuine. The more she spoke, the more I found myself thinking of Eurie's anxious face. *I can't really* make *her do anything,* I reasoned with myself. *Not even Thorn could. And if she really is in danger, does it hurt to hear her out?*

My friends had gone to wash up and change before heading

out again. Dinner theater was a big deal in Helenia, and the show Thorn had chosen boasted not only a dramatic play but also magic elements—*actors appear in the crowd! Interactive scenes! Disappearing sets!* had all been written in excited cursive on the flier we'd gotten from the bar the night before. Honestly, it sounded like a bit much. Especially on top of our brush with crime and the melancholy that had followed me all day.

When Thorn came out of her room dressed and ready, she only had to take one look at my face. She glanced at Ida. "Still not going?"

"Please," Ida said again. "I'll explain why."

"Not going," I confirmed with a sigh. "Why don't you three head to the show yourselves? You can fill me in later. If it's really good, we can always catch another show on another night."

"Fine, if that's what you want." Thorn's gaze on me was keen, but nothing was keeping her from her theater (and, perhaps, the wine). She glanced at Ida again. "We'll talk when we get back. Save all the good stuff for then. Unless you think you're in pressing danger?"

"No," Ida said, biting her lip. "Not—*pressing* danger. No one knows I'm here, I'm sure of it."

"Coming home from the theater to have dessert with a criminal," Gloria remarked rather cheerfully as she emerged from her room as well. "I should have expected this when I signed on for a vacation with you all."

"I'm not!" Ida said, looking suddenly alarmed. "I promise!"

I sighed again. "Ignore her, Ida. Come on, let's see what we can make for dinner. You might feel better if you clean up a little, too."

Thorn, Gloria, and Saki were soon on their way. While I made some veggie pasta with olive oil and garlic, Ida took a long shower and emerged in freshly borrowed clothes—though, on Thorn's explicit orders, her old clothes were safely stored in a paper bag. *Because they might be evidence,* I couldn't stop thinking. Gloria had been harsh in calling Ida a criminal, but she might not be wrong.

And still, through it all, it was as though I'd switched places with Ida at that bar and Eurie was sitting over *my* shoulder, worrying.

By the time my friends got back, I'd set up herbal tea and the last of our cookies on the veranda. Ida had finally relaxed, and fortunately, Gloria offered no more quips. We took our places while chatting harmlessly about the theater and the magic involved—it was good Ida hadn't come, Saki said, because any outside magic in the audience was suppressed, so any glamours or protection spells to keep her incognito would have been broken. I hadn't thought of such things, but was not surprised to hear Saki had.

Thorn sat on one side of Ida on our one long metal bench, while I sat on the other. In the patio chairs, on Thorn's other side, Saki and Gloria sat sharing a package of chocolate-covered popcorn they'd bought on the way home. Expectant silence settled over us.

"I know," Ida said, apropos of nothing, looking into the shifting twilight rather than at any of us. "I really can't put it off any longer. It's just, I'm terrible at talking. I try to come up with the words to say but they just get jumbled up in my head. And it makes sense in my head, but when I start to say it out loud it just all falls apart."

"We'll ask questions when we need to," Thorn assured her.

"The point isn't to be well spoken," I added. "It's just to let us know what's going on and how we can help."

"I'm not sure if I can explain it. Like I said, you've been really nice and I know I ought to try—the thing is—it sounds so silly when I say it."

Saki interrupted, pausing before she crammed another handful of popcorn in her mouth. "Are these things you told Eurie?"

"No." Ida looked surprised to hear the name. The sun had set, but in the glow from the twinkling lights strung across the veranda, I could see her eyebrows raise. The dress I had loaned her sat a little too loosely on her shoulders. She tugged at the wide straps. "I guess I never told anyone, really. Except—but. You won't understand unless I do, tell you, I mean.

"My parents separated a really long time ago," she said in a rush, before going on, "it's, um, kind of a whole thing. Like, I know, that's not a really big deal necessarily, especially not when the parents are . . . both there for their kids. But for my parents it was like, *a really big thing.* So I always figured it was, too. I guess I'm kind of just figuring out now that life isn't always so, you know, dramatic. I mean, maybe it was for them because that was how they felt, how they still feel, but like . . . it's weird for me trying to figure out what things actually are and what to tell people about my life."

I caught Gloria's eye. She was making a scrunchy face at me, but I couldn't tell what she meant. I had to admit, I was currently at a loss as to how this was going to relate to any disappearances or potential murders, but I waited Ida out.

"Anyway what I mean is," Ida said, with another big sigh, "is, it's like, not okay, you know? That I didn't go home. She's probably already . . . it's probably already . . ."

Saki leaned forward so she could see Ida squarely. "It's been less than a day?"

"Also," said Gloria, still looking very grumpy, "you're an adult, aren't you?"

"I know but like, I'm *not*," said Ida. "I mean, if you *asked* my mother, she'd probably say sure, I am, obviously. I'm twenty-six. Eurie and I were going to be roommates, starting this summer. But then there was that thing with Raffael, and Mom said why not wait. Because she didn't actually want me to, you know. I didn't even realize that until yesterday. It's just all so—restricted, and I hardly even think about it."

Ida, who had been fervently addressing the vines and lights above us, now buried her face in her hands. In the silence, Thorn cleared her throat. "As a police officer back home, I just have to say, it is good practice to report someone missing as soon as their schedule is disrupted, they're out of reach, and you have reason to worry. We'd rather it was nothing than the worst possible thing. Given the circumstances last night, it's not bad that your mother might be worried."

"No, I *know*," said Ida, a picture of wretchedness. "That's why it's so hard to explain. She—what do you mean, the circumstances?" She looked up. "Is it because they saw him there?"

I caught Thorn's eye as she settled back into a more serious pose. "Ida," I said, firmly, "I think you need to explain a little more."

"There's nothing wrong with it," Ida said quickly. "With any of it. Sometimes I think that's the worst part." She wiped roughly at her eyes again, and then continued. "I just can't— I can't even *breathe*, sometimes, when I'm there. At home, I mean. With Mom. I just can't even think thoughts. Sometimes

I don't know *what* I think until I am outside, with the flowers. I tell them things and—oh, I know it sounds so silly—but there *is* flower magic in my family, you know, that's why Mom took over the botanical garden and all. And it's so hard because home is supposed to be the place you go and you're supposed to be able to tell your family anything. It feels like—somebody made me a promise just to laugh when I find out it's fake. Just to make me hurt and feel alone. Or maybe I just *am* alone. But I'm not, at least, I don't think so, maybe. But he *did* say I should come back and—" Ida laughed mirthlessly, staring down at the stones beneath our feet, her hands framing her face—ready to wipe back tears. "I met somebody. I was going to—you have no idea—I can't say it. I went up on that trail. Not by the well, there's another spur that goes up to a higher peak. No one goes up there much. But he was coming down, and he said—" Her breath caught. "He said to me, 'the mayflowers are out,' and I just started bawling at him. Like really. You all think I'm bad now, you should've seen it." Ida wiped at her nose.

"Well," said Saki, diplomatically, "some people *do* find it easier to talk to complete strangers."

"Like us," groused Gloria.

"Enough from the gallery," I told them. "Ida, I take it this was back in the spring?"

She nodded, still not meeting anybody's eye. "He was really good about it, though. We talked about all kinds of things, but nothing, really. I never said who I was or what—what I'd meant to do. But—he gave me his card, I still have it. I went home and I told Mom and—and—and," said Ida, losing her momentum, "she was just angry I'd used the last packet of tea she wanted that morning. It was like coming back into a bubble where the real me didn't exist."

Ida paused again, and Thorn leaned down, resting her elbow on her knee. "This person was at the bar last night?"

"No, at least—I never saw him." Ida ran her hands through her hair. "I was just there for Eurie. I haven't seen him since that day—except this morning."

Both Saki and Gloria were leaning forward, staring hard at me since Ida was unresponsive to any such pressure. I laid my hand gently on Ida's arm. "Maybe tell us about that. Take us through what's happened since we left you last night."

"We walked out with you," Ida said, slowly. "We were right behind you. Then—that's all I remember. One moment I was looking at Gloria, carrying Thorn, and thinking it was neat how we met, and then the next minute, I woke up. I was in a courtyard in a villa, and nobody else was there."

"Not *our* villa," I said, reactively.

"No. A very nice one," Ida said. Saki made a face over her back, like, *what, our villa isn't nice?* But then Ida went on. "Like—*palatial*. Two—three stories at least. Trees and flowers I'd never seen before. The most amazing, happy flowers . . . that's why I didn't scream. I just went looking, and the floors were all marble tile and there was a little statue of a unicorn in gold, and I was just standing there, looking at it, wondering if it was a dream, and then he was there."

"The same person you met on the trail," Thorn clarified. "Whom you hadn't spoken to since?"

"I know it sounds so silly," Ida said, but her voice sounded wistful now rather than ashamed. "He was even more surprised than I was . . . he asked how I'd got in. I had no idea. Apparently there was a lot of security, but *I* never saw it. He asked what had happened, but I couldn't remember. Then he was worried and said I ought to go home, to talk things out with my mom and get cleaned up, but I said . . . I said," Ida repeated, sitting up, "I said I'm not going to. That's it. I'm done."

"But you didn't stay there," Saki pointed out logically.

"He gave me a ride," Ida said, a little uncertain again. "He has an enchanted carriage. He didn't want me to be on my own—things were a little woozy. But he didn't know where I live. So I gave him the wrong direction. I said it was a house by the trail and then—then I slipped away. It was very easy. It is very easy, you know," she said, closing her eyes, "to get lost in the flowers."

Thorn's open-mouthed look, half surprised satisfaction and half skeptical disbelief, mirrored my own, I was certain. Even the seasoned officer looked unsure of what to say next.

I tightened my hold on Ida's arm, vaguely worried she might bolt again. "Ida, what's his name?"

In response she slipped her free hand into her pocket, and held out a well-worn business card to me. I had to squint to see it in the dark. The paper itself seemed to be a deep matte black. It was almost as though the words, embossed in silver filigree, were hovering in shadow. *Marcus Antoine Pluto*, it read. *Merchant of rare magical goods.*

I sucked in a deep breath as I handed the card over to Thorn. "Well," I said, since Ida seemed not to be listening, "I know Ida's family might want to raise the alarm."

6

A Mythical Holiday

The next morning, my friends and I were still at a loss. Ida was deep asleep on our couch in Thorn's spare pajamas. It had been another gorgeous sunrise, but I couldn't bring myself to call Luca from the patio again: it felt odd, knowing there was a fugitive (criminal? victim?) possibly listening in from the living room. Instead, I sat at the kitchen bar with Gloria, the other early riser of the group.

The local paper Gloria hid behind bore the headline *Botanical Garden Heiress Missing, Friend Presumed Murdered* plastered over a picture of Ida wearing a pained smile and a fancy ballgown at some sort of charity event.

Gloria must have noticed me staring over my cup of iced tea. "Didn't tell us she was famous," she grunted.

I glanced through the arched doorway to the living room, where Ida was still snoring softly. "They're probably just making a big deal of it for the story. If she was *actually* famous around here, wouldn't—ah—Marcus know her by sight, and have a better idea of where she might live?"

It felt a little funny saying the name of someone I hadn't

met—someone with such a decidedly *un*-flashy business card. Thorn had expressed the opinion last night that only businesses of a very dubious nature went in for such trimmings, and I could see her point.

Saki had been all for paying him a visit.

It was quickly becoming apparent that of all of us, Gloria had the best idea of what an actual tourist on holiday ought to do. She folded her paper with an aggressive crinkle, unworried about our house guest. "We only have her word for any of this. We clearly don't know how things work here. We should drop her off at the police station and be done with it."

"Says the person who hired Maggie when she first came to town," I pointed out. Gloria could be as opinionated as she wanted, but when push came to shove, she had a soft spot for people trying to break free of old patterns. We all did.

"Exactly. I'm the expert," Gloria said. "I'm the one who got a front-row seat to Maggie and Officer White Knight-'Mina' falling in love. If she has a type, this is it, mark my words."

"Is *that* what you were making faces about last night?" I chuckled into my tea. "Thorn is devoted to Maggie, we all know that. I'm not worried about her falling for Ida."

"No, she won't *fall* for her," Gloria agreed, in what was clearly a *you don't see the point* tone. "But she'll get even more involved than she already is, which is *already* too much. Between Herc and Little Miss Heiress, we're never going to get out of here."

"Oh, we'll get out one way or another," I said dryly, thinking of the strangely unfriendly customs officers at the air station. I didn't tell her that Eurie's eyes had haunted my dreams, shifting from worried to enthusiastic over and over. "Is there something else bothering you? You seem awfully fond of weird nicknames all of a sudden."

Gloria slapped her paper on the counter, a frown creasing her immaculate make-up. "If you ask me—"

I had, and I was interested in her answer. But a knock at the door interrupted her. This time being inside the house instead of outside with a magic mirror, I heard—and recognized—Herc yelling from the front doorstep.

Gloria's mouth snapped shut, but her dark eyes blazed.

"That's in danger of becoming a habit," I murmured, sympathetic to her obvious protest. Daily visits from the police were not usually high on a *girls' trip to-dos* list. "I'll get it."

I slid from my perch on a stool and made my way through the kitchen. I didn't make it far, though. Ida was sitting bolt upright on the couch, looking like a cross between a party-goer who'd overstayed their welcome and a deer caught in the sights of a hunter. And from her front corner room, Thorn was stumbling into the hall.

"Got it, got it," she mumbled, raking her long hair back from her face with one hand. Before I could protest, she was at the door.

Sometimes, having great speed comes in handy. But that's only when you remember to use it.

"Oh no!" Only Herc's straw hat was visible on the other side of Thorn as she opened the door. "Did something happen to you?"

"*Is that the police?*" Ida hissed to me.

"Late night at the theater," Thorn told Herc, doing her best to not lean on the door frame.

I glanced back at Ida. Though I couldn't force her to *go* to the police, I didn't dislike the idea of letting the police come to her. I had sympathy for Ida, but there was still Eurie to think of—poor Eurie, only referred to as a "friend" in newspaper headlines. Her investigation would definitely be hampered if Ida managed to keep evading authorities.

"They'll need your help," I whispered back.

Ida clutched at her borrowed blanket. "But why are they *here*? How did they follow me?"

I raised an eyebrow. "Judging by today's newspaper, just about *everyone* is—"

"Come on in," said Thorn, loudly, having finished whatever conversation she and Herc had been carrying on outside. "We've got someone for you to see."

Well, that answered *that* conundrum.

I glanced back at Ida, ready to leap after her if she tried to run away. It wasn't very likely, given that she was wearing acres of silk pajama pants and didn't even have her feet on the floor, but I was irrationally tense as Herc came in.

Oblivious, Herc entered the room like a kid arriving at preschool, a bright toothy grin on his face as he looked at me, at Gloria over my shoulder, and then—and then he finally caught sight of Ida.

"Whoa," the officer said, his straw hat falling from his large hands.

Meanwhile, Ida was breathing a huge sigh of relief. "Thank the gods!"

My eye caught Thorn's. *Did I somehow imagine Ida's extreme reluctance to go to the police?* I wondered. *No; no, I couldn't have.* We would have gone straight to the local station if it hadn't been for the way she acted, like she thought they'd physically hurt her. I could see the same thoughts running through Officer Thorn's mind.

"Sit," she told Herc. He moved to obey as though he'd forgotten his feet weren't glued to the floor. Looking at Ida,

Thorn added, "Explain."

Though I was still confused, I did have to suppress a small smile. Unlike Officer Thorn, who had always seemed ready to operate at full tilt at any hour, Vacation Thorn was definitely not a morning person. Quietly, I took a seat in the armchair. Gloria was staring us down from her stool in the kitchen, still nursing her paper and her instant coffee.

"You can't tell the Chief," Ida said first, her gaze intent on Herc, as though she was hoping to hypnotize him.

Herc swallowed and then, as if he had indeed been hypnotized, he nodded. "I can't tell the Chief."

"Both of you, *explain,*" Thorn interjected impatiently.

This time, they both followed the order at once.

Officer Herc was clearly embarrassed, scratching at his neck. "See, the Chief has a kind of, um, what would you call it, that is, whenever the Botanical Garden comes up . . ."

Ida, meanwhile, was almost frantically calm. "The police chief is obsessed with my mother and if he knew where I was he'd tell her, and she'd tell him to lock me up and he *would.*"

The silence that followed was profound. A thud and a muffled curse could be heard from Saki's room.

Behind me, Gloria crinkled her newspaper again. "And you didn't just *say* that last night because . . ."

"I didn't know you knew Officer Herakles!" Ida said, still clutching at her blanket.

"And how *do* you two know each other?" Officer Thorn asked her new mentee, rather severely.

Herc burbled. "We don't, not really, I mean everyone at the station knows about the Chief and Edda—sorry, Miss Idunn—but it's true—I've just been there for a few concerts myself, just security, you know, when the Garden might need it. That's all."

I raised an eyebrow at Ida; this did not explain how she knew his name. She hastened to assure me, "I've heard the Chief talking about him. You're very new, right? You're not involved in all the—politics?"

"I've been on the force a year," Herc corrected her modestly. "I just want to do my best, Miss."

"Herc came to us yesterday about Eurie, and your disappearance," Thorn continued, looking at Ida. "He's investigating on his own at this point, and he could use whatever evidence you can give him."

"You're investigating on your own?" Ida seemed more interested in Herc than ever. She leaned forward. "I can tell you everything I remember."

"Go through your questions, and write things down," Thorn reminded Herc. She rose, and I did too, intending to leave them to a somewhat-private interview. Herc looked like he could hardly believe this turn of events, but he did as Thorn said, smiling at her briefly before she left.

We gathered around Gloria at the counter. We could still hear the conversation on the couches if we tried, and clearly, she was trying. "Let's see if she tells him the same things she told us," she muttered.

Thorn clapped her on the shoulder. "Who said we weren't here to investigate?"

At this point, at last, Saki's door banged open. She'd chosen the room closest to the kitchen, which meant that she spilled out directly into our midst. Her hair was unbrushed and her shoes, usually conjured up by a magical glamour on her prosthetic feet, didn't match.

"I got out here as quickly as I could," she panted.

I chuckled. "We're giving them a moment. No need to rush."

"Unless you want to make some proper coffee?" Thorn said hopefully.

Sakura rolled her eyes and grinned. "Okay, four orders, coming up. Are *any* of us managing to take a vacation on this trip?"

"I'm doing fine," Gloria said, retreating behind her newspaper.

It would have been more convincing if the paper wasn't upside down as she trained her attention in the interview in the living room.

7

Opening the Box

S aki was just getting started on a frittata made with more vegetables she'd bought on impulse from farm stands along the road yesterday when a strangled scream rang through the house.

Officer Thorn and I reacted first. This time, I managed to remember that I could run. I made it back to the living room before I could think. *Was leaving Herc alone with Ida such a bad idea?*

Ida was still on the couch, unharmed—but she was definitely the screamer. She looked up at me with her hands over her face, tears pouring all over. "Nobody said she wasn't *alive!*"

"Oh, Ida, I'm so sorry . . ." I had no idea what else to say. Had we really not broached the subject? Officer Thorn had been circumspect in her questions, not wanting to lead the witness, and the rest of us had naturally followed suit. We'd assumed that Ida knew what had happened—or that her knowledge, either way, might later help prove her innocence or her guilt.

Ida toppled down, leaning her head toward me over her knees. Apparently Herc hadn't been so delicate. But that was

54

to be expected: he was the official here, after all, and he'd have had to tell her at some point. I glanced at the two officers. Thorn had arrived and was standing over Herc, who looked up at her with a stunned expression on his face.

"Come and get statements from the others, relating to Ida's story," Thorn told him. "Let Red have a minute with Ida, to help her calm down. She knows better than to say too much."

Thorn lifted an eyebrow at me to confirm, and I pursed my lips at her. It seemed to me that saying too little had led to this in the first place. But perhaps it had been inevitable. Thorn certainly seemed to think so. She led Herc away matter-of-factly, like this happened all the time.

I sighed, and after a brief hesitation, decided to sit on the edge of the couch, alongside Ida's feet. Ida herself was still crying, seemingly insensible to any of these comings and goings. I *did* feel awful for her, of course. But there was something else, something that kept me from trusting her . . . *perhaps,* I mused, *I've been involved in too many murder investigations.* All I wanted in that moment was Luca's insight. Or William's. No doubt William would have plenty to say about everything we'd done in the past day, and the promise we had broken!

"I just thought," Ida said, her shoulders heaving, "I thought she just—ditched me. Maybe not on purpose, maybe she just went home or to see Raffael or something. That's all—that's all I thought. I thought he was investigating—neither of us coming home!"

"Well," I said, rather awkwardly, "that *is* what Officer Herc's investigating, in a sense, Ida. That's why your testimony is so important. But we know it must be very hard."

Two girls left the bar . . . and only one returned.

Ida was still crumpled up, like a discarded note. She hiccuped, and then her shoulders started shaking again. "My gods! And there I was, thinking it was—somehow lucky! What happened to me! But compared to her—oh, my gods, where did Eurie go?"

"Hmm." Without thinking of it, I mimicked Luca's thoughtful demeanor, even going so far as to lay my hand on her knee. I almost said *we know precisely where they found her,* but at the last minute it occurred to me that Ida might be wondering where Eurie went after the bar, during that time which Ida couldn't recall. Ida had ended up at a strange estate, but had Eurie been there too? Had she gone there, or somewhere else, and then been taken back to the bar for some reason?

Not the time, I reminded myself. I could all but hear William reprimanding me for focusing on facts rather than being sympathetic.

"And you knew? You must have known. That's why Officer Herakles came to you before? Gods! Now I see why you all were so interested in going to the police!" Ida burst, lifting her head to wipe at her eyes. "I thought it was just some weird tourist thing!"

I had to chuckle at that, if darkly. "I think we're learning that we're not very typical tourists. We didn't mean for you to be shocked like this, Ida, truly. We were trying to help by . . . not interfering too badly," I said, not sure if my vague phrasing made any sense.

Ida was distracted, in any case. She shook her head, still looking down at her knees. "She's gone! She's really gone? Eurie? Just like that?"

"I'm sorry, Ida." That was when I finally felt it, the reality of her grief.

"I have to pull myself together," she said, almost as though she hadn't heard me. "I have to—on top of everything else—but what does the rest of it matter?"

"Anything you have to say might matter," I told her gently. "Sometimes you never know what can help an investigation until it's over."

With a mighty sniff, Ida met my gaze. Her eyes were red-rimmed and her cheeks were blotchy, her skin strained by the constant rubbing. Compared to when we'd met her, dressed up in her makeup for a night out, her lashes looked lighter, and her mouth paler. The effect was heart wrenching, given the context. "We left together, but I didn't see anything. I wish I had!"

I wasn't so sure about that *not seeing anything* part, but I tried to remain gentle. "Ida, didn't you mention something to us about seeing someone come up to her? Someone you didn't want us to get involved with?"

"Did I?" Ida looked stricken.

"Even if you don't want to tell me or the others, it'd be good to tell Officer Herc," I added.

"It must have been—But everything's hazy . . . I can't believe she's gone," Ida said, shaking her head again. Her hair flopped limply. "Are they sure?"

"Yes." This time, my voice was full of sympathy. "They're sure it's her, Ida. But they're not sure why or how. Herc was the only one to think it might be murder at first—that's why he's investigating."

"Really?" Ida's brows rose, and I wondered if I'd violated Officer Thorn's caution to *not say too much.*

It was too late now, but I decided to keep things moving. "Are you ready to talk to him again?"

"In a minute," she said uncertainly. "Red—you've been so kind. You must know. What do you think happened? What does *he* think?"

"I appreciate it, Ida, but I really don't know," I said truthfully. "Remember, my friends and I are very new here. We don't know things the way you and Herc do."

"But maybe that's good," Ida insisted.

"Sometimes it can be." I hesitated, thinking of the newspaper article and how well-known Ida might be. A question came to mind, and before I thought better of it, I asked her, "Ida, if you had no idea what had happened to Eurie, why were you so determined to hide?"

"Was—was I?" This time, Ida's wide eyes looked fearful.

"Yes," I said firmly. "You ran away, remember? And you told us you wouldn't go back. Why?"

"I just—I realized some stuff. Unrelated stuff," she said. "Or, I do now, anyway."

"You did, or you didn't?"

She bit her lip.

I tried again. "From who? Eurie?"

Ida shook her head.

"From someone you were waiting for at the bar?" She *had* mentioned waiting for someone, hadn't she?

But then again—she'd been talking to us all night. When could she have had time for some kind of revelation with someone else?

"I don't know if he can be trusted," she said, increasingly vague. Then, abruptly, "Do you think I could still stay here?"

I sighed. "You need to finish talking to Officer Herc."

* * *

I was feeling vaguely like a pinball, back in the kitchen with my friends. We watched openly this time as Herc settled in for Round Two with Ida, now with Officer Thorn at his side.

"Told you," said Gloria. "Involved. Capital 'I.'"

"It *is* weird though, don't you think? On top of being tragic, of course," Saki said, leaning over the counter. She'd finished and plated her frittata. The others had eaten, and I was catching up with gusto.

"Something does feel off," I admitted, around a forkful of fluffy eggs, peppers, and onions.

Gloria rolled her eyes at me. "Something's always off about *murder.*"

"Not so," Saki chirped. "Usually it's very straightforward. Not when Red's involved, of course," she added affectionately. "But in big cities, most murders get solved quite quickly. It's usually an act of passion that isn't very well thought out."

"How do *you* find the ones that are?" Gloria asked me.

I shrugged, my mouth full.

"Have you considered that it's part of your heritage?" Saki's blue eyes danced speculatively as she considered me. I knew what she meant: as the child of Seers, even if I couldn't See the future myself, maybe I was drawn to these kinds of things. It had occurred to me before, but I wasn't sure how I felt about it; especially at a time in my life when I was about to settle down with someone else, someone I didn't want to be constantly getting into danger. Before I could swallow and protest, though, Saki went on, "Anyway, it's another one that's clearly bound up in some kind of myth, wouldn't you say?"

That distracted me. Fairy tales and legends often had a way of playing out over and over in Beyond, but with obvious twists. They weren't fate with a capital "F," as Gloria might say—it was more like they were in the water, in the air, ready to influence a stray thought, easily followed but often just as easily thwarted.

"Eurydice," I mused. "Not a happy story."

Gloria glanced between us. "I'm not familiar."

"An old legend," Saki told her. "Eurydice had a lover, a musician, Orpheus. When she died unexpectedly, he went into the underworld to save her. But after going all that way, he lost her on the way back up."

"Why name your child that, then?" Gloria shook her head.

"You know very well that names don't mean destiny," I told her. "They can be changed." Gloria had changed her own name when she took over the salon in Belville.

"You're just making my point for me," Gloria argued. "People change their names for a *reason*. Like they pick them in the first place for a reason."

"Maybe we need to find an Orpheus," Saki said, her gaze on the living room.

"The point I'm making is, you're thinking too narrowly," I protested.

"Has anyone thought about Ida?" Saki interrupted. "The name Idunn is a lore-mirror for Persephone, you know. The stories are very similar, going from flowers to the world of the dead, and staying there."

I groaned. "No, I hadn't known that." But I did know that Sakura, in her private practice, considered the ancient goddess Persephone one of her patrons. It was why she'd named her café the Pomegranate, after one of the goddess's symbols.

Gloria was still frowning about the name issue. It looked like both my friends were more involved than they thought.

As if to prove my point, Gloria declared, "Fine. We're going to the Botanical Garden today."

"Is that so?" Saki looked amused.

"Yes. And I'm going to show you that sometimes the literal answer is the right one," Gloria continued, including both of us in her challenge.

I glanced at Saki. "Are you up for another walking-heavy day?"

"Oh, I'll be fine, Red, but thank you for asking." Saki grinned mischievously at Gloria. "I love a chance to get someone to think a little deeper."

"Don't you dare try that shadow stuff on me," Gloria warned her. "And match-making won't work either, remember?"

"But that's no reason for you not to have a chance to reflect," Saki replied, looking downright devilishly smug. "If you want to put some philosophy to the test, then we will!"

I looked down at the rest of my frittata. "Guess I better eat fast. At the rate you two are going, I'm not even sure you'll wait for Officer Thorn and the *actual* investigation going on!"

8

Hiding in Flowers

In fairness, the Botanical Garden of Helenia was amazing. Well worth rushing over a belated breakfast for.

Though Ida and her mother may have moved to Helenia to run the garden, it was clear that the garden itself had existed for a very long time—centuries, even. It sprawled across an entire island, just visible from the harbor. As we rode a small ferry toward it, rising and falling with each wave, we could see massive trees of all kinds interspersed with the occasional gazebo or low roof. A lookout platform already busy with tourists rose above the treeline on the north end of the island, looking back toward the town. The island itself wasn't large, but it was lumpen and craggly, long and narrow in exactly the way that an old tree-lined road might be.

The ferry deposited us at a dock which was more a terrace of stone steps than a marina, like someone had simply left a large staircase unattended and the water had slowly crept up to meet it. Small boats jostled among each other along the water line, dropping off and picking up visitors before departing. The plants were already overwhelming. Urns as big as William lined the steps, each one overflowing with succulent vines, leafy spikes, and blooms of pink, yellow, and orange. My own back patio at home was something of a container garden, and I could have spent all morning just investigating those urns alone.

"One of us'd better watch Red," Gloria announced, as I strayed from the stream of tourists going up the sun-baked steps.

"I need a moment before I go up all those stairs, anyway," Sakura said. She followed me and sat heavily on a bench tucked next to the flower display. Her skirt poofed around her legs. She was wearing a flared sundress covered in colorful sunflowers, as cute as ever, but her face was more the color of her stark white hair.

"Forgot about you and boats," Gloria admitted. She followed Saki, so that the three of us were separate from the crowd. "You could've stayed back, you know."

"And miss this opportunity?" Saki grinned up at Gloria, recovering some of her spunk.

In fact, Officer Thorn had elected to stay back instead. She'd cheerfully appointed herself as Ida's keeper for the day, and I had no doubt she wanted to be on hand for Herc if necessary. From what I'd gathered, the young officer had spent all of yesterday questioning people from the bar with no real success, and now planned to track down Eurie's boyfriend based on Ida's information.

I poked a rounded, bauble-like succulent leaf absently, torn between appreciating the flowers and wondering about the case. Not to mention my friends' sudden competition. "It probably *would* be best if we paused here and made a plan."

Gloria put her hands on her hips. "How hard is it? We go up

the stairs, we go in, we look around. See what we hear about Ida. Done."

"Don't you want to even *try* to meet her mother?" Sakura asked.

"And aren't you both forgetting that it's *Eurie* we're really curious about?" I added.

Gloria tossed her head, her red feathers glinting in the bright morning sun. "*I'm* curious about Ida. Seems to me she's Suspect Number One."

I wasn't so sure about that, but I knew better than to start an argument. Especially while standing on the dock literally outside the garden gates. "Well, they both worked here, so we can keep an ear open for things about both of them."

"And ear, and a mind, too," Saki said, with another pointed look at Gloria. "I'm sure that once we get going, something useful will turn up, even if it's not what we expect it to be."

As if in a silent race to be the first one to discover said *something,* both Sakura and Gloria began marching up the steps. I lingered, looking at an orange blossom as big as my head, and gave one last wistful sigh. "And maybe we could also enjoy the flowers while we're at it . . ."

People don't realize how plants affect everyday life, Eurie had said.

At the top of the steps, a fabric canopy provided welcome shade. The cliff side opened up into a wide plaza lined with ticket booths, each sporting racks of maps, magical fans, and taps for refilling water bottles. The crowd was at a lull, which meant that Saki and Gloria were clearly identifiable at the booth in the corner. Gloria, tall and dressed in black, as usual, looking like a stormfront while Saki, chipper and quick as a little bird, was clearly chatting up the ticket seller.

". . . so *interested* in your programs," she was saying. As I came up, she turned to me. "Right, Red? Some inspiration from the programming they do here might be *exactly* what the Pomegranate needs."

Uh-huh. The only "programming" Saki was known to do at her café were holiday parties and the occasional matchmaking set up. I had no illusions that she suddenly wanted to put on art shows or educational talks on botany.

But her razor-sharp memory—not to mention her questionable commitment to the truth—paid off in this case. "We *had* an artist in residence," said the ticket seller, a young-looking merperson whose nametag read *Medu S. A.* His hair was wrapped up in a deep green silk scarf which complimented his olive skin and dark eyes. "But you wouldn't have learned much from *those* programs. Try looking at the conservatory exhibit instead. One of our staff put it together, Ida—she's amazing."

"Cool," said Saki brightly. "Where was that on the map, again?"

Medu leaned out of his window to show her, marking a paper map with an official Botanical Garden pen. Before I could ask another question, though, another wave of tourists came up from the dock, and Medu waved us on with a practiced smile.

"See?" Saki tucked the map into her purse as we walked out into the garden, under a canopy of broad-leafed trees. "We barely even made it inside, and we're learning things."

"Yeah, that he loves Ida and hates Eurie for some reason," Gloria muttered. "That was her, right? The artist in residence?"

"That's what Ida said when we met," I agreed, pausing to

admire a grand fountain. Water sparkled and poured off of a set of rearing horses sculpted out of pale limestone. "I wonder what he meant by saying you wouldn't learn anything from her programs, though?"

"Let's ask someone else," Saki decided, scanning the flower beds in front of us for any other unsuspecting staff members. Before Gloria or I could stop her, she'd plunged down the nearest path and was already calling out to a gardener with a dirty rake and shovel over one shoulder.

"We've created a monster," said Gloria, her normally nonchalant expression a bit wide about the eyes.

I chuckled. "*You're* the one who tried to tell her that myths would determine the mystery."

After four impromptu chats, a chase through the rose garden, and nearly getting trampled in the children's please-touch-me garden, I wasn't quite as amused. Lunchtime was right around the corner, and the sun was high and hot. Saki set off again in pursuit of a gardener with a wheelbarrow—someone she *swore* she'd seen, but Gloria and I hadn't so much as glimpsed. In short order, we were all lost in a hedge maze.

"Whose idea was this?" Gloria's teeth were audibly grinding. Even as the tallest of us, she couldn't see over the hedge walls. Her feathered crest barely reached the top of the perfectly-pruned rows of green.

I had to agree with her frustration. Though the walls were high, they did not keep out the sun, and as someone who had become accustomed to cloudy, comfortable Belville, I was feeling the heat.

"It's on the map, don't worry," Saki assured us. She gave up on her mysterious wheelbarrow attendant, for the moment at least, and pulled out her paper map. For the first time, might

I add, since we'd entered the garden!

And as if the map itself had summoned help, who should come around the nearest corner than Medu, the ticket seller. He bore down on us without any pretense, causing even Sakura to look a little alarmed. No one else was around, and though birdcall was audible everywhere in the garden, the hedge walls blocked out any other voices.

"I saw you run in here," Medu told us. "I just started my lunch break. Do you need help?"

I faltered. Somehow, that wasn't the question I had expected him to ask. "Um, well, we *did* just realize we are a little lost."

"And we still haven't made it to the conservatory," Saki added in her most innocent voice.

Medu smiled. "Come on, I can show you. This maze is no joke. You didn't read the sign, did you?"

"What sign?" Gloria remained solidly in place.

"This hedge maze is one of our most unique exhibits," Medu said. "It was designed specially, with outside consultants and everything. Unless you take a red flower in with you, you can get really stuck, until closing time at least."

My mind was instantly turning. "How would that work?"

"I don't get it, myself," Medu said with a shrug. "But come on. I do know a shortcut out—they showed all the employees, just in case."

Gloria fell into step with me, although it was clear she was half suspecting him to lead us into a trap. I was still intrigued by a living maze that could be manipulated by color. Ahead of us, Saki was the only one keeping her head in the game.

"Did Ida design that too?" she asked Medu. "Like the container exhibit?"

"No, the maze was actually Edda, who runs the Garden," he

said, his voice becoming less friendly. Something about the admission seemed to bother him.

"Edda and Ida?" Saki repeated, sweetly. "That must get confusing."

"Oh. Edda's Ida's mom," Medu said, as though surprised we didn't know.

Beside me, Gloria startled. For the second time that day, she whispered, "Who names their kid that?"

I shushed her. Medu had continued:

"Edda's been in charge since I started here. She puts on some really big exhibits, too—not really exhibits, but gardens. But Ida's the one who has the flower magic. The stuff she does is really amazing. She ought to have been the artist in residence in her own right."

"Is it a big deal?" I asked.

Medu nodded back at me. "It's huge. It can make or break your career, if that's what you want to do. And honestly," he added, almost under his breath, "Eurie never really deserved it. All her stuff is just *political*."

I caught Gloria's quick glance, but that was all we had time for before the path Medu led us down took an abrupt left, and we were deposited outside the maze. In front of us, a wide, mossy lawn extended along the front of a building made almost exclusively of glass.

"There's the Conservatory," Medu said in a perfectly normal voice again. "There's a café in there, too, if you want a snack."

"Wait," Saki cried. "See? I did see someone!"

As one, the three of us turned to look where she was pointing. At the far corner of the maze, a tall, masculine figure obscured by a wide-brimmed straw hat was conversing with someone in a white skirt that trailed over the gravel path.

"That's Edda," Medu said, sounding genuinely surprised this time. "You saw her?"

"No, the other one," Saki insisted.

Medu tapped his hair scarf thoughtfully. "I think he was the consultant for the maze. Not sure why he'd be here now, though."

"We are *not* about to go and ask them," Gloria growled.

"No, of course not," Medu said, his already wide eyes now round as saucers. "I should be getting back to my lunch anyway. You're alright now, right?"

"Thank you!" Saki said, dismissing him. But she was still staring at the figures by the edge of the maze.

"What is it?" I asked her.

"I'm not positive," she admitted slowly, "but I think I've seen him somewhere before."

9

Life Contained

When Edda and the mysterious stranger disappeared into another garden, we finally convinced Saki that we could do the same—into the café. Set up cafeteria-style at the center of the conservatory, it was the perfect balm to my fraying temper and baffled wits. The glass ceiling arched high above us, and the shade provided by leafy trees—not to mention the breeze from strategically-placed ceiling fans and even some floor vents—made the interior deliciously cool. Water features and streams set along the walkways created a soothing atmosphere. Even though the place was full of tourists who looked just as exhausted as I was, the general air was happy and calm.

I briefly lost Gloria and Saki amid a maze of food displays offering plated entrees, snacks, and desserts, but managed to meet up with them again on the other side. We were all laden with a bountiful harvest: Gloria's tray was crowded with an overstuffed hummus wrap, several containers of nut mixes, and no less than three bottled drinks, while Sakura's was stacked high with local cheese boards and an enormous piece of baklava. I looked down at my own tray of falafel salad and scones and iced tea, and I laughed.

"Okay, looks like we all needed a break," I said, already feeling better. "Anyone see a table we can use?"

Gloria marched through the crowd of diners, leading us to a small wrought-iron table at the edge of the wide indoor patio. On the other side of an old railing, a dragonfly hovered over a long, shallow pool of water which gave way to dense ferns and orchids.

"This is truly incredible," I said as I took my chair.

But somehow, I'd become the only one playing tourist. Saki had pulled out her map, it was true—but she wasn't plotting an afternoon stroll to the viewing deck or through the alpine garden. "They went this way," she said, jabbing her finger at the more showy flower gardens along the center aisle of the grounds.

"Good thing you can't read maps," Gloria said, around a mouthful of hummus and summer squash, "because like I said, I do *not* want to talk to them."

"I can so!" Sakura undermined her own confident assertion by squinting at the map, and then rotating it ninety degrees and pursing her lips. "You're a chicken. They don't have to *know* we're investigating. We can just 'bump' into them."

Despite myself, I chuckled. "Remember, right now we agreed to rest. That heat is no joke. Don't forget to eat, Saki."

"Half the garden knows we're investigating," Gloria added dryly. "You aren't exactly subtle. And I for one would like to know what Medu's deal is."

"Do you always just suspect the last person you saw?" Saki retorted. At last, she gave up on her map and began unfolding the paper on a cheese tray instead.

Behind her wrap, Gloria shrugged. "At least that's a more focused way of going about things."

"Both of you could use a little *less* focus right now," I interrupted. "Please?"

"I thought you were the career amateur sleuth," Gloria reminded me.

"That's an oxymoron, but nonetheless, I agree," Saki said. "This can't be how you usually go about cases, Red."

"Well—" I broke off, and hid my confusion by taking a long drink. I *wanted* to say that in fact it was, and that I often found that I learned something new by doing something *other* than investigating, but that wasn't exactly true. Saki and Gloria both had seen firsthand that I had a tendency to worry over each new case or danger . . . until William or Luca made me think about something else.

In that moment, I realized how much I missed them both.

But it's been barely three days, I reminded myself. *That's nothing!* When I'd left my home island to become an alchemical apprentice, I'd hardly even looked back. For *years.* Some of those years, William and I had been on the road, and I'd just assumed that travel was part of my personality, the way some people expressed themselves through art or poetry or knitting tiny hats for rescued animal babies.

Then again, the whole reason for this trip was that I was about to *truly,* publicly settle down with Luca.

And once again, I saw Eurie's worried eyes at the bar. She'd been so passionate one moment—and gone the next. A promise broken. *Is this the kind of thing that's going to keep happening, to me* and *Luca, forever? Even when we want to rest?*

"Ahh," I said, aware that I'd paused for too long. With one hand, I grasped the pendant that hung under my sundress tightly. "Um, that is, every case is different, I suppose. It depends on the other people involved. And the actual *case* itself."

Gloria scrunched up her nose and made a face, which was only partially ruined by the fact that she had a piece of lettuce on her mouth. "Could you be any less an alchemist? Any minute now you're going to start talking about 'ingredients' and 'hypotheses.'"

"Give her a break," Saki said more kindly. She also offered Gloria a cloth napkin—a peace offering of sorts. "Red, it's okay if you miss everyone back home. We're not offended. We know we're not your usual crime-solving squad."

"Because there weren't supposed to *be* any crimes on this trip," Gloria muttered. But she accepted the napkin and wiped at her face.

"You both are great," I said. How could I tell them that somehow, I'd connected my feelings about weddings and love with a strange artist's enthusiasm and then let it draw me into a downward spiral of worry?

"Obviously we're great," said Saki, grinning. "But you miss your partner in crime. In *solving* crime, of course. Why not call him?"

"I didn't bring the mirror along," I admitted, realizing now what a silly oversight that had been. With the way Saki tended to dart off after every lead, having an extra way to communicate would have been a good idea. "But I might, um, just take a walk for a minute. Clear my head. Would you mind?"

"Of course not. Go on," said Sakura. "We'll take our time resting, and we'll plan out our next route."

"To find the staff lunch area," Gloria said, but the way she smirked made it clear she was teasing.

"Okay." I smiled faintly back at them. "Thanks. I'll be right back—don't eat my salad."

It was strange. I tended to be pensive at times, sure, and perhaps annoyingly methodical, as Gloria had pointed out. But I didn't often get hit by things like this out of the blue.

Unless I am *helping with a case,* I thought wryly as I followed a thin, winding path away from the café. Hoping it would be a short loop and I'd be back with the others in no time, I let my mind wander. I'd been pestering them so much about taking a break—maybe I was the one who'd actually needed one.

Because I miss Luca. And I'm going to marry him. I sighed as I trailed my fingers over a mossy palm trunk, passing by. It was a good thing, definitely. But it was so big!

And I knew, of course, that this was probably *exactly* why Sakura had suggested we take this trip. So that I would realize just how big it was.

My parents had always been devoted to one another. I knew what love could look like, and I knew Luca and I had it. But there was something—not just about Eurie—it was something about Ida too, about her confidences and this, her garden home. She struck me as almost dangerously earnest. It was the kind of sincerity that could exist completely without solid reason or fact. It made me want to reexamine my own assumptions. It made me long for the sympathetic sounding board Luca so often provided. I had seen its like several times before—in criminals.

The path I was following widened onto a flagstone floor, and suddenly I was in a long hallway along the conservatory's front windows, looking out over the garden. In those windows, suspended on silver chains, hung a myriad of baubles no bigger than my fist.

Ida's exhibit. There could be no doubt about it. It took my breath away—the sunlight streaming through the glass, each little shape containing its own colors, its own world. It was like seeing an artful display of potions, but maybe even a tiny bit better because I knew these were *alive.*

The others would want to see this, most likely. It might give them some insight into our unexpected house guest. But— they wouldn't want to see it for quite as *long* as I did. Like so many other places in this garden, I could have spent all day here.

So I decided to linger for just a minute before going back to my lunch.

I was drawn to one nearby, a little bottle hanging on a curved wire with little tufts of teeny flowers extending up through its open top. Each glass vessel was a different shape, many of them clearly repurposed. This one showed its layers of house guest gravel, then soil, then moss and the leaves from which the flowers extended. I bent in to look at the way she'd designed it so that the flowers and the moss could coexist. There were pebbles set under the plants, the flowers' roots partially visible and thriving in the water droplets captured by the moss fronds. It was orderly and intentional, but still a bit wild.

"She knew exactly what they would all need," I mused. The gallery was so quiet, I almost didn't notice that I'd spoken aloud rather than in my own head.

Until someone else chimed in.

"I disagree," a low voice said.

I turned, curious. He'd been standing so still I hadn't noticed him at first. He'd taken off his big straw hat, but it was tucked under his elbow, and something in the way he stood, arms crossed and feet spread, identified him immediately. This was Sakura's mystery gardener, the consultant on the maze. I sucked in a breath, surprised.

"The results we see here are not the product of expertise, but of constant trial," he continued. "You can see in some of the containers that they were emptied of an older, lighter dirt, though not completely washed before they were filled again. This suggests that those terrariums are not first attempts."

He was wearing a gardener's sturdy boots, but in all other respects he did not look like someone who talked about soils for a living. His brown trousers were creased—not by use, but by an iron—and he wore a white collared shirt underneath, of all things, a brown vest that matched the trousers. He was a little taller than I was, but appeared to be quite human, with short black hair pushed straight back from his pale forehead, mussed by his hat. His face was incredibly serious as he continued staring at a suspended glass vase.

"Furthermore," he went on, "many of the larger specimens contain species that are not, technically speaking, thought to coexist. In this one, for example, there is a hybrid ladybug orchid alongside a cat's-whisker fern. This particular orchid is known to prefer dry soils, the fern proven to prefer wet. Therefore, one could reasonably say that one of the two of these plants is not going to thrive, which will in turn render the entire ecosystem a failure."

I blinked. *Failure* seemed a little harsh. And who said "furthermore" in everyday conversation?

"Just because she's experimenting doesn't mean she's inexpert," I protested.

"I didn't say she was." He turned to me at last, one dark

eyebrow mildly raised. "But for the record I do not believe she is experimenting. I see no repetition or patterns which would indicate method. No, this exhibit strikes me more as the efforts of someone obsessed with the idea of confined life, without thorough understanding of the mechanics to support it."

"Restricted," I corrected, struck by a sudden and sad thought as I glanced at the baubles again. "I think she has more understanding than you might suppose."

"Ah. You know her, then."

His voice wasn't challenging or superior, but rather quietly factual. In fact, nothing he'd said had been put out in a rude or provocative manner, aside from some general annoyance and odd word choices. I glanced back at him. His eyes, trained on my face, were gray as flint.

"You must too," I reasoned. "You're the one who helped put together the maze, I take it?"

He shifted so he was facing me directly, and swept his hat to the side in a delicate, old-fashioned bow. "Quinn E. Doyle, at your service."

10

Reason Embodied

"And you," continued this very strange gardener, "must be an alchemist, surely. Your name?"

"Call me Red," I said, a little hesitantly. It wasn't so very odd for people to identify my profession before meeting me. The goggles, gloves, and toolbelt often helped with that. What *was* odd was the way his mouth quirked back in an amused smile when I gave him the name. It wasn't the look of confusion I sometimes got from others wondering why I should be called *Red* if my hair was black and my skin light brown. No; his expression let me know that he definitely understood the reference.

"A pleasure to meet you, Red," he said easily. Now that he was facing me, I was doubting my initial assumptions: the outline of a magnifying glass in his vest pocket was innocuous enough, but it looked like he had some kind of small flare gun on his hip. "And may I ask the reason for your interest in our mutual friend and her botanical efforts?"

Now my hackles were up. He was coming across as wolf-in-gardener's-clothing far more than Medu or anyone else in the garden had. I swallowed. "Professional interest, of course."

"Of course." His gray eyes danced over my expression, which I hoped was perfectly straight. "Of course, a purely professional alchemist does not often take into account her subject's emotional state."

Darn. He'd noticed how sorry I was for Ida in the moment I saw the connection between her life and her art. But I desperately needed to avoid letting him know I was involved in her disappearance. He was too sharp by half. "Not always, maybe," I conceded, "but I would argue that alchemists who limit themselves entirely to reason also limit what they're able to achieve. It's the nature of the field to be inclusive of all kinds of experiences."

To my surprise, Quinn Doyle tipped his head back and laughed.

Just as I was considering whether I might ask him about the maze and how it was made, purely as a distraction of course, there came the sound of hurried footsteps behind me.

"Come on, you have to come back with me," Sakura called to me even before she'd emerged from the path. She burst into the gallery, panting, leaning over her knees. "We saw Medu again. Gloria's gone on ahead."

As she glanced up, I reached out for her shoulder to help her keep steady. "Did something bad happen?"

Off to the side, Quinn *tsk*ed. "Much better to simply ask, *what happened.* It refrains from leading the witness."

"She's not a witness, she's my friend," I snapped back, annoyed because normally I *might* have thought the exact same thing. But this was Saki. I knew she'd tell me everything when she caught her breath.

Meanwhile, Sakura drew herself up. "You!" she cried,

noticing Quinn. "When did you last see Edda?"

"My, my. A witness," he said, with emphasis which might have been playful if it wasn't increasingly annoying, "who asks questions in return. Not very helpful, I must say."

"Neither are you," I retorted. "Come on, Saki. Let's head back."

"No, I'm afraid I really have to insist," said Saki, planting her feet. She glared at Quinn, black sparks of magic lighting up around her silhouette. "When did you last see Edda?"

Quinn stared at Sakura for what felt like a very, very long time. Then he smiled. "Why don't I tell you on the way?"

* * *

I was wholly unsurprised when Quinn did not, in fact, tell us anything as we raced back down the path.

Instead, he started an argument with Sakura this time.

"Such concern," he observed, barely out of breath, "for someone you've never met. Why involve yourself?"

"How are you so sure I haven't met her?" Saki retorted.

"Someone with your magical capability would no doubt be able to locate someone they knew well in the event that they went missing, under normal circumstances."

"Did I say she was missing?"

"You inquired as to when I last saw her, which is indicative of—"

"You're making a lot of assumptions, mister!"

"There you are." Gloria sighed with relief as she met us back on the café plaza. "Medu and the other staff are checking the conservatory, but it's already been done twice with no luck. Someone said they saw her headed back outside—into the maze."

I skidded to a halt and thought quickly. Much as I didn't like to, I agreed with Quinn: it was now obvious that Edda was missing, and Medu had most likely been the one to notice. The fact that Gloria was trusting him to take part in a search—even if it was a rather low-stakes one, given that the previous ones had failed—probably meant that he had come to Saki and Gloria to enlist their help for some reason, and he must have made a convincing appeal.

But I hadn't been gone all *that* long! Time was apparently of the essence, but I hesitated. "Hasn't it only been half an hour since we saw her with Quinn?"

"You Quinn?" Gloria narrowed her eyes at the man, who made another stately bow, despite being a bit breathless—as we all were. Sakura was glowering at his side. To me, Gloria went on, "You can explain *that* later. But yeah, it hasn't been long. They haven't called police or anything. But they're worried—apparently she was supposed to be giving a talk at noon."

"Right as we were sitting down," Saki added for emphasis. "But she never turned up to the presentation room, which is at the other end of the conservatory. Medu came this way looking for her, and ran into us. He asked if *we* had seen her since then, and we offered to help," she added, looking pointedly at Quinn.

"She's not answering her radio, or anything," Gloria recited. "It's all very unlike her, he said."

"She does run the place," Quinn commented. "My impression is that she does not take that responsibility lightly."

"We can search the maze," I realized. "We have the literal maze-maker right here."

As one, the three of us turned to look at him. Quinn didn't seem ruffled by the attention. In fact, he put his free hand into his vest pocket and said, "Maybe I should wonder why you three apparent strangers are so very concerned about a person who's been missing less than an hour."

"Maybe you could just ask," Gloria said, frowning. And also forgetting that we had something—something very big and Ida-shaped—to hide. I did everything but stomp on her foot, hoping that she would remember and that Quinn wouldn't notice.

"I could," he agreed, perfectly friendly. "But so far, I've found your two friends very unreceptive to direct questions. Perhaps you'd like to fill me in?"

"No," I said for her, "you wouldn't. She doesn't have anything to tell you," I added to Quinn. "We're just meddlesome. It's a bad habit. Are you going to help us with the maze or not?"

His gaze alighted on me for a second, clear and quick. "I'd be delighted. My thanks for the invitation."

Rather than risk getting into yet another argument, I turned on my heel and led the way out of the conservatory. Fortunately, Gloria fell in next to me, leaving Saki and Quinn to ignore each other behind us.

"What's his deal?" Gloria whispered.

"I can't tell, but he knows Edda and Ida and doesn't seem as friendly as he acts," I said, dodging a family that sprawled out across two tables.

"Did he know Eurie?"

"Oh." I hadn't thought that far. "That I don't know. We didn't talk very much—just about the garden. What happened to our lunch, by the way?"

Gloria chuckled. "Saki magicked it. Don't worry, you can

still have your gross salad later."

"Thanks a lot! You sound just like William," I complained, as we spilled out into the summer air.

"I can't help it if he's right sometimes," Gloria replied. Her grin disappeared, though, as she turned back to Quinn. "So what's up with your maze?"

"Ah. It isn't *my* maze," the man said, reaching into his vest like some kind of stage-show magician, "but I do happen to know its secrets."

From the perfectly flat inside pocket of his vest, he pulled out a dewy red rose.

Saki gagged.

Clearly amused, Quinn strode forward, taking the lead. We immediately lined up behind him. As we entered what technically should have been the exit for the maze, I did have a brief shiver of doubt. As the maze consultant, he surely knew his way through it—but he might also know ways to get us stuck in there. Now I was more resolved than ever to keep him in sight.

We took the first few turns in quick succession. The noise of playing children and botanical tour guides faded with each new direction. Just like before, the maze was unfailingly the same—every single hedge looking exactly like the one we'd passed before. Quinn was holding the rose up at chest height as he walked ahead of me. He was, I realized, twirling it.

I hopped a step forward, so I could poke my head up next to him, and asked the question that had been on my mind for ages now. "How did you do it?"

"Keep a rose in my pocket?" For once, his gray eyes looked a little startled.

"Not that," I said, exasperated. "The maze. How did you

make the maze respond to color?"

"Ah! A fellow technician," he declared, turning slightly to beam at me. "You want to know how it was made?"

"Technically an alchemist, as you well know, but—yes," I said, left to run after him for a moment as we rounded another corner.

"You will be well-suited to understand it," he went on, almost as though I hadn't spoken. "I approached the matter purely as a question of intention. The intent of the maze must be, at all times, to confound those who are unfamiliar with it. Meanwhile the intent of the maze-enterer is—?"

"Where are we *going*?" Sakura called from behind me.

"Not exactly," Quinn continued. "A person who enters a maze expects to solve it. Otherwise, they would not—"

"No, really," Gloria called from the back of the line. "How is this helping find Edda?"

"How?" Quinn came to an abrupt halt, and I had to duck to the side to avoid getting a faceful of his straw hat. "Because she'll be at the center."

"How do you know that?" Gloria asked. She looked vaguely annoyed, but next to her, Saki was staring daggers at Quinn.

"It's the only place on the island where a person beset by political machinations whose child has recently gone missing under mysterious and, dare I say, murderous circumstances to have a hope of enjoying a moment alone," Quinn said, matter-of-factly.

I winced. *So he* does *know about Eurie.* Somehow, that did not feel reassuring.

Gloria shook her head. "This is starting to feel a lot less maze-consultant-gardenery."

"Did I say I was a gardener?" Quinn's bland expression

stretched into a wide smile, as though this was truly amusing.

"I've got it!" Saki burst. Without waiting for us to inquire curiously, she stepped forward, pointing one finger at Quinn. "I *knew* I'd seen you before. You were on the front page of the newspaper at the air station!"

Quinn shrugged one shoulder. "An occupational hazard I do my best to avoid."

"What *is* your occupation?" I asked, though I had a feeling I wouldn't like the answer.

And in the end, Quinn did not provide one. Sakura answered for him. "He's a local private detective!"

11

A Little Tea Can't Fix

Gloria reeled. "Just what exactly are you investigating?"

"If we're being accurate," said Quinn, looking only very faintly abashed, "I am *the* private detective on the island—Helenia, that is. Until you and your friends showed up," he told me, rather graciously. But the gesture left me cold, wondering, *Does he actually know who we are? How could he?*

"But I only began this line of work in the past year," he went on. "Before that I was an inventor of some little repute, and it was in that capacity that Edda engaged me to work on the maze. Perhaps you'd like to ask her about it yourself?"

The fact that *he* had to remind us of our actual purpose in the labyrinth only made me more annoyed at him. But still, he was right. I strongly suspected he made a habit of that.

"One thing at a time," I reminded Gloria, grudgingly. She nodded.

Quinn, too, nodded, and began walking forward once more.

We followed at a more leisurely pace. Sakura was still obviously displeased, and I was just gearing up to ask her what her thoughts were when we rounded yet another corner and the maze opened up.

We weren't outside it—no, the walls still surrounded us. But they stretched out to encircle a clearing as big as our rental villa. Roses had been planted around the clearing's edges, and in the center, a stone patio was topped with a deep red, fringed canopy. Under that canopy, at a small tea table, two people sat—and judging by her long skirt, one of them was definitely Edda.

The other, I hadn't seen before, around town or in the garden. Nonetheless, Quinn strode up to them with easy familiarity.

"Edda," he said, as we got closer, "your staff missed your lunchtime 'Container Gardens' presentation. They even went so far as to enlist some guests to look for you."

"We weren't enlisted, exactly," I hastened to add, worried suddenly for Medu's future. "We just offered to help. We tend to—do things like that. We didn't realize we'd be bothering you."

"My stars!" Edda cried, lifting the back of her hand to her forehead. "Was that today? I forgot all about it. And now I've disappointed all our guests!"

I stopped short at the edge of the patio, glancing surreptitiously at the others. Gloria was frowning again, and Sakura was obviously scoping the entire place out. Quinn looked completely impassive. Either he had a great poker face, or this was something Edda did a lot.

I was willing to bet both were true. On closer inspection, Edda's long white skirt turned out to be a drapey, gauzy dress, like four sets of sheer curtains gathered together and thrown over her shoulders before being tied round the middle.

She had Ida's golden hair, but hers was impossibly long and piled atop her head in a massive bun, from which artful curls escaped to frame her wide blue eyes—and possibly obscure the slight wrinkles which framed said eyes. A wide gold necklace performed the same function for the flushed, pale skin around her neck. She was a solid lady—the drapery of her dress didn't hide that—and she was acting like the merest wind would knock her over.

And where her daughter had blended in well with other locals and tourists in a popular bar, Edda had clearly chosen to stand out.

"You poor dears," she went on, addressing myself and my friends. "You were hoping to learn about gardening? How you must look down on me for missing the appointment! But the simple truth is, I've been so overwhelmed that I completely forgot!"

I almost wished Thorn had come along with me instead of Saki and Gloria in that moment. Of all the residents of Belville I could have traveled with, these two were perhaps the *least* likely to respond patiently to such a performance. Officer Thorn at least had her training to fall back on.

I cleared my throat. "Uh, actually, we were mostly just worried about you. We didn't mean to come across as—dramatic."

I hadn't *meant* to give the word emphasis, but it would have taken someone much more diplomatic than I to manage it. Distinctly, I saw the corner of Quinn's mouth quirk up.

And now, I added silently, *I think I see where Ida gets it from.*

Edda had either not noticed a thing, or didn't care in the least. She continued, "I can't *believe* I scheduled our tea for the same time as a presentation, Hestia. Normally I am so much better than that. Normally, I have Ida to help me—"

While Edda broke off into a literal sob, which sounded quite dry, I glanced at her companion. *Hestia?* The name rang faintly of local folklore. Perhaps I'd read it in a guidebook. But this Hestia was very real. She looked to be sheepkin, with rounded ears poking out of a curly mass of hair cropped close to her head. The tips of the curls were black, but the roots were gray. She wore large round glasses that all but obscured her olive face, and though they had a tea laid out in front of them, she was clutching a file folder almost as big as her torso. Hiding behind it, perhaps? She had to be half Edda's size. They made an odd pair.

Neither Hestia nor Quinn made any move to speak, and Edda kept talking, now solely addressing me. "Town hall wants me to agree to be advisor on botanical matters. But how can I even think of it? You've heard, I suppose? My daughter is missing! My *only* daughter. Presumed—oh! I can't say it. It's too much to bear. But I couldn't let the Garden go on without me."

I looked at Quinn again. I hadn't heard anything about Ida being presumed dead, but then again, if only Herc knew her whereabouts, perhaps the rest of the police force wasn't optimistic. Still—wasn't it strange, to leap to such a drastic conclusion?

It was hard to tell, but Quinn seemed to be clenching his jaw. He finally spoke again. "Edda, if you are *quite* well, perhaps my new friends and I should return to the conservatory, to call off the search."

"Heartless! That's what he is," said Edda to me. Looking back at him, she added, "Won't you introduce us first?"

Gloria stirred at my side. "There's really no need."

But on my other side, Quinn's eyes had taken on an odd glint, just for a moment. He smirked directly at me. "Certainly. Edda, please meet—in order—Sakura, owner of the Pomegranate Café, Gloria of Hair and Beauty, and renowned alchemist Cinnabar Sunset, who would no doubt prefer you to address her as Red. They have achieved a measure of fame," he said, each word deliberate and terrible, "for aiding the police in solving crime."

Not a single person was looking at Edda. Gloria's fists were clenched so tight I half expected her to burst into flame. Saki had almost stepped out of line to interrupt him. And Quinn was still regarding me with that insufferable smile.

Had William been present, the man would have found himself pulverized by approximately one ton of angry magical dog.

"An alchemist! And detectives!" Edda cried, clapping her hands. It wasn't correct, but it was enough to reclaim everyone's attention. "My stars, how *perfect*! This is fate. You have to help me. Please—aren't you moved in the slightest by a mother who spares nothing to search every length of Beyond for her daughter?"

Gloria snorted. Her resolve was clearly wearing dangerously thin.

"We're on vacation," I said, my voice strangled.

"You were *drawn here* to investigate," Edda corrected.

"Shortly *before* the disappearance took place," Quinn noted wryly under his breath.

I contemplated kicking him.

"We really couldn't interfere," said Saki, sounding much more resolved than I did.

"Not to worry!" cried Edda. "You'll have Quinn to guide

you. He can tell you everything you need. Can't you, Quinn dear?"

One look at his face and now I was contemplating laughing at him. Vengefully.

"There's no need. We're on vacation," Gloria said, echoing my words in a much less apologetic tone.

"Why doesn't Quinn just solve it himself?" Sakura added, her voice innocent and saccharine.

"He's not so good with disappearances," Edda said airily. Quinn sidled for the first time. But he said nothing, and she was already continuing, "You girls are exactly what we need. Someone to *understand* her. You'll be able to relate to my Ida. Quinn simply can't."

I glanced down the line at my friends. Should we simply tell this woman no and walk away? She was certainly rude enough. But on the other hand—

—she was, in a way, right without knowing it. Without knowing a single thing . . .

In a flash, I saw the use in this ridiculous situation. "Edda," I said, firmly, "the truth is we wouldn't be allowed to take on another case. It's very bad practice. Because we already have an investigation going . . . into Eurydice's death."

Edda blinked at me. I wasn't sure if my attempt at vague, arbitrary legalese was going to go over, but that wasn't my primary concern. What I really wanted was to see her reaction to Eurie's name.

And here she was looking at me like she'd never heard it before.

For the very first time, Hestia stirred. "These are all *local* matters," she said. "Not something tourists would understand, anyhow."

Edda regained her speech. "Hestia, dear, I *told* you, Ida's abduction isn't related to the others. That's a totally different affair. Now, girls, I'm so *glad* you're looking into poor Eurie's death. Someone has to. We have to know for sure if she did it herself, right? But surely that won't take all your time. And you might still want Quinn, mightn't you?"

I glanced at the man in question. *What is he, her personal assistant? Why does she keep offering to foist him on us?*

"The two could be related," Edda added, leaning forward. "Have you thought of that?"

"We've thought that Ida might have done Eurie in," Gloria said bluntly.

Inwardly, I groaned.

But Edda took it in stride. "It's so true! Terrible, but true! You can't imagine the throes of doubt and worry I've seen as a mother. Ida's been so awfully *distant* lately. I'm worried her head's been turned. She's fallen into a terrible crowd. She needs to be found and taken into custody, for her own safety!"

Before Gloria could switch sides and chew Edda out for being so callous about her daughter—because I knew full well she was going to—I jumped in. "What do you mean, 'a terrible crowd'?"

"Do you know," said Edda, her wide eyes opened to their fullest, "I don't have a clue how it happened, but she's in close contact with *Marcus Antoine Pluto!*"

She said it like it was a curse and a shock, but we'd already heard his name before. My friends and I glanced between ourselves, unimpressed.

"He's the leader of the underground market in magical artifacts," Hestia told us, a bit huffily. As though our ignorance was a personal affront. "Town hall's been trying to get him for years, but we can't ever pin anything on him."

I glanced at her with more interest. *Is she part of the local government, then?*

Saki crossed her arms. "I've yet to see what's so scandalous about this unsanctioned trade." Apparently, it was her turn to lose her temper. And while I personally thought that the "scandalous" part might depend a great deal on *what* he was trading, not to mention how he procured it, I was even more interested to see Hestia stiffen and clutch at her folder.

"My dear, you don't *know* him! But nobody does," said Edda quickly. "Except his *gang members.* They want to take over the island! *Most* unsavory. Who knows what he made my Ida do?"

"Go home," Gloria muttered under her breath, "which, it turns out, *is* pretty unsavory."

Fortunately, only I heard that particular comment.

<h1 style="text-align:center">12</h1>

<h1 style="text-align:center">Allies, and Worse</h1>

By the time we'd extricated ourselves from Edda and Hestia, I didn't have the heart to suggest we see the rest of the garden. Gloria looked more like a storm cloud than ever, and I judged that Sakura was just as likely to start some kind of tax payers' rebellion as she was to continue asking sly questions about Ida and Eurie.

"Your tickets are good for two more days' entry," Quinn said tactfully as he escorted us out of the maze.

Gloria was having none of it. As soon as we emerged onto the grassy moat around the maze walls, she rounded on him. "You just got us involved, and now you want us out of here?"

"Who do you think you are?" Saki added, hands on her hips.

He looked at me, and I crossed my arms. "What they said. What *was* that back there?"

For a moment he paused, like he was considering his options. Then he looked up with that quirked-up smile and another half-shrug. "I didn't want you to walk away under the misapprehension that I don't know who you are."

"More like you wanted *us* to investigate for her rather than you," Gloria declared. "But too bad. We're not."

"How *do* you know who we are?" I asked, more curiously. Fortunately, the afternoon was hot and no other visitors seemed interested in going in or out of the maze.

"Modesty may be a virtue, but surely you're not unaware of public interest in your cases," Quinn said, now fully smiling. The monotone, even hedge behind his head just made him stand out more from our surroundings. It was strange to think we'd ever thought he was a gardener.

"*All* of us?" Saki asked. "We've *all* been in the papers?"

Gloria glowered. "I'm going to talk to Leo the moment we get home."

"The tenacity of *Belville & Beyond's* local reporter is, ah, commendable," Quinn said, with a polite but amused cough. "I followed her reports of your investigation into a cold case last fall with great interest."

"But most of her articles stay local. Do you read *all* the papers in Beyond?" I couldn't fathom how he had the time. But Quinn was smiling like a sphinx, unlikely to give a straight (and non-annoying) answer, so I shook my head and moved on to other matters. "Well, anyway, you have all your answers about who we are and why we're interested. Why are *you* interested? Are you really investigating on Edda's behalf?"

At that, his face clouded. "I have various professional interests in the case."

"And personal ones." Whatever the moment of weakness was, Saki had seen it. She leaned in, that too-familiar gleam of *I know you're trying to hide something but I can see it!* in her eyes. "So who disappeared before?"

Quinn's mouth pressed into a firm line. He didn't even try to hide the fact that he wasn't going to answer her. "Shall I accompany you back to the ferry landing?"

***

Predictably, Saki was still pondering the question when we went out for dinner that evening.

Gloria had taken over as Ida's companion, and the two remained in our villa with all our café leftovers and, rather unexpectedly, some black nail polish. Not that it was surprising that Gloria had brought some with her—her nails were always perfect, and *always* black—but I found it cute that she was now willing to get to know Ida. I was very curious to know what would come out of that conversation.

However, that meant that Thorn was now our third party, and she was even less interested in Quinn than Gloria had been.

"We'll ask Herc," she said. "He'll be sure to know about any investigators on the island." And as far as she was concerned, that was that.

This evening we'd walked down almost to the harbor level, and all the way across town, in search of a hole-in-the-wall restaurant Saki had demanded we try. It was famous, she insisted, though no one else had ever heard of it. (Then again, Quinn's familiarity with all three of us had undermined my idea of fame!) It was also tiny. In fact, it was as if someone had seen an alley between two villas and decided, *perfect!* And then proceeded to install an oven and build a roof over the neighbors' walls. Between the cobblestones, the floor was actually grassy. No windows lined the brick walls, which had long ago lost their white-washed brightness. It was dark, and close, and it smelled divinely of garlic and rosemary. After an interrupted lunch and a tea time spent rehashing the days' events for Thorn, I was dying to eat.

Fortunately, we'd managed to get a table at the back before some live musicians—and all their entourage—filled the front of the restaurant.

"I still think it could have to do with the case," Saki said, raising her voice over the musicians warming up.

"Then we'll find out about it in due time," Thorn insisted. She glanced across the little round table at me, shaking her head. "These deputies of yours! Distracted by every new thing!"

"That's *Gloria*," said Saki primly.

I laughed. "Nobody's a deputy here, remember. For as annoying as Quinn was, it's probably a good thing he's looking into the murder too. Did Herc have anything new to say?"

Thorn leaned her elbow on the table and her chin in her hand, making our utensils slide in her direction. Saki rescued her iced lemonade and held it close to her chest. "He only stopped by once. Said he'd told the boyfriend and got his alibi, but needed some help figuring out how to check it out without letting everyone know what he was up to."

"Couldn't he just not tell whoever's asking?" Saki asked, her white eyebrows scrunched. "After all, he *is* a police officer protecting an investigation."

"It was a little more complicated than that. Turns out, the boyfriend was playing a private party on a yacht in the harbor—some bigwig event. Which," Thorn went on, pointedly eyeing Saki, "your friend Pluto was at. Sounds like nobody got back to dry land until dawn."

"He's not *my* friend," Sakura said easily. "He's Ida's. So her mother thinks, anyway. What did you make of that, Red?"

I had given this thought and had an answer ready. "I'd guess that Ida keeps that business card in her pocket all the time. It certainly looked worn enough. Seems most likely to me that her mother found it there—nothing more. Ida certainly doesn't seem to have any political agenda or antipathy, so I doubt she's actually been inducted into some kind of 'gang.' She wouldn't be able to keep something like that down, would she? I mean, we've been with her constantly."

"More than that, she *wants* us to be," Saki added, agreeing. "I thought it was all nonsense, myself."

"Going through another adult's pockets?" Thorn tugged at her pointy ear, a clear sign that she wasn't liking what she heard.

"Could have been while getting the clothes ready for laundry," I said, to be fair. But then I thought of the fineness of Edda's accessories. "Or, maybe not. I suspect someone else does the housework."

"Let's make a list," Saki said brightly. She sat up in her chair and pulled out a little notepad and pen from her purse. Both were adorned with some sort of pink, poofy material. Thorn's eyebrows were almost lost in her hairline, and I grinned to myself as Saki went on, "Known people in Ida's life—her mother, most likely some kind of staff, the gardeners, Eurie, and Pluto. Known people in Eurie's life—Ida, the gardeners, the boyfriend, family—?"

She glanced at Thorn, who leaned in. "Raffael is the boyfriend's name. Family is from a remote town on the other side of the island—mother passed away, but there's a brother and father remaining. They're on their way to town now to make arrangements."

"She was living on her own," I put in. "Since Ida was planning to move in with her. Right?"

Thorn nodded. "Turns out, though, that she had some high-powered friends. Ida was telling me today she did some commissions for town hall, murals and the like. One of her contacts there, a young secretary named Wharton, is one of the people who has disappeared."

"What?" Saki put down her pen, her blue eyes round as saucers. "You waited to tell us that until *now?*"

"She's also been found out lying at work," Thorn added, smug.

"*About* her work, you mean?" I frowned, even as our food arrived and we all had to lean back to make room for plates and bowls of shareable pasta, chopped veggies, and grill-charred cheese. It smelled heavenly.

But Thorn wasn't distracted. "No, not about her art. Ida let it slip that sometimes Eurie would lie for her—telling her mother she was busy when she was trying to get out alone, that kind of thing. Ida insists Eurie never minded, but it sounds like it was giving Eurie a certain shifty reputation around the garden."

"I can imagine Edda wouldn't react well to it," Saki admitted, exchanging her pen for a fork. "But does that explain everyone else? Like Medu? He seemed to have some other problem with her. He mentioned politics."

"That I don't know. Ida showed no interest in current events—aside from her own." Thorn took a bite of cheese and closed her eyes in blissful appreciation.

I had to agree with her, having just finished my own first bite of pasta. "I think all we can say for sure, Saki, is that you definitely made the right choice about where to come for dinner."

Around a forkful of cucumber and tomato, Sakura beamed.

As we fell silent, eating to our hearts' content, the restaurant noise filtered into my awareness. The musicians turned out to be a singer with a guitar along with a drummer and a bass player in the background. They finished a sad ballad to great applause. Another voice took over, yelling to the crowd that Orpheus would now take a short break before playing again.

Funny, I thought. *That's another name I've heard before.* It wasn't odd for folkloric names to hang around in a certain region, of course: they were often family names, or even considered lucky by local communities. But this one felt like it had come up recently. I just couldn't remember why . . .

And with my head down in my plate, I missed the gleam in Sakura's eye.

"Oh, excuse me!" she called. I looked up to see she'd addressed a young man walking past. "I just wanted to say, you're an excellent singer."

"Hey, thanks, that's really nice of you," the man said, slowing down. He had wavy brown hair that anyone might envy, with just the tips of elvish ears poking through. His voice, warm and melodic, did sound like the singing I'd just heard. I watched Saki, surprised.

"You must know lots of people in the music scene around here, right?" she went on. "It's just, we were looking for someone. Do you know Raffael?"

The man shifted back on one heel. His eyes, one gold and one brown, caught a shaft of light from the sconces on the walls. "But, that's me. You're looking for me?"

"It's you?" I looked at him with more interest. *How in Beyond did Saki do that?* It was as if she had conjured up a witness for us. "I thought the announcer said your name was Orpheus."

"That's my band's name," he said, one hand in front of his dark tunic, as though he was missing his guitar. "I started using it in honor of my girlfriend. Her name is—was—Eurydice."

13

A Ballad of Woe

Officer Thorn was now fully engaged, too, though her back was to our visitor. She turned to talk over her shoulder. "How are those connected?"

"Oh, you haven't heard the story?" Raffael ran his hand through his hair, then sighed. He grabbed the nearest free chair—actually a stool which had been propping open the back door—and pulled it up to our table, and sat. "Orpheus and Eurydice were these amazing lovers, a long time ago. They had the most beautiful wedding, the kind where *everyone* was there. But on that day, somebody poisoned Eurydice and took her from Orpheus, so . . . he went into the realms of the dead to free her."

His eyes were cast down, a fact accentuated by his long lashes. His voice had become distinctly melancholy. I cleared my throat. "I'm sorry—we didn't mean to bring up unpleasant things."

"No, no, it's good to talk about it. That's how I figure it all out, by putting it into words," he said, offering us all a faint, helpless smile through the shadow. "You knew Eurie?"

"We met her a few nights ago," Saki said. "That's why we were looking for you. Just to say, we're thinking of you. It was awful when we heard the news."

"It's hard," he replied honestly. "I wanted to take some time off, you know, just—feel it. But I've got to keep paying the bills, and I have my bandmates to look after. And in this town, if you're not playing every night, they forget all about you. It's a rough business. You have to spend money to make it, they say—and if you haven't got money, you've got to spend your time."

I didn't know much about the music world, but the picture he painted did seem grueling. I hesitated, feeling pretty terrible for him.

But Officer Thorn clearly did not. "Did you hear they've connected it to Pluto somehow?"

"I did hear that, yeah," Raffael said, nodding. "It's not what I would have expected, but, it kind of makes sense."

"Why wouldn't you have expected it?" Saki asked, leaning in, her dinner forgotten.

"I wasn't really sure they knew each other," he offered. "I mean, a lot of high-up people know *of* Eurie, because of her art, but she's kind of reclusive, you know? Or—she was. And of course everyone's heard of Pluto, but no one usually *sees* him. The police officer said there was some kind of connection through Ida, though, which makes sense. Eurie was really protective of Ida and, like, involved in her life. So she could definitely know him that way."

The more I watched him, the more Raffael really did seem miserable. But it didn't show up in his words: it was small things, like the slump in his shoulders and the deep circles under his eyes. Things that wouldn't impact an artist's performance, I supposed. Still, he was giving us a lot of information. Ida had been practically incoherent when she heard the news—though, granted, Raffael had had a day to ponder it all. Even so, I decided to ask, "How long had you and Eurie been dating?"

"Just a few months," he said. "Since summer started. I thought I was so lucky when she agreed to go out with me. And I was—she was an amazing person. Beautiful inside and out."

Hmm. A few months wasn't very long. I couldn't help but think of Luca—at this point, we'd been best friends for years. If he was suddenly gone, I wasn't sure how my world would keep going. But maybe the newness of the relationship explained why Raffael was alright talking about it.

Saki chatted to him for a few minutes about his music, and then it was time for him to get back on stage. Thorn turned to watch him go thoughtfully, sticking a massive forkful of twisted pasta in her mouth.

"Most people murdered are done in by their partner," she said as she chewed.

"True, but a partner of three months?" Saki was quite pragmatic about the dangers of love—especially given her reputation as a matchmaker back in Belville.

"Somehow, we always end up investigating the ones that aren't," I added.

Thorn swallowed and was already ready to take another bite, but she paused to grin. "That's 'cause they only call you in for the contrary ones, Red."

I rolled my eyes, but she didn't deter me from asking my real question. "Saki, did you *know* he was going to be here? Is that why you wanted to come?"

"I wanted to come because they have the best garlic sauce on the island," Sakura replied, innocently swirling her glass so that the ice cubes clinked. Then she grinned mischievously. "And because I knew that, as a true tourist trap, they'd be sure to have live music. I honestly thought we could just ask the musician to lead us to the boyfriend—I didn't think he would *be* the boyfriend."

"Must be a pretty good gig, playing here," I mused. Maybe that also explained why Raffael hadn't wanted to give it up.

"The kind of thing musicians might kill for," Saki agreed. Then she stuck out her tongue at Thorn's startled reaction. "What? Just a turn of phrase. It's impossible to *completely* stop being morbid at the drop of a hat, you know."

"Yes, it is, if you're respectful." As though Thorn knew we were silently counting up all the puns and in-poor-taste comments she'd made throughout her career investigating crimes, she hurried on. "Funny how willing he was to think Pluto did it, if they both have the same alibi, eh?"

"Sounds to me like everyone thinks Pluto would be the one to *hire* someone to do it," I suggested, over another bite of cheese.

"And hire them also to take a person to his house, just so he can ineffectively deliver her home later?" Thorn shook her head.

"Maybe his hired help is not very smart," I said, now invested in this idea. "Or maybe he was trying to make some kind of impression on her. Maybe Eurie was in the way."

"Maybe we can find out tomorrow," Sakura interrupted, in her most singsong, smug voice.

Officer Thorn paused, her drink midway to her mouth. "You have another restaurant idea? Is it as good as this one?"

105

"Even better, but no," Saki said, beaming. "I've got an appointment with him tomorrow morning to look at some *very* expensive magical goods. Now, aren't you glad you brought a shadow witch along?"

* * *

"Okay, seriously," I said, the next morning. "You're going to have to walk me through this. *How?* And—what are we going to tell him?"

Saki beamed, stretching her hands over her head in a gesture of satisfaction as we set out from the villa. She'd positively refused to tell us anything else about her meeting with Pluto while Officer Thorn was around. She hadn't even allowed Thorn to come—on the basis that even an on-vacation police officer "acted too much like a police officer," and we all had to admit she was right on that score. It had worked out well, anyway. Thorn was watching Ida and waiting for Herc's now-daily report while Gloria took another hike above town. She had my mirror so that she could reach Luca, at least, in case she needed help. None of us were particularly good at carefree travel any more.

Except, of course, Sakura. She looked pleased as a cat, and she was wearing her fluffiest skirt—a mess of white tulle and deep blue flowers that matched the tiny hat perched on her gleaming hair. Not exactly an outfit that screamed *I'm going to meet with a lord of the underground*, but perhaps that was the point.

"It starts with when we got here," she said, strolling down the lane past other villas like she'd grown up here. "When you travel, as a magic practitioner, you usually let the authorities where you're going know who you are and what you can do. Isn't there something like that for alchemists?"

"No, though I did have a bit of a fight this time," I admitted. *About tariffs. On botanicals.* Suddenly, that conversation was making more sense, in light of what else we'd heard about local politics. But I set that aside for now. "It's not a bad idea though. Unless it's some kind of weird tracking thing?"

"Oh, no," Saki said lightly. "Usually, it's Witches traveling, you know, and they're only too glad to help out other Witches or meet up and have tea parties or whatever it is that they do." Leaving aside the fact that she was making fun of official Witches for doing precisely the kind of harmless thing it was her actual job to do, Saki went on. "It does get a *little* uncomfortable sometimes, as someone whose training was . . . less *sanctioned,* but when we got here they basically just waved me through. I was a bit surprised, honestly, but of course now I see why. I wonder," she added impishly, "how much of their tourist trade Pluto is responsible for? And meanwhile they're trying to arrest him!"

"Not very hard, or not very well, apparently," I commented.

"True. Well, anyway, from what we've heard, I was certain he or his company was monitoring those records somehow. And I was right! I stepped out yesterday afternoon and did a little scrying, and with basically no trouble at all I was talking to one of his secretaries."

I was amused to think of a secretary "scrying," that is, using a reflective surface to magically "see" someone or somewhere else. It wasn't too different from my mirror, in fact, except that Saki as a witch was able to search for whatever she wanted to see, rather than simply connect with a paired object. "Okay, points for initiative," I said. "Dubious points, mind you, since it does mean we're going to somebody's lair."

"Ida went and she was fine," Saki said, tossing her head.

"He obviously likes her though," I pointed out.

"Obviously," the incurably romantic witch agreed. "And who's to say that where Ida went was actually his house? She didn't even see the inside. It could have been some strange set up, like you were saying last night. That's why I did it this way. I thought of doing a tracing spell on his business card, but eventually decided this way would be better to avoid any traps."

"Plus, if it *was* his house and you traced it, it'd be harder to explain why we just showed up there," I admitted. "Alright. You've thought this through. So what are we looking at?"

"Thaumaturgy," Saki said, grinning at me.

"Ugh." She had me. Thaumaturgy was a very old form of magic—a form of magic which often relied on alchemical methods to create spells, or what might be called "miracles." It was a high-stakes practice that tended to be a little dangerous and extremely fascinating. I couldn't say no now. Sakura had apparently thought of *everything*.

"And that's why you're my business partner," she confirmed, cheerfully. "And before you ask, yes, I am actually quite interested in making a purchase. *If* he has something I like. But I had to be sure to request something unique enough that he would be the one we dealt with."

"Sakura," I interrupted, ducking as we passed beneath a branch that hung low over the road, "it's all very well and good to be a shadow witch, or interested in thaumaturgy. But have you thought about the fact that he might be an 'underground' dealer because his methods are truly unsavory? What if the artifacts are stolen, or counterfeit? What if you end up involved in—or supporting—a really unethical business?"

"I can handle myself, and so can you," Saki said confidently. "And if you have any other doubts, I suggest you keep them to yourself."

"What? Why?" I was confused—she had never been the kind of friend who didn't want to talk something over.

"Because, silly," she said, turning in the street, "we're here."

"*What?*" I glanced up and down the road. It looked exactly like our neighborhood, which we had barely left. The house in front of us could have been a carbon copy of all the others. White wall, wire gate hung with vines, a tiled roof clearly visible beyond. It was nice, don't get me wrong, but it was nowhere near the opulence Ida had described. And it was also definitely not a business or a store. It looked like somebody's aunt lived there. And besides—we hadn't been walking very long at all. "You're telling me he's *right down the road?*"

Sakura laughed. "Did you really think I was going to take you traipsing all over town again, after last night?"

She stepped toward the gate and, as I watched, speechless, placed her hand on the bell that was set on one side. Indigo magic flared, then black. The gate swung inward. Saki stepped one shiny black shoe through. Both shoe and white stocking disappeared.

Looking over her shoulder, she winked at me. "If you're coming too, then you better come quick."

14

Going Underground

The little tiled roof and mess of vines were gone immediately. The actual house loomed over us, even from a distance, and the garden was *exactly* as Ida had described. So much so that I almost mentioned it to Sakura. *Wow, these carefully pruned trees and fancy water fountains are just like Ida said! Wonder if we'll find the unicorn?* But fortunately, at the last minute, I thought better of it and shut my mouth. If Pluto was so concerned about safety he had a magical glamour spell hiding his entire house, he probably had some kind of listening spell in his garden.

I had to admit, though, as eerie as it was walking deeper into an estate which I knew no one outside could find, I had to admire his style. Where better to hide something than right in the middle of an innocent neighborhood?

The path from the gate was wide marble tiles, and it led down in small, graceful steps toward the front door. We crossed a little creek running over smooth black stones. *Is the air growing colder, or is it just me?* Saki was in front, so I couldn't check her expression. She was focused on the house,

110

which to my non-magical view was obscured behind tall white columns.

When we stepped between the two nearest columns, we were on a porch of sorts that wrapped around the house. It seemed far too elegant to be called a porch. The door was just ahead, in deep shadow, and beside it sat a statue of a dog, so realistic I could almost imagine the stone breathing.

"Aren't you the cutest thing," Sakura said to it. She reached out, a little sparkle around her fingertips, and booped its smooth nose. "I hope your name isn't Cerberus. You ought to get your own identity."

To my amazement, the stone guard dog blinked. Its carved, foreboding expression became one of puppy-like adoration. When its tail wagged, I half expected the stone to crack.

"Her name is Flora." It wasn't the dog who spoke, but the voice was so ponderous and deep that for a moment I might have believed it was. Instead, a person appeared out of the shadow to our left. There was no question in my mind that this was Pluto.

"Much better," Saki said, now scratching Flora behind her floppy stone ears. As though all of this was entirely normal. I stuck my own hands deep in my pockets and did my best to keep my cool.

"She thinks so." For a fleeting moment, Marcus Antoine Pluto smiled. When he did, he looked rather sweet—like someone tourists such as ourselves might encounter in a museum telling meaningful tales, or behind a bar serving up soulful drinks. But then he slipped back into his initial, probably habitual, countenance. Now that my eyes were adjusted to the shadow, it was easier to see him. But he wasn't trying to make it easy—that much was certain.

His skin was slate gray, much like Flora's stone. He was wearing a black silk shirt and black trousers, and something else—something almost like a second skin of magic. It shimmered over him constantly, like he was under a very thin film of water. His eyes were dark and his features sharp, set into an impassive mask, but other than that, it was difficult to describe him. But the tone of his voice was distinctive. "Forgive me if I startled you," he went on. "It amuses me to see how new guests respond to my garden."

He didn't look remotely amused. But Sakura did. She was perhaps two feet shorter than him, and she looked up with a careless grin. "Very nice, but it's all rather *on the nose*, don't you think?"

He moved a little bit, shifting on his feet. His hands, I realized, were clasped behind his back. "I have found it is best to be comfortable."

The way these two were going, between Saki's playing with the dog and Pluto's slow-moving speech, we were going to be here for a year. And I had things to do. Eurie's murder wasn't going to solve itself. But even so—something told me that any bit of rudeness would be a *very* bad idea.

"Of course," said Saki. "We're all drawn to what we like. Flowers, dogs . . . streams that remind us of the river of the dead . . ."

"Thaumaturgy," Pluto added, still entirely straight-faced. "Yes. Though your friend has scruples." He shifted to face me directly. "Do you still think I might have stolen my wares?"

Ack. Maybe when Ida had met him on a hillside he seemed friendly, but here, on his own turf, in deep shadow, with a magical stone guard dog nearby, his presence was overwhelming. *Just how much of us talking did he overhear?* "Erm, well," I scrambled to collect my thoughts, "to be fair, I haven't seen them yet."

"You seek to judge for yourself." He turned to Sakura. "Come inside."

Then the door swung open for him and he simply began walking away.

In the brief second we had alone, I made a face at Saki. She laughed silently and waved my disbelief away with one hand. Flora the stone dog stayed mournfully in place as Sakura turned to follow our host. As I followed, I did my best not to act like I was skirting past what seemed like a very friendly pup. I'd seen William pounce on enough people to know that appearances could be deceiving.

The inside of the house was, predictably, dark. Not because of some architectural oversight or necessity—it was clearly by choice. We turned this way and that through doorway and hall, every space as shadowy as the last. Perhaps he didn't want us to see what was there, or find our way out again? It wasn't a comforting thought. *Maybe,* I told myself instead, *it's just been a really long time since he dusted, and he doesn't want his guests to know.*

There was also no sign of anyone else present, even though Saki had said she'd dealt with a secretary. The place was silent, not at all like a hub of magical trade. It felt like we were simply walking through room after room of impenetrable empty space.

And then, abruptly, we were in a long room. There was torchlight here—or what I strongly suspected was *magical* torchlight. Enough that we could make out bookshelves lining the walls, disappearing into the gloom above us, and the shadows of desks and chairs. The thick carpet swallowed up every footstep. It might have been a library or a study, in a normal house. Apparently, Pluto had *very* good vision in the dark.

"Here." He made some gesture I couldn't follow, and a lamp on a nearby table illuminated the space around us. On the table an indigo velvet cloth had been laid, and on that cloth was a collection of glass bottles, wire contraptions, a cauldron, and a tome or two—all dusty and fractured with age.

It was all I could do not to immediately pick up the nearest bottle.

Sakura, fortunately, was more circumspect. She looked up at Pluto. "I suppose you allow others' magic here?"

"In this room, yes," he said, inclining his head.

Saki lifted her hand, and the nearest bottle rose, held aloft by black sparkles much as she had been cushioned while floating up the mountain a few days ago. She let it drift closer to us and trapped it between her hands, still not touching it, but concentrating on it in such a way that I was reminded of William working his protection spells. More black sparkles flared around her bobbed hair and in her eyes. After a tense moment, she grinned and levitated the bottle to me.

"Cool." I caught it in my gloved hands, my goggles already in place. Though my glass lenses couldn't do everything Saki could, they *did* show me faint magical auras, as well as magnifications of the bottle's scarred surface. It was a unique shape and had obviously been through a lot of experimentation, leaving it with physical marks and a faint purple hue, but that was all I could tell by mere sight. I glanced up at Saki. "Can you do that on one of the books?"

She laughed and looked at Pluto. "You don't mind?"

"Please." He remained impassive, watching us from the edge

of the circle of light.

Sakura repeated the process with one book, and then another. One was a handwritten journal of spells and experiments—the other a reference book from centuries ago. Having set the bottle gingerly back on the table, I juggled the books to look inside their front covers before doing anything else. They both had the same name scribbled on the upper left corner in faded, spidery ink. *Hermes Trismegistus.*

Much as I was trying to be Sakura's unobtrusive, level-headed assistant in this particular endeavor, I couldn't contain my amazement. I looked back at Pluto with my jaw practically on the floor.

"It can hardly be a surprise," he said. "Why else would an alchemist such as yourself be in Helenia, if not to look for relics from your profession's past?"

"I—I'm not a collector," I admitted, shaken into honesty. "When Sakura suggested thaumaturgy, I didn't think—I thought maybe, a few antique baubles that have come down through the years—not—"

"Neither am I a collector. I do not care for baubles," Pluto said, supremely unimpressed as my words ran out. He shifted to face Sakura. "*You* know."

"I do, but I like confirmation from time to time," she replied lightly. She turned back to me. "Red, he isn't just named *after* Pluto. This *is* Pluto. So you can return home saying you've met another deity now—other than our meddlesome friend at the Pomegranate Café, that is."

To buy myself a moment, I stared at the handwriting—*the handwriting of Hermes the Great!*—on the page in my hands, not reading it but thinking furiously. Sakura calling anyone else "meddlesome" was a laugh, but I knew the person she was referring to—Hunter, a roving nature deity who had recently settled in town. Until he'd shown up, I hadn't thought much about the concept. But just like there were characters and creatures in old folktales, there were many, many deities: some elusive and evasive, like Hunter, while others were involved and downright terrifying. Some still had active temples and followers, while others opted for a quiet life or let their titles slip away. Ida was named for a goddess, but from her age and limited sense of self-worth, it had seemed pretty clear that she might have divine blood but was not herself divine—not in the *I have a house no one can find, I knew one of your philosophical heroes personally, and now I show off relics from past ages like it's nothing* sort of way.

Nor the *I once ruled death and the Underworld* sort of way, either. I gulped. My understanding of divine power was limited: it was something more often studied by priests and sorcerers, not alchemists. *I hope Saki knows what she's doing . .*
.

As if on cue, she laid a hand over mine reassuringly. Addressing Pluto once more, she said, "Why bother selling things?"

When I looked up, Pluto was watching me. He seemed to shimmer. "I enjoy it when these old memories go to new homes. The right homes."

"And why bother with other names?" Saki pressed.

"To live a long life is to accumulate many." Pluto looked at her thoughtfully. "You mean to ask, why hide."

"That *is* what I asked," she retorted. "You just didn't answer directly the first time."

Pluto continued to think about this for a moment. "It's in my nature."

"Seriously?" I couldn't stay quiet any more. "That's all?

That's it? Everyone's running around thinking you run an illicit market and you're some kind of crime lord and you had your girlfriend abducted, and all you can say is, you like streams in your garden and having old stuff? If that's the case then why do you sound so sad all the time?"

From a deep pocket of shadow nearby, there came a familiar—and highly annoying—laugh.

15

Falling from the Sky

Quinn Doyle stepped into our circle of light. Just the look on his face had me thinking of hitting him over the head with a tome.

But the tome I was holding *had literally been written by Hermes the Great,* so I thought better of it.

"Aren't you going to answer?" Quinn asked Pluto, standing with his hands in his pockets behind the table of thaumaturgical goods. He'd left behind his straw hat and his vest and trousers today seemed to be gray—it was hard to tell in the gloom. But he was undoubtedly the same. And there was still that glint of a strange device on his hip.

Pluto frowned slightly at Quinn, which was the most expression I'd seen him make since we'd talked about his dog. "I don't have to answer. What does she mean, a 'girlfriend'?"

"She means someone female whom you happen to have feelings for," Sakura said, her blue-eyed gaze fixed on Pluto, an inscrutable expression on her face. "Does that ring any bells?"

Pluto's gaze hit the floor. He actually stepped back, out of

118

the light, as though he was hoping we might forget he was there.

Unable to make sense of this, I turned to our next problem. "What in Beyond are *you* doing here? Do you work for him too now? Or are you just following us?"

"I was here first," Quinn replied, with a distinct air of smugness. "But no, I'm not here on a case. To answer your primary question, I am here because Marcus told me there was someone else interested in my artifacts."

"*Marcus?*" Saki asked.

"*No,*" I said, at the same time. "You are *not* Hermes Trismegistus. No way. Not possible."

"Agreed, since the person in question disappeared in an ill-fated experiment," Quinn said, grinning. The lamplight caught only the bottom half of his face, turning his expression ghoulish. "You can call me Daedalus if you like, *Little Red Riding Hood.*"

"Oh." For as annoying and surprising as he could be, this made perfect sense—and it made me soften. Daedalus's tale was not a happy one to identify with. In ancient legend, he had been an inventor, commissioned to build a giant maze. He and his son then were trapped inside his own creation, lest he show people the ways in and out. They finally escaped by flying away after Daedalus invented wings made of wax and feathers—but, overjoyed with freedom, his son Icarus flew too close to the sun, and the wax in his wings melted. He fell back to the ground and perished.

Saki and I were still standing in the light, and no doubt Quinn could read our expressions. When he spoke again, it was in a gentler tone. "Mind you, I'm not being entirely literal. I am an average and boring human, on the whole, and I never had a son—but—I did have a sister. A sister who, as you may have surmised from Edda's comments, disappeared one year ago, shortly after I completed my work with the Botanical Garden.

"Since then I'm afraid I've made a nuisance of myself around town," Quinn went on with a wry, sad smile. "Marcus will no doubt attest to that. We met while I was turning this island upside down. I have always had a special interest in these particular things," he waved a hand at the table, "but never the money to purchase them. Marcus was good enough to hold them for me . . . until someone asked him to see them," he added, with a speculative look at Sakura. "But he did at least give me some notice before the sale."

"No sale has been made, and if you keep hiding in the shadows, then I don't see how one could be," Saki told the darkness pertly. Pluto stepped back into the very barest edge of light, looking—if possible—a bit chagrined. His face was impassive once more, but his shoulders slumped.

I had other matters on my mind, though. "Your sister's disappearance," I said to Quinn. "We heard there have been other disappearances in town—maybe related to politics? Was it part of that?"

"I have considered it," he replied levelly. "If it was, then it would have been the first one. The next disappearance, or rather the first confirmed politically-motivated disappearance, occurred six months afterward, and there have been four more since then."

"At regular intervals?" I asked, trying and failing to understand the math.

"No," said Quinn. "It's accelerating."

"And does Eurie and Ida's encounter fit into the timeline?"

Saki asked.

"None of it was me," Pluto intoned.

"That isn't what I asked," Sakura replied, a warning in her voice.

"As a matter of fact," said Quinn, stepping forward fully into the light, "it does. I would have projected the day afterward, had anyone asked, but given that nothing else occurred that day—"

"Technically it did happen in the early morning hours," I interrupted. I couldn't resist the chance.

Quinn acknowledged the correction with a quirked-up smile. "Nevertheless, the other disappearances took place in broad daylight, usually at the victim's place of work."

"And they didn't turn up in your garden afterward?" Saki asked Pluto. "You didn't, for example, drive them anywhere?"

"None of them have been found," Quinn answered.

"I appreciate your dedication to the facts," Saki told him, "but I expect your friend to answer for himself this time."

The three of us looked at Pluto, whose mouth was pulled down slightly in a distinctly pained look. "No," he said, managing to sound both dutiful and mournful. "None of the others turned up in my garden."

"Wait." Quinn peered up at his enigmatic "friend." "The *others*?"

Saki glanced from Pluto to me. "Sorry," she whispered.

I sighed. If she couldn't see any way out of it, then I didn't either. And maybe it wouldn't be such a bad thing to bring Quinn into our confidence—in part. "You might as well know," I told him, "if you didn't guess it already, but we've talked to Ida."

Quinn was very still, attentive. "Since her disappearance?"

I nodded. "We met her on a trail above town. It didn't really make sense to us at the time—she was basically feral, and refused any kind of help. Said she wanted to 'disappear into the flowers' and that that was how she'd gotten away from Pluto."

As one, the three of us turned once more in his direction. I buried my momentary guilt at my half-truths under interest in *his* take on his encounter with Ida.

Pluto's sigh was sepulchral. "I told her," he said, staring into the darkness above us, "that she ought to go home. Face her mother. Say what was on her mind, and be done with it."

"Not bad advice," said Sakura appreciatively. "Tell us more about why she had your card and how she could have gotten into your very protected house."

"She wasn't in the house."

Sakura put her hands on her hips.

Pluto turned to Quinn. "I didn't know she still had my card."

Quinn crossed his arms.

"I didn't mean for it to happen," Pluto told the air over my head, sorrowfully. "I give people cards sometimes. If I meet them and they seem like they need help. It never works out quite right."

"Particularly if someone then gets murdered," I suggested.

Saki bit her lip, as though trying not to laugh.

"I take it very seriously," Pluto said, addressing her as though he could see that she was not. "But I didn't have anything to do with that lady's death. I came across someone while I was walking in the spring. She was very sad. I gave her my card. The card can make the house appear. I thought she might find it if she needed a place. But she did not. Then, two days ago, I find her in the garden. She has no idea where she is. She obviously didn't mean to come here. So there's no need for her to *stay* here, I think. I offer her a ride home. Then she gets out and runs away."

"You *saw* her and you didn't say anything?" Quinn asked.

"You knew she was in trouble and you let her go?" I asked, a question that had puzzled me since I first heard Ida's tale.

"You just go around *giving out keys to your house?*" Saki demanded.

Pluto looked down at her, his dark eyes faintly startled. "Just the garden. There's Flora. That's how it's always been." To us, he added, "I didn't know her name. I don't like to go chasing people."

Quinn shook his head and rounded on Saki and me. "You two know an awful lot about the matter, as it turns out. Is that why you came here in the first place? To see if Marcus is behind the abductions?"

"Or worse," I pointed out.

Pluto glanced at me, then at Saki. "*Is* that why you came?"

"No," she said. "First, I wanted to see if I could. Second, I'm going to buy that cauldron, just to spite you both. Third, I wanted to see what kind of tea they serve at a place Ida described as 'palatial.'"

Pluto gazed thoughtfully into the shadow for a moment, as though not sure if any of this was true—or perhaps trying to remember what "tea" might be. Then, very faintly, he smiled. "I could make you a cocktail."

"Close enough," Saki decided. "And I want to drink it in the garden, where I don't have to use magic to see your faces."

Pluto bowed swiftly, and departed. Clearly interpreting this as a sign to follow, Sakura strode off in his wake.

I glanced at Quinn. "I don't think she actually means it," I said, in a fit of sympathy. I knew what it was like to have a research love. "If you want the artifacts, really, then you can have them. I still can't believe I even touched them. Or that they even exist!"

Quinn grinned. "That's what I thought when I first saw them. Don't worry about me, though—I've already copied out everything from both books, and made a copy of the cauldron at home."

Chuckling, he left behind the others—but not before seeing my eyeroll.

"He just has to be one step ahead," I muttered. Trailing after the others, I tried to imagine what Luca and William would say.

I had a sneaking suspicion they'd say that it served me right!

16

From the Chorus

I stepped out of the house into the daylight and had to pause for a moment to adjust, feeling very much like a mole emerging from hibernation. Once the glare had subsided, other more pleasant sensations came in. The sound of the stream and the faint smell of honeysuckle. Sakura's voice, and then her little blue hat and shrug: she'd settled herself on a stone patio beyond a few garden beds. Quinn was already there, talking to her.

I glanced around at the garden as I made my way over. I was determined to enjoy some scenery on this trip—even should it be the death of me—although, that seemed like bad luck to think when in a god of the afterlife's yard.

Pluto, god of the underworld. That was going to take some getting used to. Saki and Quinn seemed to think it was perfectly normal, but then, Saki was a shadow witch and Quinn was obviously lacking in social graces, so they didn't count. Thorn and Gloria would have much more reasonable things to say about it. Probably starting and ending with, *you went* where?!?

The garden was nice, though. Around patios and fountains and, of course, the stream, the beds were arranged naturally, curving and rising in free-form banks of soil and plants rather than adhering to brick-lined, rectangular beds, like we'd seen at the Botanical Garden. There were far fewer blooms here—really just the honeysuckle, which draped over a trellis that provided shade for Saki's patio. Everything else was most likely grown for its foliage or, in the rare case of an ornamental tree, its fruit.

Odd for someone who named their dog Flora, I thought. And I kept thinking about it. Sakura and I had assumed that Pluto was in love with Ida. That was how the story tended to go, and Ida herself had been so vague that it was easy to fill in the spaces. Now, though, I wasn't so sure. Either he was concealing something from us, or he really didn't care much about the whole affair. Or he was just *so* blasé that he couldn't express his emotion, even if he *did* love her . . .

Quinn, on the other hand, obviously did care deeply about his missing sister. And therefore stood to gain a lot more from getting the police to seriously investigate the disappearances.

"Red's never told you?" Quinn was saying to Saki as I came up. He smiled lazily from his wrought-iron bench, and I did my best to ignore him as I sat beside Saki across from him. He went on, "Hermes Trismegistus is one of the great, some might say *mythical* figures of early alchemy."

"It wasn't alchemy then," I said, rather stuffily, I'll admit. "That was thaumaturgy."

"My point exactly," Quinn said, settling back against the bench with his hands behind his head. "But when you're trying to think of heroes of the field, who left behind mysteries and secrets to unravel, he's the one who comes to mind . . . along with a certain Paracelsus. But Red already knows all about *him.*"

Irrationally annoyed by Quinn's knowledge of my teacher and my training, I asked, "If you're so interested in alchemy, why didn't you become an apprentice?"

"I might have, but I make a terrible student," he answered easily. "I only study in fits and starts. It's a personal failing."

"More like a personal choice," I retorted.

Quinn beamed benevolently. "Precisely."

Watching us, Sakura laughed. "You'll have to watch out, you know," she told Quinn. "Red's engaged to a scholar. If he was here, he'd tell you himself: 'if there's anything we love, it's study!'"

"And *each other,*" I added, swatting at her. Though her impression of Luca *was* pretty good. No doubt he would have found it very funny, but I doubted our present company understood.

But she was not to be deterred. "And amateur sleuthing, and a big fluffy dog, and getting into danger . . ." Sakura counted off items on her fingers.

"Now you're just being mean!" I protested, laughing. *Trust Saki to make light of something that's secretly been bothering me all this time.*

A slight rattle of glassware caught my attention, and I turned to find Pluto at the edge of the patio, a tray of drinks in his hands. Each one was a different shape and color, and even contained its own stirring stick or straw—*no wonder they made noise,* I thought. I couldn't help but be reminded of Ida's hanging terrariums. At my shoulder, Sakura was looking too, clearly curious.

"You're lucky," Quinn told us. "This is Marcus's real talent, if you ask me. He knows peoples' favorite drinks without a second thought."

"It's experience mostly," Pluto said, his voice quiet in comparison. He served Saki and I first. My drink came in a rounded glass, the liquid inside layered—an earthy green on the bottom, clear on top, topped off with a sprig of rosemary and a long glass spoon. Sakura's, on the other hand, was in a long-stemmed glass that flared open in her hand, the fluid a deep purple—with pink glitter. *Who keeps edible glitter on hand, aside from Saki herself?* I had to wonder. Saki looked appreciative, stirring her drink with a delicate glass stick adorned with a butterfly.

Quinn's drink was amber, in a plain glass with large ice cubes. Pluto sat beside him and took the smallest glass for himself, a narrow cylinder full of something that got darker and darker toward the bottom.

Without a word, he held his glass up in a toast, and the rest of us followed suit.

After a long sip, Quinn said lightly, "I didn't know you were engaged to be married, Red. It seems I've focused too much on criminal reports in the papers."

"I have always told you that," Pluto reminded him, though again in comparison he sounded downright gloomy.

"The ring is often under my gloves," I admitted, only half paying attention. What I really wanted was to know what was in my drink. I swept the spoon up through the green layer, watching it swirl in the layer above. The green layer, I decided, had to be a kind of juice or syrup: it was sweet and herbaceous. The clear layer was carbonated and light. Between the two, there was a perfect balance.

"We came here to celebrate," Sakura explained.

"How long are you staying?" It was Quinn who asked. Over the rim of my glass, I was dimly aware that Pluto had drained his and set it on a nearby table.

"Only three more days." Saki faltered as she looked at me, then grinned across the patio. "Barring anyone's attempts to get us embroiled in a case that can't be solved."

"This case *can* be solved. Or it could be, if you were more forthcoming," Quinn returned, though his voice was friendly.

Sakura laughed. "Forgive us for not being more trusting after the way you tried to get us all roped in by Edda."

"Ah. There are worse things," Quinn said, though he didn't sound too sure about that. "Speaking of, have you been to the town hall yet?"

"No." I looked up from my drink at last. "Though I thought yesterday Saki was going to show up there and start a petition."

Quinn looked interested—Pluto was looking at the stones under our feet. Sakura blushed. "Not on anything relevant to the murder, and anyway, a town hall wasn't exactly high on our list of tourist sights to see."

"You might find it illuminating," said Quinn. "Don't you think so?"

He was looking at Pluto, who looked up at Saki and me. "It is helpful sometimes to understand," he admitted vaguely. "Do you like your drinks?"

"Yes," I said promptly. "But I want to know what's in mine."

"Tarragon syrup with rosemary bitters, half a lime, and sparkling water," he answered, his expression lightening a little. "You can keep the stirrers, if you like." He looked at Sakura. "And you?"

"Butterfly pea flower," she said. "Very clever. I like the sparkles, and I *will* keep this butterfly, thank you. But the dark rose extract can be poisonous, you know."

"Never when mixed with nectar from the same plant," Pluto replied, holding her gaze. My eyes were probably wide as saucers, and I could see surprise on Quinn's face too. But Pluto was as inscrutable as ever.

And Saki, for her part, laughed. "Well, it certainly was delicious. But it wasn't quite my favorite."

* * *

"You went *where?!?*" was the sum total of Thorn and Ida's reactions when we met them at the villa. Gloria returned from her hike shortly afterward, and joined the chorus without delay.

Ida had started making lunch for everyone, working busily behind the kitchen counter. It must have felt a bit like being on stage, with us all arrayed along the bar watching her. She didn't seem to mind that part, but I couldn't help but notice she wasn't quite the chef that Sakura had become.

"I didn't know Quinn knew Pluto," she said, scrunching her nose—perhaps in thought, perhaps in concentration—as she sawed a lump of goat's cheese into chunks.

"Neither did we," I told her. "Although, when you think about it, it does kind of make sense for a detective to know someone who literally r—ow!"

"My foot must have slipped," Saki said cheerfully, not looking at me as I nursed my kicked shin. "Anyway, what Red means is, I'm sure Quinn knows everyone. It's really much more interesting that *you* know him, don't you think? By the way, did he make you a drink?"

"Pluto?" Ida's hands hovered hesitantly over a head of lettuce and a pile of cucumbers. "Um—no? Does he do that kind of thing? I don't drink much. Usually."

She peeked up at us guiltily from under her messy topknot—as well she should. She'd been drinking quite a bit at the bar when we met her. But, perhaps that had been a special occasion? The glass spoon from my own drink was tucked into a pocket on my belt, so I hardly felt like calling her out on any hypocrisy.

I was distracted, but Saki wasn't. She pressed on. "You're sure he didn't offer you anything? Did you meet his dog?"

"What dog?" Ida just seemed more and more confused.

From the end of the counter, Gloria chimed in. "What's with the interrogation?"

"I'm just curious," Sakura insisted, her gaze bearing down on our house guest.

"What's the dog got to do with anything?" Thorn chimed in, leaning past me as she drained her iced tea.

"She's named Flora," said Saki. "The dog."

"That's—nice?" Ida, in the middle of nervously chopping lettuce, nearly nicked her fingers.

I laid a hand on Saki's arm. "I agree with everyone else. What are you getting at?"

"If you're saying he named his dog after his one true love, that's just weird," Gloria added.

"I'm just wondering," said Saki, undeterred, "why Pluto has apparently never been to the Botanical Garden. Because if he had, he'd have recognized Ida, right?"

"Maybe he doesn't get out much," Gloria suggested, stretching one hamstring at a time as she balanced against the counter. As the spokesperson for the opposition, she was aloof and unimpressed.

On the other hand, I was close enough to see Saki's jaw clench. "Oh, he gets out, alright. He has unusual floral essences which he uses for *entertaining*, of all things, and he named his dog for a love of the natural world. Doesn't it seem odd to you that he hasn't been to the biggest natural attraction in Helenia?"

At that, Ida broke.

"Okay! Alright!" She held up her hands, half a cucumber in one, a large knife in the other.

"Tell us about it," Thorn told her, as she took away the knife and vegetables. She settled the chopping board in front of her and began doing the salad prep herself.

Ida steadied herself with one arm braced against the counter. With the other, she wiped at her face, smearing bits of cheese and cucumber seeds over her cheek. I handed her a handkerchief, moving my legs just in time so that Sakura couldn't kick me "accidentally" again. *What is* with *her?*

Clutching at my handkerchief, Ida began, "He *has* been there. He used to go there all the time, I guess. I mean, he was always there. What I mean is, before it was my mom's, it was *his*."

"Excuse me?" Of all the answers I had expected, this was not it. Gloria had stopped stretching and Thorn had stopped chopping, even. Only Sakura looked unsurprised.

"He used to live on the island," Ida said, in one very long sigh. "The whole thing was his garden. People could go there, I guess, but it wasn't exactly an attraction like it is now. There weren't any programs. But people would go because there were rumors there were hidden things, like his house was hidden there, and people figured other things were too, and everyone knew he was super rich. So they would go and try to find things, until it became a real problem and fights broke out. So the mayor, the old mayor, came in and got him to agree to sell the land and move, and that's when we moved in."

"'Got him to agree'?" Gloria echoed dubiously.

"I don't know," Ida replied, waving her hand, smudged handkerchief and all. "This was all years ago. I don't think anyone cares any more. Mother would never tell me about it, and people mostly don't talk about it any more. Except his cards are still supposed to be keys—according to the rumors."

"That's why you were carrying around his business card?" Thorn asked, her knife still poised over the cutting board. I took it from her, along with the last of the cucumber. If we were *ever* going to have lunch, someone needed to focus on getting the chopping done.

Meanwhile, Ida nodded mournfully.

"Why?" Saki pressed.

Ida shrugged, looking down. "I thought there might still be a hideaway on the island. I didn't think there was treasure, or anything. I just wanted—a place to be alone. I thought I could find one this way. Then Eurie said maybe wherever the card opened was the place where the disappeared people were being kept."

Officer Thorn whistled, long and low. "You're telling me Eurie knew about *all* of this before she was killed?"

17

Leading is Lonely

"Oh, my goodness." My chopping slowed down and a cucumber section rolled away as the weight of Thorn's words hit me. "She knew someone who had disappeared. She had an idea how to look for them. She was involved in both the garden and local politics—and Quinn said—we didn't tell you this yet, Thorn—Quinn said a disappearance *should* have happened the day after she died, assuming they were following a pattern . . ."

"They were," Officer Thorn declared. "We didn't tell *you* this, Red, but while you were out Herc came by. Apparently, you lot asking questions yesterday in the garden caught the attention of the government. Your friend Hestia is a secretary there. Came back with a fire under her to get the local officers to solve the disappearances before you could—apparently she has a particular dislike for tourists. So Herc had been given a whole file on the disappearances. They've been happening in a spiral pattern—the time between each one is halved."

"But *why?*" I wondered, trying to puzzle it out. What point was someone trying to make? And why make it in such a destructive, frightening way?

"Well, *I* found out about Pluto," Saki declared. She took the cutting board and knife from me. "And now I want lunch. The rest is up to you."

"At least now you know everyone involved," Ida said, her voice small and wobbly. "The police—Pluto—the detective . . ."

"Not hardly," said Gloria, leaning over the counter. "Sounds to me like something shady's going on at that town hall."

"I agree it's worth a look," Thorn mused, her chin in her hand, her eyes faraway. "Poor Herc can't be left on his own to swim upstream like that."

I had to agree too. Quinn's words were echoing in my mind—and for as annoying as he could be, he *had* been right quite a bit so far.

"Well, you can all go on and investigate to your hearts' content," Sakura said primly, "*after* we eat this salad. And while they're out, Ida, you and I are going to have a very long chat."

* * *

Helenia's Town Hall sat proudly at the center of the road around the harbor. It was a wide road, paved in smooth white stones, and full of happy tourists shopping, chatting, and posing for pictures drawn on the spot by street artists. A few signs indicated local political matters—slogans like *add your name here to the advisor petition,* or *experts help keep us safe*—but on the whole, the place seemed made for visitors. Parks dotted the seaward side of the road, giving clear views of the harbor and the boats—not to mention the garden isle on the horizon. Glimpsing it made me think of Pluto's sad expression, and the people who had disappeared. Suddenly Edda's dramatics seemed more out of place than ever.

That said, there was something calming about Helenia itself. The mountain rose on our right, clusters of white walls and tile roofs clinging to every ledge. A continuous line of shops and cafés lined that side of the street, broken only by the proud expanse of the town hall building. It, too, was white, with carved columns lining its front and huge double doors of dark wood. More carvings could be seen, just barely, under the protective lip of the three-story-high roof. It was impressive, but honestly, it too just made me think of Pluto's home.

But I couldn't express the unsettling sense of recognition—or imitation?—to Gloria and Thorn, who hadn't been to Pluto's house and frankly seemed *very* uninterested.

"The question isn't what it looks like, Red," said Thorn, rubbing her hands together. "The question is how do we get *in*."

I cast an eye over our little group. Gloria, in a black tunic and tights, looked like she ought to have melted under the hot sun even before we set out from the villa. Her gaze was ice cold, as usual. Even her small black backpack looked too cool. Thorn, in a flower-printed button-up top and shorts, wasn't fooling anyone: she still stood exactly like a police officer, her feet spread and her hands behind her back. Also, her straw hat was giving me flashbacks to Quinn in the garden. I winced. My own yellow dress and water bottle belt ensemble wasn't quite going to carry off the impression that we were casual tourists intrigued by town government on its own.

"There," said Gloria, pointing.

She'd spotted a ragged group winding its way through the

building's columns. The people were of all shapes and sizes, but at their head was a rounded figure in khaki. *Perfect,* I realized. *A tour group.* On our own we couldn't disguise our seriousness and curiosity, but if we could get lost in a herd of tourists, maybe we stood a chance of not alarming *every* employee.

Thorn was already marching ahead. Gloria and I hurried after her, just in time to hear the guide cheerfully inform her that the tour was free and that *of course,* we could join in.

The transition from bustling, dusty street to the cool shade under the columns was worth it on its own. I drifted in among the other tourists, listening with only half an ear to the discussion of types of columns and types of carvings. The brief mention of types of *stone* caught my attention, but it only confirmed what I already knew: that the prevalence of marble in the island's buildings was due to a mine at the other side of the mountain. With that glossed over, we were heading inside.

And in the main entry hall, we were met with what could only be Eurie's art.

It was a mural that stretched all the way up to the ceiling, three stories tall. Colorful whorls and larger-than-life flowers dwarfed the reception desks and stanchions around us. It made my heart hurt just to look at it. Not because it was sad—not in the least: it seemed to be a map of local flora, a joyful expression of all the things Helenia had to offer. What made my chest tighten was exactly what I had thought when I first met Eurie: the contradiction between the promise of her work, her love of her art and the anxiety in her face, the terrible and abrupt way she'd left the world.

Looking at that mural, completely oblivious to the tour, I

knew I *had* to solve this case. And it wasn't about Ida or Pluto or Quinn or even all the ways my friends had become involved, too. I just had to believe that this kind of love wasn't as fragile as crime made it seem.

"I say we ditch the tour as soon as we can," Gloria muttered in my ear. The crowd was already moving again. I let myself be swept along, Thorn coming up behind my other shoulder.

"We're bound to find a lead," she agreed.

Unfortunately for them, they never had a chance. Our hawk-eyed tour guide navigated the group deftly down halls and up staircases, through open meeting rooms and across ancient stages, keeping up a steady stream of historical anecdotes, architectural notes, and *make sure we stay together, everyone! On to the next stop!*

I was half ready to throw in the towel and let myself be shepherded along until the inevitable gift shop when fate intervened.

"Oh, look who it is, everyone!" Our tour guide cried, stopping our procession midway down a hall on the third floor. "This never happens. You must be very lucky!

"Everyone, meet the leader of our beautiful island! When he accepted his post as our mayor two years ago, he took the title Theseus, as a symbol of his dedication to leading the people of Helenia. Normally he's in meetings and studying new laws all day long. He has a very busy job overseeing trade and tourism here, as well as local politics! Maybe if you're very lucky, he'll shake your hand!"

"I bet he stops in on *every* tour and they always say that," Gloria whispered in my ear.

From the look of Theseus, I was inclined to agree with her. He was an older man, his skin a deep brown and his hair stark white, rising straight up above sparkling blue eyes. He wore sleeveless traditional robes of white, and as he shook hand after hand, the muscles of his arm were very much in evidence. His teeth, too, flashed ostentatiously white as he grinned. He seemed to be a person who was most comfortable when someone was looking at him.

But for all that, he looked genuinely kind as he exchanged a greeting with each tourist. As he neared us at the end of the line, I glanced up at Thorn uneasily. She wasn't known for *not* making scenes.

As it turned out, though, she didn't have to. Right before he got to us, the person beside Gloria leapt out with a pencil and a clipboard in hand.

"Theseus, sir, this is Pandora from the Hermetic Herald, pronoun 'they,'" the apparent reporter-in-tourist's-clothing announced in a single breath. "What's your comment on the most recent disappearance of Idunn Skaald and the murder of her friend Eurydice?"

Theseus leaned back, up to his full height. It became apparent that he'd been stooping to meet everyone. Now, he stood about as tall as I did, and he looked like he might fight rather than shake someone's hand.

"And what are your thoughts on the pattern of disappearances, which Idunn and Eurydice fit into according to my calculations?" Pandora pressed.

Tourists—*real* tourists—were beginning to shift nervously. The tour guide was obviously trying to shoo people along, but no one was listening.

"There is a time and place for those questions," Theseus said, loudly, "and it isn't now."

"Can you comment on why you have *not* held a press

conference?" Pandora asked, leaping immediately into this opening.

"We will share information when it is time to do so," Theseus said, his perfect teeth clearly gritted.

Pandora wasn't intimidated in the least. "Do you know that that's not reassuring for citizens to hear? Do you mind that rumors are flying about the case? What would you like citizens to believe, when it seems Town Hall is doing nothing about the matter? Do you really believe that bringing in advisors will solve it?"

"I can't help the rumors," Theseus protested, looking back at the tour guide as if to say *this is your fault, fix it!*. The tour guide began weaving through the crowd as if to bodily remove the reporter. "Any notes taken on this tour are prohibited," Theseus added. "You'll have to surrender your clipboard!"

I glanced up at Gloria, who nodded.

From behind me, Thorn stepped up, literally pushing her way past Pandora. She began shaking Theseus's hand vigorously, his fingers swallowed up in her large green palms. "Mister Theseus," she said, in her very best country-farm tones, a voice that reminded me strongly of her mother, "I can't tell you how much I've been looking forward to meeting you. My friends and I just *love* Helenia. We've had the most interesting trip—"

Meanwhile, Gloria rushed at the tour guide and I tapped Pandora on the shoulder. The reporter looked startled—they'd been too focused on the interview-that-wasn't. I grabbed their hand and bolted down the nearest corridor.

"Did—did you just attack the mayor?" Pandora wheezed, pulled along at my heels.

"No," Gloria answered as she came up behind us. "I just

scared the tour guide a bit. Don't worry, it's good for them."

"Tour guides are people too," I reminded her, dragging Pandora down a back staircase.

"You can let me go," Pandora said. "I want to get out too. I can't let them take my notes. Do you know where you're going?"

"No. Just *down*," I confessed. The staircase twisted on itself, plain and empty, but echoing with alarmed voices above. I was glad Pandora had caught on: the smooth stone steps were difficult to manage at speed.

"Follow me," Gloria told us, overtaking me. "*I* at least was paying attention." She took us down another hallway on the second floor and darted through an open door, leading us straight through a meeting in progress.

"Does 'paying attention' mean planning escape routes?" Pandora panted at my side. Gloria led us neatly into another staircase before most of the committee members had even stood up.

"She's not really one for guided experiences," I replied, focusing on my feet as we tumbled down the last flight to the ground floor.

Gloria turned one way, toward the main hall. We all could see—and hear—a secretary already yelling. Without another thought, Gloria rammed into the exit door set demurely into the outer wall of the staircase. Whatever lock was on it gave immediately, and we spilled into an alley housing a café.

Pandora skidded outside and nearly knocked over a bakery cart. "What kind of tourists *are* you?"

I grabbed the reporter's arm again, leading them out toward the crowded street. "Really, really bad ones."

18

On the Outs

In a matter of minutes, we were sitting at a streetside café a few blocks down the road. We'd carefully chosen a table that was as little "streetside" as possible, tucked into the shadow of the café's awning. It hadn't prevented Thorn from finding us and, once she'd collected a very large smoothie from the café window, joined us. Fortunately, no one else actually seemed to be looking.

Pandora, however, was looking at us with undisguised curiosity. Our newest friend-in-crime had mastered the art of looking unprepossessing. They wore a classic tourist outfit of white capris and an orange blouse, but on close inspection, little details gave them away: their skin, for example, was pale, without trace of vacationer's sunburn. Their eyes, too, had dark circles underneath, and their short brown hair was unceremoniously squished back under a visor. Now, doglike ears poked up over the visor's rim—personal details which had been hidden before, perhaps in an effort to be incognito.

The reporter was also small and slight, but seemed completely at ease surrounded by myself, Gloria, and an officer of the law who looked rather smug.

"Could give them a few pointers on security," she was saying, mostly to herself, as she sipped pureed strawberries and mangoes through a charmed paper straw. "Herc said someone was stationed there—never saw them! Now I see *why* they think they need the force there. Weakest presence I never saw!"

"Probably you didn't see them because you walked out the front while they were chasing us out the back," Gloria informed her.

"Maybe *don't* tell Herc about this," I added, sipping my own iced matcha with local honey. "Just a suggestion."

"I can be sly if I need to be!" Thorn retorted. "I thought I did pretty well."

I eyed Pandora, whose iced tea was untouched and whose pencil was poised over the still-present clipboard. "We don't do this kind of thing very often. Sorry for all the excitement."

"'This sort of thing' being breaking out of government buildings? Or saving reporters in distress?" Pandora asked, turning a speculative gaze to me.

"Neither, really," I answered, thinking of Leo back home. Whenever she was in distress, it was usually because she wanted to be. "Um, sorry if we, ah, misread the situation. But it didn't seem like you were getting anywhere—except into trouble."

"And the whole reason we were there is because we're interested in the case too," Gloria said, unceremoniously spilling the beans. She didn't have Saki's subtlety, but she did have her love of pastry: she'd opted for a truly enormous scone with cream. Should any wayward police officers find us, it could have made a good projectile, actually.

Pandora accepted the admission with a brisk nod. "That explains it, then. You're from an out-of-town paper?"

"No, we really are just supposed to be tourists. But we have a history of getting drawn into things—it's a long story," I said, glancing at Thorn and Gloria to make sure they weren't about to start telling it. I was far more interested in what Pandora might have to say. "Did you manage to get anything useful from the tour at all?"

"More from the escape, when you get right down to it. Have you heard the rumor that the kidnapped victims are being housed in the town hall itself? No? It's out there, trust me. But it seems like a bust. We went through most of the hidden doors during our exit, and I didn't see any indications the building has a basement. So it's back to square one." Pandora set the clipboard on the table and took a sip of tea. If they'd been reserving judgment before, it seemed now that they'd made their decision. We were, apparently, trustworthy.

"You have the evidence to disprove the theory, though," Thorn said appreciatively, looking at the clipboard sideways. Pandora had sketched out a plan of the building as the tour wound its way through the halls. "That's a good schematic. I'm guessing they don't go around handing out plans of Town Hall?"

"No." Pandora smiled briefly—a flash and then it was gone. It seemed the reporter was always willing to turn on a dime. "I won't do anything nefarious with it, though, Officer."

"Told you you're too obvious," Gloria murmured from across the table—and over her scone.

"I'm off-duty," Thorn informed them both. "And I don't see the harm in it. Especially if they've got *security,* though I still have my doubts on that."

"That's part of the proposals to appoint governmental advisors." Pandora settled squarely into their chair, as though getting ready to make a presentation. "You all really don't know much about it?"

"We sort of got interested in the case from the other way round," I said cautiously. "We met Ida and Eurie on our first night out here."

"That explains it." Pandora nodded. "They were the latest in a series. There've been six others. I've been tracking it—here." They flipped through the papers attached to the clipboard, dislodging a collection of tour tickets, newspaper clippings, and drawings before pulling out a sheaf of notes. All four of us leaned in over the paper. Pandora kept talking, tapping certain lines on the page with their pencil for emphasis. "The first one was Harley Doyle—there's some speculation about that—it depends who you ask, but *I* say, why would it fit into the pattern if it wasn't related? But that was one year ago. Then there was one six months later—a lot of people forget about that one—then one three months after that. And *they all were associated with town hall.*"

As one, we leaned in further.

"The first one," Pandora said, assured of a captive audience. "Harley. Had just started working in the records department— hadn't even been there four months. The next one, Tangerine, a lot of people don't know this but he had just picked up the night shift on the janitorial staff. Then Winter was a tour guide, for tours like the one we just were on. Still a student and planning on continuing courses in the fall. After that there was Pokey, who was the head of security and had just retired. After he left was when they put in the police guard. But they tried to keep it really quiet, so a lot of people don't know about that one either. The next one caused a big stir—Wharton, who was a secretary there. Lot of people interested in that one. It kind of overshadowed the following disappearance, which was a street artist who used to work on the corner, Vesta. And then, right on the dot, Ida—and Eurie. But nobody'd ever been murdered before. At least, no one has ever been *found*."

"How are you connecting Ida and Eurie to town hall?" I asked, while also glancing over at Thorn to make sure she kept any comments about a security guard apparently named "Pokey" to herself.

"Didn't you see it?" Pandora didn't wait for an answer. "That big mural the tour guide was going on about, with the whole island and all the local flowers and farm products over each region. That was Eurie's work. She spent several months on it, and Ida would often come to help her as her assistant."

I glanced at Thorn again, this time more sharply. She shook her head, just barely. *So Ida never mentioned that to Thorn, either . . .* Gloria, too, was looking surprised.

"The way you put it, it's obvious," she said to Pandora.

The reporter preened. "I'm glad *you* see it, but not everybody does. It doesn't help that Theseus won't comment one way or the other. He just acts like none of it exists—he'd rather talk about hiring advisors, or *not* hiring them, or whatever tariff is up for debate. And a lot of people agree with him."

"Why?" Thorn asked.

"It's bad for tourism, one," said Pandora, sitting back and tapping their fingers with their pen for each point. "Second, it's not what they think voters want to hear. Third, it's not *really* confirmed that all these people disappeared. That is— some of them, like Pokey, might have just decided to leave."

Gloria's eyebrows were knitted together in disbelief. "Surely there's a way to tell the difference between kidnapping and skipping town."

"You would think so, but it can be very complicated," Thorn broke in as the expert. "There's not usually any spellwork that'll give an answer, so the officers have to rely on interviews and physical clues. And when nobody's seen anything and there's nothing out of place, that gets tricky."

"Exactly," said Pandora. "And that's the case for Pokey and Tangerine, too. Winter never showed back up at school, which is a bad sign. Wharton, everyone knew that was a disappearance—it happened literally in the middle of a workday. He just went out for lunch and never came back."

"And—just to be sure—there hasn't been any trace of magic at all?" I asked.

At that, Pandora finally lost a little steam. They paused to take a long sip of tea. "I can't find anything that says there was," they said at last. "I would've tried searching Town Hall, but there's so many spells on the building already that my magitech detector was going haywire even while we were standing outside."

Catching on something that I hadn't, Officer Thorn tilted her head. "Are you the only one you know of investigating this?"

"For now," Pandora admitted. "Right this moment—yes. Everyone right now's pretty distracted with the stories of Ida being held for ransom."

"There was a ransom demand?" I looked quickly at my friends, wide-eyed.

"No," Pandora said, their mouth twisting bitterly. "It's not proven. It's just people's imaginations getting away from them. It doesn't help that Edda gives interviews every day saying something new."

Gloria picked up crumbs of scone one by one on her long finger. "Why hasn't anyone else connected Ida with the others?"

"They have, sort of," Pandora answered. "People on the street have, at least. But Ida herself is such a big story. The daughter of the director of the Botanical Garden, you know. That's a big deal around here. Especially since Edda and Rhea began dating."

Thorn and I glanced at each other. Gloria was still fixated on the remains of her scone. "Um, who's Rhea?" I asked.

Pandora looked surprised. "Wow, you all really *are* tourists. Rhea's basically a local hero. She arrived here as a baby decades ago and since then has made her fortune on a chain of bakeries."

Something *ping*ed faintly in the back of my mind. "Wait, do you mean those bakery carts that are all over the place?"

"Minotaur Bakeries," Pandora nodded. "That was her first business. Rumor is, she likes to work at them now and then. But she's usually gone before the press can get a confirmed sighting. Anyway, she and Edda have been dating, oh, since winter, probably. Society stuff isn't really my beat. But it's the sort of thing people love to gossip about."

"She was in the theater show, too," Gloria said, looking up at last.

"It's a courtesy role, really. Like I said, she's kind of a local hero. People in Helenia like to think that *anyone* could be a hero. They've posted a reward," Pandora added. "Rhea and Edda have. For any information related to Ida or, by extension, Eurie. Honestly, it's just muddied the waters."

"Rewards can help in the long run," Thorn cautioned, in the

clear tones of a police officer trying to reason with the press. Though it was a serious situation, I smiled at her strength of conviction.

"But that's not why you are in it," Gloria observed.

"I've been on this case since the beginning," Pandora said. "Well—since Tangerine. He was my running buddy."

For a moment, reporter-Pandora faded, and the real person underneath was visible—and vulnerable. I touched them gently on the shoulder. "I'm really sorry, Pandora. I hope you find answers—find Tangerine, if possible."

"Thanks. But I guess I should tell you," Pandora said, smiling briefly, "Pandora's just my pen name. For the paper. Seemed fitting, right?"

"Just mind it isn't *too* fitting, especially in this case," Thorn told them.

Gloria, meanwhile, stuck to the point. "What's your real name?"

"Tilia Pepper," they answered, holding out a hand to shake. I gave my name, and so did Gloria and Thorn.

"Now we're officially partners against crime," Thorn joked as introductions concluded. "And speaking of, you mentioned Harley Doyle. Is that any relation to Quinn Doyle?"

"His sister," Tilia—still Pandora, in my mind—said, nodding. Briefly I felt guilty for having forgotten to tell Thorn about that part of the morning's revelations, but Pandora went on. "I interviewed him after she disappeared, actually, but I didn't make anything more of the case at the time. I was a little put off by him honestly."

"Put off?" I prompted, interested.

"He was really intense about it," Pandora said, widening their eyes under their visor. "When Tangerine went missing, I understood it better, how it really feels, but still. It was almost scary. He vowed revenge not just on whoever took her, but basically on the whole world."

19

Above the World

Quinn, vowing revenge? He was insouciant and aggravating, sure, but I wouldn't necessarily have thought him capable of violence. *Still,* I couldn't help but think, *if someone you love goes missing . . .*

. . . anyone can be a hero, even a baker or a botanist. Is the opposite true? Can anyone be a villain? I pondered it as we started cleaning up our impromptu tea. If Luca or William disappeared—or even Saki, Gloria, Thorn, or any of my many friends back home—what would I be capable of doing?

"You wouldn't bother with revenge," Gloria said, clapping a hand on my back as we wove our way through the tables out to the street. "You'd just find them."

"Is it so obvious what I was thinking?" I smiled back at her ruefully. "I don't know. You haven't seen as much of Quinn as I have—I wouldn't say we're friendly, but I do think he's probably a good investigator. If he couldn't find her, then the case must have been *really* hard. And in a situation like that . . ."

"I get it," Gloria mused as she settled her small backpack on

151

her shoulders. "It's easy to say what you would do until you're in the situation and have to actually do it."

"Exactly," I said. We made it to the street and lingered for a moment with Pandora, who had flagged down someone from the restaurant across the way.

Someone familiar—*Raffael,* I realized. He had his guitar slung over his shoulder, and smiled wanly at the reporter. "Oh, you all know each other?" he greeted us, as we formed a casual circle on the street. "Pandora's been a real help."

"Raffael gave me an interview, about the incident," Pandora told us delicately.

That helped explain how well-informed Pandora was, then. Some remaining doubts I'd had about our new friend eased, and I smiled at them both.

"It helped we knew each other already," Raffael told us with a shrug. "Through Tangerine. I used to go swimming with him, he was a great coach. Even when he was gone, though, I didn't take it seriously, the disappearances. I—I didn't think I would, but I get it now, how worried everyone is."

"Seems like it's been a rough time around Helenia," Thorn said sympathetically, looking down at reporter and musician.

"We can get to the bottom of it," Pandora said stoutly.

"And in the meantime, the world plays on, eh?" Raffael patted Pandora's shoulder, though his eyes looked sad. "Just finished the afternoon gig myself. Are you all out sightseeing? You should try the gondola ride, if you haven't already. Everyone always says it's worth it."

"It's on our list," I promised him. "But, Pandora—thanks for taking the time to talk to us."

"Thank you," the reporter replied, looking up at me. "And here—take my card. If you learn anything else, come to me first."

In that way, all reporters may be alike, I thought, smiling to myself. "Sure, will do." We waved off the two of them, who soon disappeared into the crowd. I turned to smile at my friends. "So. what now?"

"Now, we be tourists," Gloria said firmly.

"We've got time before we have to head back for dinner," Thorn agreed amiably. "What did you have in mind?"

"Exactly what was suggested." Gloria turned and pointed up the mountain. For a moment I thought she wanted to go on another hike, and the thought of climbing up out of the city only to then climb *further* up a hillside made my knees wobble. But then I saw what she was actually pointing at. High in the air, dangling from cables that looked far too thin, gondola coaches were slowly moving up and down above the roofs of town.

Thorn whistled. "No one here's afraid of heights, I hope?"

I thought of the tower Luca and I had most recently investigated back home, and gulped.

"It'll be fine," Gloria insisted. "Hundreds of tourists go up and down every day. There's dozens on it right now and they're fine. See?"

I *did* see, I had to admit. And the gondolas were taking said tourists to and from a very famous outlook point over town, known for the carvings in the rock face below it—carvings only visible from the gondolas, and the viewing platform they reached.

It *was* one of the biggest tourist attractions in town. If I returned to Luca and admitted to him that I hadn't done it, what would he say?

I sighed as I turned back to Gloria and Thorn. "Oh, alright.

Gondola ride it is."

* * *

Once the tickets were bought and we were duly shuffled onto the gondola with our new closest six friends, I'll admit, there was a moment—just a moment as the gondola took off, with a rumble and a shake through the air—when I *deeply* regretted my decision.

But then the roofs of Helenia came into view, and all my nerves were forgotten.

It was *incredible.* Before we'd come on this trip, I might have said that I wanted to go to Helenia to see the ruins, the hikes, the old wells. Even the rock carvings high on the hill, which I'd heard of time and again. But it was the view of the city that really captured my heart in that moment. The streets and buildings so white, and the people so colorful, moving along the paths like a multitude of planets through the sky—it was nothing short of exhilarating.

And beautiful. All those people, going along living their lives! And here we'd been so drawn into Ida's life, Eurie's life, cut short as it was. We'd been focusing on some pretty dark things. But there was still so much joy in Helenia, too—and, I reminded myself, there was so much joy in my own life, too. And even if it wasn't permanent, it was beautiful.

As I rested my elbows in the open window of the gondola, looking down, I just knew that William would adore this perspective. And Luca, no doubt, would have a whole series of books prepared for me when I got home, wanting to know if any of them captured the view just right!

"Aw," said Thorn, settling next to me. I tried not to think

about the way the gondola seemed to rock under her weight. "You're such a softie. I saw you smiling there."

I chuckled. "You got me. This is amazing. I just—" I turned, looking at Gloria on my other side. "I know this hasn't gone as planned. But thank you, both, so much for agreeing to come along on this trip."

Gloria smirked. "It's about time. I've been waiting for you and Luca to get together since that castle business."

"It has been a long time coming," Thorn agreed.

"Hey!" I laughed at them both. "Not all of us are as decisive as you, *Mina*!"

"Your loss." Thorn grinned complacently.

"You all are sickening," Gloria declared. But even she, our stoutly aromantic friend, was smiling.

The gondola continued on its path up, over town and then past the ruins we'd explored on our first day. They were visible as light patches of stone through the scraggly brush, dotted with sunhats and resting hikers. But by then, the real attraction was the carvings in the cliff above us.

Everyone in the gondola shifted forward to get a good look, but this time, I didn't notice the change in weight distribution. In a rare, bare rock face in the mountain, a scene unfolded before us. Though Helenia and its surroundings were serene, this scene was warlike—a battle between a warrior in armor and a mythical beast. The beast itself was so huge, and the stone so worn, that it was hard to tell exactly *what* it was. Local legends were full of all kinds of monsters, including the minotaur which now apparently served as a symbol of power for a local business leader. Arrayed behind the monster and the warrior were a dozen more figures, each representative of an ancient god. I didn't know enough myself to differentiate them, but I wondered if Pluto was among them.

The mural had been carved centuries ago—so long ago that its creator had been lost to time. *Most likely, creators,* I thought. *How could one person make something so huge?* For a moment, the thought reminded me of Ida helping Eurie paint her murals. But I wasn't sure what to make of it, and I let the thought slip away.

The gondola hesitated, then lurched up, past the carving. Now the landing site was in view, along with a sizable crowd of people enjoying the scenery and walking down a set of steps to look at the carving up close. The passengers of the gondola began shifting, getting ready to disembark in an orderly fashion.

"Remember," Thorn told Gloria and me as we joined the standing line, "we can't be staying up here all night."

"What, you're already ready to hop the next gondola back down?" I teased. "I just want to get an up-close look, just for a few minutes. I think I see a souvenir stand if you don't want to take the stairs."

"*I'm* taking the stairs," Gloria added. "I didn't come all this way to not see the famous carving."

I was still chuckling as we made our way to solid ground and let the crowd push us in different directions. Thorn went with the visitors who were making a beeline for the souvenir and café stands set into the side of the mountain. They streamed across the wide, flat plaza, dispersing to look at iced drinks and postcards and beaded keychains. Meanwhile, the gondola was reloaded with visitors heading down. Gloria and I followed a larger portion of the crowd, plodding across the plaza to a set of stairs at one side.

"I didn't know you were such a fan of ancient art," I told her over my shoulder.

"What I am is a fan of the awning that I saw down there," she replied. And she made a very good point—the plaza itself was unshaded and felt hot enough to scramble eggs on. "The only way to get some shade is to look at the carving. Don't tell Thorn that, though."

"Your secret is safe with me." I grinned as I turned forward to focus on the steps. They were well-made, wide and shallow with a railing on one side, but the sheer number of people trooping down to look at the carvings made them a little perilous. After running down two flights of stairs already that day, I was happy to take things easy. Gloria, too, seemed perfectly content as I slowed down, letting the family in front of us have more room.

With everyone focused on climbing down alongside the cliff, the air was quieter. Instead of shouting and laughing, there was focus, with most of the voices now being those of birds in the nearby woods. I looked over the railing. The mountainside was steep, but thin trees and brush were dug into the soil, smelling of sage and warm bark. The trees were crowned in deep green leaves, while the herbs and shrubs around them sported silvery green; and there was a glimmer—

I stopped short. "Gloria, did you lose something?"

"What? No. Why?" From behind me, Gloria peered down the stairs.

"Over there," I told her, pointing between the trees. "I thought I saw something curve through the air and then fall. Something gold." I craned my neck to look behind us, but most of the other tourists from the gondola were already passing us by. "Someone's probably going to be missing it, once they realize it's gone."

"That's *if* there was something there," Gloria said.

"There definitely was." On impulse I reached up to my forehead—only to find that, instead of my goggles, which would have been able to zoom in on the forest, there was only a sunhat. Good for preventing sunburn, of course, but not so good for confirming the existence of lost artifacts. "I'm sure I saw something."

"Well, if you're going to go . . ." Gloria glanced around. Most of the crowd was already at the bottom. Her point was clear: now was the best time to potentially break a rule.

Another set of rules. Lamenting to myself that we really did seem to be terrible tourists—but determined to alleviate that by rescuing someone's prized ring or toy, or whatever the gold object had been—I slipped under the rail and into the woods.

I didn't have to go far. A few steps through the underbrush, winding past a tree trunk. There was a crash behind me. When I looked back, I saw that Gloria had decided to come too.

"In case you start sliding down the mountain," she muttered.

"I'm not going to do that. See?" With just one more step, I lunged forward, right into a dewberry bush. I emerged with something round and golden clutched in my fist. "Weird," I said, mostly to myself. "Why would someone bring a golden apple up here?"

A stick snapped in half as Gloria, too, lunged forward. She made contact with my shoulder just as the apple began to shimmer. It was so very, very pretty. Bright and shining in the sun—

—until, abruptly, the sun was gone.

20

Mere Mortals and Heroes

The next thing I knew, Gloria and I were alone in empty white space.

"Gods above," she muttered. "What have you done *now*?"

"I didn't do anything! I . . ." I watched the apple in my hand dissolve into nothingness. Precisely like an incriminating object whose purpose has been fulfilled. A terrible feeling settled in my gut. "Yeah. Okay. I was tricked."

Suddenly, the idea that mysteries were somehow attracted to me seemed *especially* dangerous.

"We can think about that later," Gloria said. "Right now we need to get out of here."

"Out of where?" I looked around, but all I could see was white. Pure whiteness, Gloria, then more whiteness beyond her. I did my best to keep the panic at bay, but it was tough. "Where *are* we?"

Gloria looked around too, clearly bewildered. "Empty space? A magical dimension? A dream?"

Even without knowing the answer, this was far too much

for me to wrap my mind around. I shook my head. "Do you still have the mirror? If you can get it to connect with Luca's, then he and William can get a message to Saki. She'll be able to do something—probably?"

While Gloria reached into her small backpack, rummaging around, I took a deep breath and tried to focus. The ground beneath my feet felt solid and flat. The air was cool. There was no sense of the space getting smaller, nor any kind of danger . . .

And then a faint, deep laugh echoed through the place.

Gloria met my wide-eyed gaze. "I've got it, but I can't get it to do anything," she whispered.

"Did you hear that?" I asked, preoccupied.

"Yes! We need to get out of here *yesterday!*"

"I agree, but what do you propose we do?" I hissed back. Another laugh sounded, seeming to come from all around us. "Would it do any good to run?"

Gloria didn't waste time pondering the suggestion. "Let's try it. Go!"

Together, we launched ourselves haphazardly into the whiteness. I had no idea which direction to go, but as another laugh sounded, I was perfectly happy following Gloria's lead. I was only worried I'd outpace her in my panicked state. *Should I hold her hand and pull her along? She'd hate it. But if it's a choice between that and getting left behind with some weird invisible laughing creature—*

Together, Gloria and I smashed right into a wall and fell backwards.

"Oh. Ow." I sat up first, putting one hand gingerly to my head. "We're . . . in a room? A white room?"

"How did we not notice a *wall*?" Gloria grumped, sitting up next to me. Her feathered crest, usually sleek and beautiful, was fraying in all directions. She looked a bit like a surprised fountain.

"What is going *on*," I agreed. "Ugh. Okay. New plan. We're in a white room. Something's making noise. Um—let's move around the walls. Wall. I mean, who knows, right? It could just be one weird wall in the middle of nothing!"

"Calm down," Gloria insisted, peering around us. "It's a good plan. You go one way, I go the other."

"But not too far," I added hastily. Maybe Gloria was the one who *looked* like a shocked plume, but I certainly felt like one. This was a far cry from being on the hillside looking at art!

We helped each other up, bumping into the wall as we went. It certainly was solid. It didn't look any different from anything else around us, but when I put my hand on it, I could feel something rough and cool. In a rush of discovery, I gestured for Gloria to do the same. "Keep feeling it as you move around," I told her. "Maybe we can find a door or something. Maybe this is all some weird mistake."

"Yeah, and the ghost who haunts the place thinks it's funny?" Gloria rolled her eyes at that.

Still—instinctively, we both held our breath for a moment. No more eerie laughter sounded.

"Okay," I said cautiously. "Let's go."

Gloria nodded at me, then turned and began walking slowly away, leaning into the wall as she went. It was like watching a mime. She looked like she was holding both hands flat against nothing. I almost laughed.

But then I reminded myself that I'd better do the same if we wanted to learn more about this strange and potentially terrifying situation. I adopted the same pose, keeping as close to the wall as possible. No matter how hard I stared at it, I couldn't see a thing. But I could feel that same cool roughness as before—like the wall was, in fact, old and slightly damp stone. When my fingers ran into a clump of moss, it was so startling that I shrieked and dropped the harmless fronds onto the floor.

. . . Where they promptly disappeared.

"What? What happened?" Gloria asked.

"Nothing. Moss," I corrected myself. "I found some moss. But I don't understand. Why would it be growing on the wall and we wouldn't be able to see it? Even now. I can't see it. But I know what I felt."

"Obviously there's magic at work," Gloria said, sounding both matter-of-fact and like she was about to ask for the manager at any moment.

"But *why*?"

"Focus," she retorted.

"Fine," I agreed, returning to the wall. "But, you know, sometimes understanding *why* does help."

"Think while you wal—ugh."

Gloria's voice stopped short, and now it was my turn to look around. "What?"

"Corner," she reported after a moment of waving her hands in the air. "I found a corner."

Somehow, I found this heartening. She was only a few yards away, which meant we definitely weren't trapped in some unfathomable expanse. "Okay, well, keep following it, I guess," I told her. My fingers hit something else different—something that wasn't moss. "I've got something weird here too. It's not stone any more. It feels like—sort of lumpy metal—and maybe—definitely—wood," I said, pleased with myself for not shrieking this time. "Lumpy metal and w—"

Without any ceremony at all, I found myself smacked in the face a second time.

I stumbled back. What I'd taken too long to realize was, in fact, a *door* was now open. Blissfully, the space beyond it wasn't white, but instead was a dark and refreshing black. Confusingly, though, the person standing in the doorway was Pluto.

"What?" I asked, for what felt like the millionth time.

Pluto's dark gaze roved right past me and to Gloria, who had run up behind me. "Who's that?"

"Right back at you," Gloria growled.

Pluto kept scanning the room. Like he could actually *see* the room. "Is it only you two?"

"Who were you *hoping* to capture?" Gloria retorted.

I shook my head gingerly, willing my thoughts into order. "Gloria, Pluto. Pluto, Gloria. She's a friend with us on the trip. What are you doing here?"

"What are *you* doing here?" the inscrutable deity replied.

For a brief moment I seriously contemplated screaming. It was only my brief encounters with Hunter's unique and *forceful* brand of divine magic that made me think twice and carry on civilly. "Gloria and I, and our other friend Thorn, were up on the mountain. We rode the gondola. But then I saw something flash in the trees, and Gloria and I went after it—"

"Technically I went after *you*," Gloria added unhelpfully.

"—and, as soon as I touched it, it brought us here," I concluded. "We have no idea where we are, and Thorn is probably looking for us, and this has all been extremely unpleasant. So if you could let us out now—"

"Why didn't you call Sakura?" Pluto interrupted. He was still standing squarely in the doorway, looking down at me with an impassive expression. "She would be able to undo this."

Behind me, Gloria was clearly exasperated. "Why does he keep saying things you've said already?"

I decided it was best to ignore her; I really didn't have an answer anyway. "Calling Saki was my first thought," I informed Pluto through a clenched jaw. "But we couldn't get our magic mirror to work."

"Ah." Pluto looked around the room again. "Interesting."

"I am two seconds away from head-butting him and running out," Gloria warned me, very audibly.

"Could you explain why you'd suddenly be loose in the Garden?" Pluto asked her mildly. The two of us stared at him. I crossed my arms. After a brief pause, he coughed. "Ah, yes. You're in my old store room. I had it made specially to contain magical artifacts . . . like the ones you saw today. I wanted to be sure no spell or side effect would leech out into the isle. I had no idea the protections had lasted this long."

At my side now, Gloria was not-so-quietly seething. As the one of us who was slightly more used to Pluto's disconnection from anything to do with *haste,* I put my hand on her shoulder in what I hoped was a reassuring gesture. "You used to live at the Botanical Garden," I supplied, addressing him. "We— er—just learned that today, after leaving you. So you're saying this is what, the basement of your old house on the island?"

"In a manner of speaking," he said complacently. "The house was torn down. But I left somewhat abruptly. It seems I did not effectively seal everything off."

"We were pretty effectively sealed *in,*" Gloria observed.

"Yes." For the first time, something approaching confusion flickered across Pluto's face. "You don't know who did that?"

"Shouldn't *you* know?" I asked him. "It's *your* old basement. And how did you know to find us here?"

"I knew to find *you* here," he replied. Then he pointed at the pouch on my hip. With a deep sigh of understanding, I opened it—and drew out the small glass spoon. "I heard about the incident at Town Hall," he went on. "I was worried. I checked where the glass stirrers had gone. One was here on the island and not moving. So I decided to investigate."

"You just happened to hear about that?" Gloria's nose scrunched.

"I have a contact there," said Pluto, uninterested in the matter.

"Our new friend Pluto has a *very* strange concept of being helpful," I murmured to Gloria. Putting away the offending spoon, I added more clearly, "Okay, you've investigated. What can you tell us? Can you get us out of here? Do you know who got us here in the first place?"

"Presumably you would know," Pluto returned. "Who gave you the teleportation key that brought you here?"

"It—um—no one—that is, I didn't see them," I admitted, much to my chagrin. "It didn't look like a key or anything. It looked like . . . a golden apple."

Pluto tilted his head to one side, as though intrigued by my obviously guilty conscience. "You did not remember in time."

"No," I confirmed. For Gloria's sake, I added, "There's some local myths about people, um, getting lured out of races and being generally hoodwinked by . . . golden apples."

"Gold apples from who?" she asked, watching Pluto steadily. "That's how it works, right? Someone in these old stories is always handing out those relics."

"A very good question," Pluto said, looking more interested than he had yet. "In the original, I believe it was Aphrodite."

"We haven't seen her," I said, a bit shortly, I admit. "And while that's all great to know, can we leave now?"

"One thing." Pluto glanced over our heads. "Does the room look white to you?"

"Yes," said Gloria, sourly. "And there was a ghost in it. Laughing."

"Was there?" Very briefly, very faintly, Pluto smiled. "How amusing."

"We didn't think so," I informed him.

"Ah—yes. I can see that," he said. Turning away, into the darkness, he added, "I suppose that's all we can do here. If you'd like—"

"Wait," Gloria said. "So you don't know who had the keys? You can't, I don't know, trace them or something?"

Pluto settled back into place to look at her. "No. I do not have that kind of magic. Perhaps your Sakura could. But I do not advise you bring her here."

"*Our* Sakura?" Gloria sounded bewildered again, on top of her frustration.

I was more interested in the end of his sentence, though. "Why not?"

"Because," said Pluto, once more turning to leave, "it's very dangerous."

21

Gods and Flowers

Pluto hadn't been kidding about *dangerous*. (Did Pluto *ever* kid? I had yet to find out, but I doubted it.) The moment Gloria and I stepped over the threshold and into the darkened hallway, there was an ominous rumble.

"Hold on to my sleeve," Pluto told me levelly. "And hold on to your friend. Do not, for any reason, let go. And do not acknowledge them in any way."

"*What?*" said Gloria.

"Don't make noise," Pluto replied. "If you're in contact with me, they won't notice you. Just walk forward until we're in the sunlight. Simple."

It was at this point in the retelling, when we were all safely at the villa and crammed onto the veranda explaining our adventure to our friends, that Sakura turned with pursed lips to Pluto. "Do you often find that telling people *as little as possible* works out for you?"

"It did work," he said mildly, looking at the vines trailing on the trellis above our heads.

I shuddered. The shock and confusion of getting stuck in

some kind of magical storeroom had been one thing. But that walk up through the ground under the Botanical Garden was one I did *not* want to remember. "They" had been shapes of all sizes, shadowy and undulating, which howled in search of us until Gloria and I had finally emerged into a rose garden. I hated to think of what might have happened if we had left on our own.

"What would have happened if you hadn't been there?" Gloria demanded of our resident deity.

Pluto looked thoughtful. He was dressed in the same dark clothing he'd worn that morning, and now in the twilight on our patio, he was just as difficult to make out. By the time we'd emerged into the Botanical Garden, it had been late afternoon. Pluto, to my surprise, had escorted us to the boat station and accompanied us all the way to the villa, where Thorn had recently returned to recruit Saki's help in looking for us. I'd half thought he'd teleport us or something—if he was really so interested in seeing us back to safety. But in all things, he seemed content to take his time.

"I'll assume you would have been able to open the door eventually," he said, looking at me as if half suspecting I had a bottle of acid in my purse. I did, actually—just for emergencies. He swirled the glass of iced tea in his hand and went on, "You would have found the corridor extremely unpleasant."

"But—" For the first time, Ida stirred. She was sitting on the wall in the corner, behind Thorn. "But—you mean that's been under the Garden all this time? And nobody found it?"

Pluto glanced at her. "Nobody was supposed to find it."

"Somebody *did* find it," Sakura corrected. She was sitting next to me on the bench seat, directly across from Pluto, whom she glared at. "Somebody had to have been there before in order to make the key that took Red and Gloria there."

"I agree with your assessment," Pluto said calmly, holding her gaze as he swirled his iced tea again. "But as I told your friends, I do not have the kind of magic that would allow me to trace their signature."

"I do," said Saki.

"I know," was the response.

She leaned forward. "So take me there and I'll do it."

"No." He sat back.

Thorn broke in, her voice carrying all the authority of a concerned police officer. "Has it occurred to anyone else that the other kidnapping victims might have found themselves in the same situation as Gloria and Red?"

"Yes," we all answered.

All except Ida. When we turned as one to look at her, she quivered in the shadow. It didn't help that she was wearing Gloria's one sundress, which was, predictably, black, and far too large for her. "Um, that makes sense I guess? I hadn't thought about it yet. I'm just surprised. How did—how did someone find it? I thought nobody knew where any of this was!"

"*Pluto* knew," Gloria said pointedly from the other end of the patio.

The man in question chose to contemplate his iced tea. *He really is savoring that,* I thought, bemused. I'd downed my own glass immediately after Saki had offered it, and was already thinking about our overdue dinner.

"You didn't leave any kind of alarm spells on any of this?" Sakura asked him.

He looked up at her. "That's what *they* are for."

"Yes, but condemned souls of the dead don't *tell you* when

someone's trying to get into your old house," she retorted.

He shrugged. "Do they need to?"

Sakura's eyes blazed.

"I think in this case we can all agree that you could have been more cautious," Officer Thorn broke in again. "However, I can appreciate how unlikely it must have seemed that anyone would find the place at all."

Sakura rounded on her. "Why are you defending him?"

"Let's focus on what we *can* do, in the present," I reminded her. And Pluto. "You showed up at the door really fast. So you must have some kind of shortcut or magic to get there, right? Why not take Saki?"

His gaze skimmed over me and settled back on her. "No."

"Why not?" asked Thorn.

"Because you don't *want* us to know who's doing this?" Gloria suggested.

"Um," said Ida in the corner. Her voice quavered. "Wouldn't it be *really dangerous*? What if you found—whoever it was? The *murderer*?"

"That's the idea," Sakura said, exasperated. She turned to Pluto. "And if you don't agree to take me there, I'll find a way to get there myself."

"No," said Pluto, again, "you won't."

"Oh yes, I will," she retorted, standing. Black flecks of magic began sparking around her.

"*No,*" Pluto replied, setting aside his tea, "you won't."

"Watch me!" The magic was crackling through the air now. Just to be safe, I edged away along the bench. *Or—should I be trying to catch her?* Much as I appreciated Saki's initiative, it really wasn't a great idea for her to go into danger alone.

"Stop." Pluto stood, lifting his hands. I couldn't see his magic the way I saw Saki's, but the shimmery effect that covered him shifted, flooding the air around his palms. For one brief moment, I could see his face in perfect clarity.

Then he and Saki spoke at exactly the same time.

And with an unintelligible wail, Ida launched herself between them.

Thorn leapt to her feet, as did I. Ida was caught in a shimmering shadow in the middle of our patio. Sakura was shouting with all her might.

"How DARE you! You really thought that would work? Get out. Get out of here right NOW! I hereby banish you and all your magic from my sight!"

Before Thorn or I could reach Ida, the magic around Saki expanded. It formed into a sparkling black sphere, floating in front of her, so menacing I stumbled back. For a moment it blazed there, darker than night. Then it exploded, sending a shockwave rippling over the patio and beyond, leaving sparkling glimmers and dead silence in its wake.

Ida fell to the floor, released. Pluto was gone.

Behind me, Gloria swore creatively.

Thorn knelt beside Ida, and finding that she was fine, looked up at Saki. "I agree with Gloria. Did we know you can do that? What exactly *did* you do?"

Saki fainted.

* * *

After I caught Sakura—barely—practicality took over. Thorn carried Ida in to the couch while I helped Saki to her room, leaving Gloria to clean up. Not that there was anything to *clean* exactly—the magic had left everything physical, aside from Saki herself, untouched. But the air around us certainly felt different. Maybe it was sheer shock.

For her part, Saki certainly seemed to feel it. She collapsed onto her bed. "Oh, my head. Oh, dear, I'm going to regret that. But wasn't he just being the *worst?*" she said, a bit hazily, as I rummaged through my pack for medicine and found a glass of water on her bedside table.

"Well, the jury might be out on 'worst,'" I told her evenly, thinking of the kidnapper and murderer we still hadn't caught. "Here, take this for your head. Has anything like this happened before? Is there anything you know of that we can do for you?"

"You mean me losing my temper?" Saki giggled. "It's okay, Red. All I did was banish him. It's very simple really. It just took a lot of willpower because he's very—very strong—and—oh!" she yawned. "I *am* very tired . . ."

"Okay, well, you get some rest," I decided. "I'll go check on Ida."

"Go on. She just got caught in his magic," Saki added as an afterthought, already sliding down onto her pillows. "It wasn't anything bad. Just containment, trying to hold someone in place . . ."

As I closed her door, I raised an eyebrow to myself. *"Wasn't anything bad?"* And yet Saki had been willing to perform one of the biggest spells I'd ever seen her do in response?

Something to talk to William about, I resolved. I was overdue a call to Belville anyway.

I found Ida sitting on the couch, rubbing her arms absently. From the sounds of banging and muffled arguing, I assumed Thorn and Gloria were in the kitchen—doing their best to be quiet.

"Hey," I said to Ida, taking a seat next to her. "How are you feeling? That was pretty intense."

"I'm fine," she said, meeting my gaze and then looking away. "Physically fine. Just still a little . . ."

Though I wasn't a healer by any stretch of the imagination, I did my best to appraise her. She did look unharmed, but—she was shivering, constantly. Hesitant, I set my hand on her shoulder. "Just a little what?" I asked, more softly.

"Oh my gods," she burst, dropping her head into her hands. "Oh, gods, I'm so silly. I'm sorry. I didn't mean to cause trouble. I just get—like this—when there's arguing. My throat closes up and I can't breathe. I don't know what I was thinking. I'm so sorry."

She was sobbing now, well and truly, and while I didn't have a medicine for that, I at least knew what to do. I shifted closer to her and put my arm around her shoulder. I hadn't recovered my handkerchief from her earlier, but fortunately, she pulled it from her pocket.

"It's fine," I said, as she dabbed at her face. "I don't think you made anything worse. I think—I think he was aiming for Saki, but I'm pretty sure she put up some kind of protection at the same time. And then, uh, chased him off. I would bet that's all stuff she would have ended up doing anyway."

"I had no idea he would be like that," Ida gulped. "I didn't know you all would find him. I'm so sorry I got you involved."

"Don't worry about that." I mused on her words for a moment, trying to remember what they made me think of—and wondering what, *really*, Pluto was like. What had we just seen happen? "Everyone's surprised, believe me. I don't think we know what to make of it yet."

"I'm just the worst at that kind of thing." Ida was speaking more smoothly, but she was still shaking. "I can't handle it."

"Conflict, you mean?" Struck with sympathy, I squeezed her shoulder. I couldn't help but think that Edda's world would not be a comfortable one for someone so easily affected.

Meanwhile, Ida nodded. "I'm so sorry. I know I must seem like such a hassle. I *am* a hassle. I'm trying to be better, but—it just gets me out of nowhere, and—"

"Hey," I said, gently, before she could start crying again. "You can stop apologizing now. We don't mind. Everybody's a hassle sometimes." When Ida's head jerked up, I chuckled and went on, "You think it's not a hassle that Saki just literally banned an important witness from sight? Or that *I* wasn't a hassle when I fell for that apple trick? We all do things on an impulse that we probably wouldn't do if we had a moment to think it over. The goal is always to take a breath and calm yourself down before you react, but the real trick is not to hide away in shame when you make a mistake." I squeezed her shoulder again. "This wasn't even a particularly big mistake. If the rest of us hadn't been riveted, we might easily have done the same."

Ida sighed softly as she handed my handkerchief back to me. "I guess, like I told you, sometimes it's hard to tell when things are a big deal or not."

"I get the feeling you come from a place where everything was a big deal," I told her. "But most of the time, I find that things aren't as big as you think, especially when you have someone to face them with you. And especially when you aren't already tired, hungry, confused, or all three. On which note—how about dinner?"

22

Calm in the Chaos

The next morning settled in with pastel softness. Our patio was now a refuge, an idyllic place for a vacation—just like it had been on our first full day, before Herc showed up. It was hard to make sense of how much we'd learned and done since then.

Fortunately, I didn't need to make sense of it alone. I set a glass of lemonade and a croissant I'd pilfered from the kitchen on the little patio table and took a chair, sighing contentedly as I held the mirror up in front of me. I knew even before the call started that it would help.

It didn't start off as expected, though. Instead of a sleepy or bookish Luca answering, the mirror's glass glowed blue and then filled with a close-up of a black snout. In the background, there was audible yelling.

"William!" It was a guess, but an easy one. I laughed. "You *made* these. Why are you using it wrong? Stop holding it so close to your face! What's going on?"

"Sorry," he replied, his face coming into focus. "But it's been so long since anyone called that no one here remembers how these work. Luca was using it as part of his morning beauty routine. Who are you, again?"

I laughed again, doing my best not to spit out lemonade. "You think you're *so* funny!"

"Red!" Luca's face came into view, sideways, as if he'd launched himself across William's back. The mirror lurched and adjusted once more, revealing both of them sprawled on the couch in the apartment above the potions shop. "Don't listen to him. We're so glad to see you!"

I grinned at him, still chuckling. "Well, I *am* sorry it's been a while since I called, for the record. You'll understand when I tell you what's happened . . ."

As I caught them up on Ida, Pluto, Pandora, and Sakura's remarkable display of temper, I could hardly believe it all myself. They both listened attentively, Luca's expression varying wildly, William's deepening in disapproval. As a familiar, he somehow managed to be more expressive than a dog covered in so much fur had any right to be. I knew even before I wrapped things up that I was due for a lecture. It bothered me very little, though. William's lectures usually wound up in useful insights. And maybe, just maybe, I missed him.

I missed them both. As I finished telling them about Ida's remarks in the aftermath of the night before, Luca was already leaning forward, squishing William's ear with his elbow. "You can see why she'd be worried about conflict—you all are lucky banishment is all it was! Have you *seen* the way Saki deals with Hunter?"

"She does have a definite lack of disrespect for divinity," I remarked, amused. "Which I don't really understand, because she's made it clear she has a deity she follows herself. I honestly find it all kind of confusing—alchemy is easier."

"That much is obvious," William broke in. "You've gotten yourself head over heels in something you *should* have avoided at all costs. Do you have any idea the kinds of things a literal *god of death* could do—"

"Good morning," Sakura broke in, coming around the table to sit next to me. She covered a yawn haphazardly with one hand, smiling at me over a steaming mug of coffee. Her usually sleek hair was sticking up in the back. With a shrug, she explained, "I went to bed so early last night, I woke up just now *starving*. Can I have some of your croissant? Thanks. You're talking to William and Luca? I thought so. Hi. For the record, I only was mean to Hunter because he was distracting my business partner. We're fine now."

"And what did Pluto do?" I asked, giving up my croissant with resigned humor.

"You were there. It's more like what *hasn't* he done." Saki's face momentarily darkened. She addressed the mirror. "Also, I do hear you, William. And Red knows very well—she saw some entrapped souls yesterday herself."

Luca, sweet soul that he was, looked horrified. I was pretty uncomfortable with the idea myself. "Um, Saki—is that actually what we saw?"

"Well, I wasn't there, so I couldn't say for *sure*," she said, finishing off my croissant. "But in general, those are pretty standard guardians for gates of the underworld, you know. Given his interest in *tradition,* I wouldn't put it past him."

"But also . . ." I hesitated. While I didn't necessarily want to take up arms as Pluto's defense, there were pieces of the puzzle that just didn't fit. "We weren't in the underworld, we were just in a storeroom. And doesn't he seem kind of, I don't know, bland to go around doing things like that?"

Saki's eyes narrowed. "He didn't seem particularly bland to me last night."

"Right," I agreed hastily. "Although . . ."

"What is it, Red?" Luca prompted. At this point he had both hands on William's head, almost as though he was holding William back from whatever rant he wanted to go on.

"I saw Pluto's face for a moment when he was getting ready to do his spell last night," I said slowly. "Normally I can't see him very well—I don't know if you have that too, Saki. Usually it's like he's wearing some kind of magic mask. But all his magic sort of went into his hands, and for about a second, I could see his expression really clearly. He looked—honestly, he looked terrified."

Saki shifted beside me, blue eyes alight. "I didn't see that, no. That's very interesting."

"But why?" Luca asked the question I'd been puzzling over. "Who would he be afraid of?"

I raised my eyebrow at Sakura.

"Oh, no," she said, shaking her head emphatically. "Not *me.*"

On the other side of the mirror, William freed himself from Luca's restraint with a mighty shake of his ears. "Never mind the fact that you clearly bested his magic!" he barked.

Sakura grinned lopsidedly at him. "Are you worried about us not being able to do enough, or are you mad at me for doing too much?"

"Both!" William growled, his frustration evident. I hid a smile behind my hand, even though I knew he was right and that the situation was serious.

"Well, you shouldn't worry so much," Saki replied. "I'm not sure it needs to be a big deal. I certainly didn't *intend* to do it at first—actually I wasn't sure I *could* do it—and I don't think he would have thought I could do something like that, either. It was only because I was so spun up at him that I was able to. I don't see how he could have seen it coming to be that afraid. And if that was how he felt, then why argue at all? And furthermore, since he *is* so bland, as Red says, how would he understand shadow magic anyway?"

"I kind of figured it just came with the territory," I said mildly.

"Clearly it doesn't," Saki sniffed. "He's certainly the worst god of the dead *I* ever met."

I glanced back at the mirror. William had his paw over his nose. Luca, however, was starting to look rather intrigued.

"Are you saying you don't think Pluto is what he claimed to be?" he asked Saki. "Only, I can't help but notice you haven't referred to him by name at all."

Sakura's eyes widened in surprise. "Oh. No—no, I think he is who he says he is. He wasn't the one to tell us, actually. I was. I could just—sort of feel it. Like you can with Hunter."

"*They* can't," William said shortly, clearly referring to Luca and me. The non-magic users of the conversation. "But I know what you mean."

"I just noticed—Quinn called him Marcus," Saki reminded me. "It sort of struck me. Maybe he doesn't *want* to be called Pluto all the time. Not that that's any excuse for shirking his responsibilities," she added, sitting up again. "It's perfectly obvious that some kind of crime ring is being run out of his old house now, using *his* old spells. And he's content to do nothing about it!"

"It'd be *more* obvious if he was the one running the crime ring," William grumbled, making it clear that this was the explanation he thought more likely.

"Then why let me and Gloria out?" I asked.

"So that you don't suspect him," William replied.

"But then Saki *did* suspect him," Luca added. "Of being unhelpful, at least."

"I didn't say he was a god of reason and logic," William snapped.

Sakura giggled. "No one's saying *that*. Unfortunately, if we want answers, my spell will prevent me from questioning him or his magic at all until I figure out a way to undo it. Or if I want to. In the meantime, we'll have to send Red."

"No," said both Luca and William at once.

I laughed—I knew Saki didn't mean it. "I think we have plenty of other people we can talk to."

"Would it even be worth it, at this point, to try to go back to the storeroom?" Luca asked.

"Not really," Sakura admitted, as William growled at the thought. "Any trace of the key that brought Red and Gloria there is long gone by now, I'm sure. And I have no idea how my banishment magic would take to me being in a room he literally *made*."

"In that case, you could see more sights," Luca said brightly.

I rolled my eyes at him. "You knew the answer before she said it. I'm sure you know all the magical theory behind it. You were setting us up!"

"Maybe a little," he admitted. Though he smiled, his green eyes were worried. The sight gave me a pang. My promise to make this a safe and restful vacation was definitely broken. "Can you blame me for trying?"

"Don't worry," Saki assured him. "We'll make sure Red gets back in one piece."

"Hopefully we *all* will make it back in one piece," I corrected. "But for today, I'm sure Thorn will want to—"

"'Thorn will want to' what?" Thorn herself poked her head out of the window behind Saki and me, her hair half brushed. "If you were going to say 'go to the police station to report an attempted kidnapping,' then you'd be right. Who're you talking to?"

"Not Maggie," Saki said, amused.

"Luca and William," I said at the same time. "Say hello. And yes, that is what I figured."

"Technically it was a successful kidnapping," Saki pointed out. "It was just thwarted after the fact."

"You're really not making either me or William feel any better about this all," Luca's voice reminded us from the mirror.

"It'll be fine," I promised them both. Again.

"Hello. Sure it will," said Thorn through her window. "Say, has it struck either of you as odd that Officer Herc hasn't shown up yet?"

23

Heroic Tasks

We made it through getting ready, breakfast, and hitting the road without seeing hide nor hair of our friendly neighborhood police officer. By this point, Thorn was looking around corners and under bushes as we walked.

"I doubt he'd be hiding," Gloria said dryly.

Privately, I had to agree with her.

Sakura had opted to stay behind with Ida, saying that she wasn't up for too much adventure after her exertions the night before—and perhaps hoping that if we *did* run across Pluto, we'd be able to talk to him. Ida herself was more determined to stay in our villa than ever. Thorn had made a hard pitch along the lines of "we're going to the station, you can too," but it might as well have been a summer breeze for all the convincing it did.

"Something's wrong," Thorn muttered. She stopped peering at every villa we passed, but she picked up her speed until I nearly had to jog to keep up with her.

And, once more, I had to quietly agree. The strange

new feeling in the air last night had lingered, banished only temporarily by seeing Luca and William's faces.

We cut down to the town center via a series of staircases set between buildings. By the time we got down to harbor level, the sun was fully risen and already hot. I was ready for the shade of the police station.

However—when we found the building, led partly by signs put up for the benefit of tourists and partly by Thorn's sixth sense for police work, it was clear that shade was the only inviting thing it offered. Helenia's police station was fairly large and square, set back from the main road by two blocks— and adorned with swords.

"What's that?" Gloria frowned as she looked up at the line of weapons hung under the building's roofline the way other local buildings sported carvings. "Some kind of 'lost and found'? All the weaponry they've confiscated?"

Thorn, too, paused, looking up from the street. "Hoping to make an impression on the tourists, maybe," she said. She squared her shoulders. "Good thing we're not impression-able."

"Speak for yourself," Gloria muttered, catching my eye as we fell into step behind Thorn.

I chuckled, if a bit uneasily. "Let's just make our report and head out. Easy."

* * *

It wasn't easy.

It wasn't quick, either. The clerk at the front desk was more interested in Officer Thorn's experiences in Belville than in our report, and once an officer finally came around to talk to us, we had to be separated and go through the story several times. Much as I understood best practices in policing—to a modest degree, as informed by my association with Officer Thorn—my head was spinning and I was decidedly grumpy by the time I was released from my windowless interview room. I rejoined Thorn and Gloria in the lobby feeling like a criminal reluctantly released.

"I don't think they believed a word of it," Gloria announced, not quietly, either.

Thorn was pacing across the tile floor. "It's true we don't have physical evidence."

I thought back to that little bit of moss I'd found in the wall. *Should have saved a sample!* But I doubted even that would have helped. "Maybe it's because we're tourists. We don't fit the pattern."

Gloria snorted. "Maybe it's because they don't care about anything but *town hall.*"

I glanced around surreptitiously. Given the ruckus we had caused yesterday, they might have had reason to care. I'd been very vague about my day prior to the apple incident in my own report. *Maybe Gloria was easier to recognize, and they gave her a hard time about it.* I resolved to ask once we were out of the building. Possibly over a refreshing tea and sandwich.

"We've made the report," Thorn said, though the usual firmness in her voice was absent. She glanced once more at the clerk, ignoring us from behind a heavy desk. There was no other furniture in the lobby whatsoever. Just white walls and tile. "Nothing else for it," she decided, rubbing her hands together. "We're done here for now. Although between us, I never did see . . ."

The door to the street opened, and sunlight streamed over

our shoulders. Thorn's voice trailed off as she surveyed the newcomers. They were only shadows at first: one large shape, one thin one.

My heart stopped—at first I thought, *Pandora!* But the thin shape was too tall to be our new friend the reporter. Any gratitude for that was short-lived, though. The two newcomers stepped forward and the light settled around them, revealing Officer Heracles . . . with Quinn Daedalus handcuffed and in tow.

"Now this I *have* to hear," Gloria murmured.

Though I did share her curiosity, I was torn with my desire not to linger. We hadn't just overstayed our welcome—we'd barely been welcome the moment we stepped through the door. I knew Officer Thorn was itching to leave, too, probably to give vent to her thoughts outside.

Before either of us could speak, however, Officer Herc clocked our presence in the otherwise vacant lobby.

"Officer Thorn!" he cried, gladly. He came to a full stop in front of us, a broad grin stretched across his face. His straw hat was hanging over his shoulders by a lanyard around his neck, its frayed edge giving his face a half-hearted halo effect. "I mean, good to see you. Too bad I'm busy."

Then, in an almost hilarious pantomime of looking around surreptitiously, Herc kicked Quinn.

Just *lightly.* Not enough for anyone but Gloria, Thorn, and I to notice. Quinn himself wore a pair of manacles, no straw hat, and an expression of bone-weary resignation. "Oh no," he drawled, standing stock still with his shoulders rounded forward. "I seem to have dropped something on the stairs outside."

"Great. Thanks. I mean, let's go grab it," said Herc, raising his voice for that last bit. "Here, we'll see you folks out while we're at it. Wouldn't want you to trip."

And just like that, the massive young officer herded Quinn, Thorn, Gloria, and I right back out the door.

The station door hardly swung shut behind us before Gloria drew breath, and I knew she was about to give him a piece of her mind about the lackluster policing we'd seen from his comrades. If Thorn didn't get to her concerns about his morning activity first.

But with characteristic initiative, Herc beat them both to it. "Officer Thorn! I got him! Did you see?"

Thorn and, in fact, *everyone* turned to look at Quinn, who was doing an excellent impression of Pluto.

"Right," said Thorn, noncommittally. "I see that you got . . . someone. Were you sent out for him?"

"No," Herc admitted quickly. "I was on my way to see you, and he stopped me in the street. Said he wanted to make a complaint, but then it came out that he was the last person who saw Eurie, and—"

"What?" Gloria and I spoke at once, both turning to glare at Quinn again.

Quinn shrugged, gazing off into the distance.

"—but actually," Herc continued, "Officer Thorn, I was wondering if you knew . . . . the procedure I should do? Because—everyone in there's going to be gone—I mean, they're all out looking for Ida . . ."

Ah. Another reason for our lackluster experience, maybe, I thought. And yet another reason to step carefully. I caught Thorn's eye: from the serious set of her brow, she was obviously thinking along the same lines.

"Step down to the corner with me for a minute, Herc," she

said. "Maybe we can give each other some directions."

It took a moment, but Herc's face visibly brightened. He trotted down the steps with Thorn. After a beat, Gloria nodded at me and then followed them. Apparently, complaining about the police took precedence over guarding Quinn, as far as she was concerned.

And given that she'd last seen him at the Botanical Garden with Edda, I didn't blame her. Nonetheless, I had *plenty* of questions. All I had to do was turn to him with my arms crossed.

For the first time, Quinn's weary expression broke into a small smile. "Let's have it, then," he said. "But if you don't mind, I'm going to sit."

He promptly dropped down to the steps, sitting in a patch of shade cast by the overbearing roof. I glanced at Thorn, Herc, and Gloria; they did actually look like tourists getting directions—or giving them. All three were waving their arms in various degrees of frustration and emphasis. Their conversation was only faintly audible, but it was clear they'd be at it for a while.

So, I sat down an arm's length or two from Quinn, close enough to watch him without being in any kind of danger. If he was dangerous? He did still have his weird flare gun-like device in a holster. But he'd seemed more *dangerously annoying* to me so far.

"Maybe start by telling me what happened," I suggested. It was, honestly, a little difficult not to sound smug. At that moment, I didn't especially believe Quinn was the killer, so it was amusing to see him brought in by the police.

"You'll be even more amused to know why I hailed our friend the officer," Quinn remarked, a knowing look in his gray eyes. "I was just leaving Marcus's and on my way to the police station, to do my best to get Sakura arrested for practicing baneful magic."

I sat bolt upright. "You *what?* That isn't funny!"

"No, but it's possible," Quinn replied. "Perhaps not entirely *practical*—you must have seen yourself how motivated Helenia's police force is, with the exception of Herakles—but I was willing to do my best."

"But—" I frowned. "Why?"

Quinn tilted his head back, looking at the clear blue sky above town. "Marcus asked me to."

Oh my goodness. I shook my head. *Can this get any more complicated?* With a breath, I reminded myself to focus on the big picture. Aloud, I said, "Okay, we'll get to that—trust me, we'll definitely get to that. But for now, how about explaining everything, from the beginning?"

"You're assuming I owe you any kind of explanation," Quinn observed. There was a slight but unmistakable twinkle in his eye as he looked back at me. "But I'm certain you will make a much better listener than Officer Herakles, and we seem to have reached a stalemate, so here you have it.

"Over the past year, Marcus has found it helpful to occasionally call on me. You can imagine that he meets people of all kinds, not all of them savory—or particularly forthcoming. If he had a buyer with nebulous intentions, he would contract my services to look into them.

"For that reason, and for the purposes of being discreet about it, I have a bell in my study which rings when Marcus wants to see me. Last night, very late, that bell rang. When I went round this morning, I found him in quite a state."

"'Quite a state' how?" I asked, intrigued. "Not hurt? I

suppose he told you what happened?"

"He did, but I would be interested in your assessment of the proceedings," Quinn acknowledged. "I do not believe he was physically hurt. Would you and your friends be upset if he was?"

I frowned. "Of course. Argument aside, none of us meant for *that* to happen."

"Argument aside, you say, but can you also lay your suspicions aside?" Quinn was looking like a sphinx again, asking leading questions. I just stared at him until he said with a slight, crooked grin, "He told me in no uncertain terms that I should prevent Sakura from discovering his old storeroom."

24

Great Theater

"I'm impressed that you *did* find it, by the way," Quinn added, while I sat quietly processing this.

It wasn't a shock—not exactly. But the lengths these two were willing to go to in order to keep their secrets *was* getting suspicious. Very much so. I pursed my lips at his comment. "You're the one who's currently arrested, so I don't want to hear anything about how I fell for a golden apple trick."

"No, I thought it was quite brilliant, really," Quinn insisted genially. "Nobody else has even come close to figuring out where the kidnapping victims went. You did put those dots together, of course?"

"Of course," I agreed. "And that's why Saki wanted to see it, to see what more we can find out. So what's with this campaign from Pluto all of a sudden? He abandons the property for years, so much so that he claims he has no clue who's using it now, but he suddenly cares if a shadow witch goes there?"

"I think you might find it depends *which* shadow witch,"

Quinn remarked. "In any case, he didn't give me his reasons. He was very agitated about it—which, for him, is saying something, as you can imagine. I'd just agreed to try the police when I stepped outside and, lo and behold, a police officer was marching down the road."

"Saki really chose quite a neighborhood to stay in," I muttered, distracted. I ran my hands through my ponytail as I did my best to think it all through.

"Some," Quinn said, his nose cheerfully in the air, "believe in fate."

I didn't quite grasp his meaning, but I knew one thing for certain. "Well, if she finds out he tried to get her arrested, she'll do worse than banish him." I had no clue what *worse* was, myself, but had unwavering faith in Sakura's ability to figure it out.

"And he might deserve worse, if he was indeed trying to keep his secret because he is the kidnapper," Quinn agreed. His grin, for a moment, had a vaguely wicked tinge. Then he went on conversationally, "But it was, in all honesty, my own idea to try the police. Marcus himself didn't have much direction to give, only a pressing need for her to stay out of it."

"Okay, so *you're* the unscrupulous one," I said, shifting on my step to face him more squarely.

"Hadn't you noticed?" Quinn asked. His innocent act was nowhere near as good as Saki's: he looked too much like he was enjoying himself. "I'll have you know I do have a few scruples, but what they are I prefer to keep to myself. As you yourself have observed, my attempt did not go as hoped."

"Tell me about that part," I said, eager to get back to actual facts. All this talking about what people were or were not willing to do was making my head spin. It was not unlike being led through the Garden's maze, in fact. "How did you go from accusing Saki—and how did you have any proof, anyway?—to getting arrested?"

"On the whole, I think my biggest failure was not realizing that Officer Herakles was *familiar* with Sakura," Quinn said, his eyes thoughtfully settled on the buildings across the street. "It was rather more difficult to convince him that someone who had served him breakfast and tea was a public danger than it would have been otherwise. I ought to have known you four would have found Helenia's one useful police officer," he added, briefly and lopsidedly grinning at me.

"To be fair, he found *us*," I said. *Or more correctly, he found Thorn!* That trio was still talking animatedly on the street corner. Herc, when last I glanced, had been taking notes. "But go on. You walked up and said 'oh no, a shadow witch is on the loose in the villas?'"

"More or less." Quinn nodded. His wrists were still bound, but he seemed completely at ease. "I did my best to keep Marcus out of it. But when I mentioned your address, Herakles began acting very nervous. He asked me what is, in retrospect, a very interesting question." Quinn eyed me from under one arched brow. "He asked me when I'd last seen Idunn."

I pretended my lips were glued shut.

"Marcus hadn't said anything about Ida," Quinn went on slowly, still watching me speculatively. This came as a surprise to me—after all, he'd accidentally trapped her and everything!—but I continued picturing a potion bottle of super-glue. A very large one. I had some back in my shop. Maybe I needed to experiment with a temporary version, safe for facial application . . .

"And in my surprise," Quinn continued, more in his normal, light voice, "I told him the truth. I saw her at the Elysian."

Super-glue or not, my mouth dropped open. "You were there? That night?"

"That night," he confirmed. "Just *after* you saw her, I fancy."

"We basically walked out with her," I protested.

Then it hit me. The thing Ida had said last night—*didn't want to get you involved.* She'd said that before. She'd said that back on the mountain trail, about the last person she saw talking to Eurie. She'd said she knew who it was, but didn't think that she should tell us—for our own safety!

Quinn was watching as my eyes grew wide. My fingers, twisted in my ponytail, slipped free as I slapped my hands on my knees, leaning in. "*You* were the last one to see Eurie alive?!"

"That's the conclusion Herakles came to," Quinn conceded. He lifted his bound wrists. "And now here we are."

Jumping from revelation to arrest *was* very Herc-like, and I understood now why Thorn had been talking to him for so long. She was probably trying to talk him down. But all the same—I couldn't entirely blame him. "Well," I said, still working through my surprise, "if you want him or the rest of us to come to any *other* conclusion, you have more explaining to do!"

"Certainly. I did my best with the officer, but I'm afraid he only heard every word as being more incriminating," Quinn said, quite genteel for someone in handcuffs on the police station's front steps. "I have faith you will see it more clearly. While I can not say for certain that I wasn't the last person to see *Eurie* alive, my actual target was Ida."

My eyes narrowed as I untangled this. "That *is* incriminating, since Eurie ended up dead and Ida ended up free."

"Suggesting that I thought one was expendable, and one was not," Quinn agreed. "However, that was not exactly my thought. For the past several months, I have been following Ida—on Edda's orders."

This was news, but I had to admit—it wasn't actually surprising. It explained quite a bit about Edda's performance when we'd found her in the maze. "Why?"

Quinn shrugged. "Edda found Marcus's card in Ida's pocket and became concerned. I have, by now, a certain reputation around Helenia for solving little problems."

"So she hired you to follow her daughter—for months?"

"Not every moment," Quinn corrected. "Ida spends—or spent—the vast majority of her time at the Garden, for reasons you no doubt appreciate. She and her mother live there as well as working there. She only had express permission to leave on the afternoons she helped Eurie with the mural at the town hall; otherwise, her time was accounted for. It was for those specific excursions I was hired."

The more I learned about life at the Botanical Garden, the more I found myself second-guessing how idyllic I'd thought it was. "Weird, but, I follow you. So, when we met them at the bar, had they come from Town Hall?"

"As a matter of fact, they had," Quinn said, eyeing me appreciatively. "The mural is done, but Eurie had a small award to accept for its completion, and she made an effort to include Ida in its reception. An unusual effort, I thought," he added—more in an undertone, to himself. His gaze dropped to the stairs beneath us as he recalled it. "I found much of Eurie's behavior to be uncharacteristic that day. It was also very uncharacteristic for either of them to remain at the bar so long. That was why I decided to approach Ida as they left."

"To just ask her right out why they'd been waiting there?" I raised an eyebrow, but it did actually sound like something I might do. "How'd that go over?"

"Not as poorly as you might think," Quinn told me. "Not immediately, anyway. Ida had known for some time that I was following her."

That made me tilt my head at him. "Really? You're admitting that you're not very sneaky."

"I could be," he said, "if I wanted to be, and in this case, I did not particularly care. When I introduced you, you seemed to find Edda laughable, if bewildering. Extrapolate that out across two years, and you might have some sense of how *I* approach Edda's requests."

"Why accept the job if you weren't going to do it?" I asked.

"You sound like Marcus. And I *did* do it," he retorted. "Just not especially well. It's not as though there was any real danger involved."

"Not until the end," I pointed out.

At that, finally, he looked chagrined. "Yes. On that point, I miscalculated. Eurie had never been my focus, but I *did* notice her demeanor change. I should have known to anticipate something out of the ordinary. But I did not."

I settled a little bit closer, fascinated. "So what exactly did they say?"

"Nothing much," Quinn admitted with a shrug. "Eurie asked why I was there—much more fearfully than I thought necessary. Ida rushed to her defense. She tried to explain it to her, I think, but Eurie did not listen—another strange deviation from normal. In the end, Ida told her, 'I'll take care of it, don't worry.' She lifted her hand, and pollen filled the air. The next thing I knew, I was waking up at the side of the road in front of the bar, just before dawn. Not a soul was in sight."

"And—did you—" I faltered, but had to know the answer before I asked anything else. Had he noticed Eurie, lying on the cliffs below?

Quinn shook his head. "I had no reason to look. Or so I thought. Believe me, next time I wake from a magically-induced stupor, I will be more circumspect."

"Right, so, wait," I said, pouncing on that. "Ida can do magic?"

"Flower-related magic." Quinn looked rather sly. "She didn't tell you?"

"She *did* mention she used it to get away from Pluto," I mused, not caring if he knew that part or not. I'd assumed that was all she could do. She hadn't done a lick of magic at all since staying with us, not even in her own defense the night before. *Has that been on purpose?* I wondered, with a growing sense of foreboding.

"Ida is not quite as helpless as she appears," Quinn commented.

I knew he was needling me, so I responded in kind. "And *you* can't be as calm as you act. You have to know that story is never going to convince Herc, or any of the rest of them. Your alibi for the murder is that you were unconscious in the road because of flowers?"

"My motive is just as weak," Quinn replied, remaining aggravatingly calm. "What did I gain from Eurie's murder? Or from the disappearances, for that matter?"

"It could be a negative gain," I realized suddenly. "It could be that everyone who disappeared was about to reveal something you wanted hidden. Maybe you were trying to prevent them from speaking out."

Quinn's gray eyes widened, just for a second.

And then without any ceremony or warning at all, Sakura appeared at my side—and fell over on me. She was heavy, and panting hard, trying to catch her breath. Black sparkles went haywire around her. "Red," she said. "Had to come check. With you. Did you know. Ida just disappeared?"

25

To Go Deeper

I had *not* known that fact.

Or at least, I hadn't known that *we*, as Ida's elected guardians, believed as much. Before I could parse this out, Thorn and Gloria had noticed our newcomer. They ran up the steps toward us, with Officer Herc trailing behind, doing his best to jam his notebook into his pocket as he went.

"Saki!" Thorn called. "Are you hurt?"

"What are you doing?" Gloria added, a little less concerned. She beat Thorn to us by a few strides and helped Sakura off my lap.

"Wait," Herc panted, bringing up the rear. "You *are* a shadow witch?"

"I don't see that it matters. The authorities are aware," Saki said, panting, patting her ruffled lavender dress back into place. Then she noticed who was asking. "Yourself excepted, until now. Yes, Herc, I'm a shadow witch." She turned to glare over me at Quinn. "Is that why *you* are here? Did he send you?"

Quinn shrugged blandly.

"We'll get to that as soon as I finish this," Saki said, her eyes narrowing to slits before popping back open, her air of alarm returning. "Officer Thorn! Herc! You have to start a search for Ida. A proper one. I—"

She faltered, and fell sideways again, this time onto my shoulder. Again, she was breathless and unable to speak.

"Okay, something drastic has happened," I concluded, shifting her onto the step next to me. "It must have really worried you, because you've used too much magic and are on the verge of passing out. Right?"

Saki smiled at me, but rather than her usual chipper brightness, her eyes looked hollow. "Full points," she panted. "I'll tell. William. That you've learned."

"I've learned enough about magic to know you need to rest immediately," I agreed. "But that's probably obvious to everyone here. So take your time. One more minute could mean a lot more trouble for *you* in this state than it might mean for Ida."

"That's. The thing." Saki took my advice, though, and didn't say anything more at first. I offered her water from my bottle, and she took small sips. Thorn, Gloria, and Herc shifted to stand in a line before her. Quinn was acting nonchalant on my other side, but I could feel him trying to listen over my shoulder. "I was in the kitchen," she said finally, sounding more like herself. "I had just taken the sun tea pitcher out of the window to wash it. Ida was on the patio, shielded from the road, reading one of the books from the lending shelf. I had just boiled more water and was ready to set up the next batch of tea. I wasn't busy more than two minutes, I swear. But when I went back to the window to put the tea in the sun, Ida was gone."

"Did you hear anything?" Thorn asked immediately. She was physically restraining Herc with one hand above his elbow.

Saki nodded. "One thing—a scream. Right after I looked and saw she was gone. Then nothing. I even started calling for her and got no reply. Not even from the neighbors. I went outside to look, of course."

"For evidence of shining apples?" Gloria tilted her head, feathers waving gently. As usual, it wasn't totally clear if she was being helpful or just wry, but her question deserved to be asked.

"Nothing there," Saki confirmed. "No apples. No broken things. Nothing upset. The book was lying on the table with a bookmark inside. I tried to trace her but I—I just kept getting—flowers."

"Apparently," I informed her, my own voice rather dry, "Ida has a lot more capability than we thought."

"Oh, I knew she did," Saki said, her eyes earnest and confused. "You can sense these things on other magic users—unless they're trying to hide it, or are repressed somehow. I knew she could do more than she was doing, but that's not saying much. What I didn't know was how much she *knew* she could do. I kept trying to learn about her training, but she just said she had always spent all her time in the garden."

"With flowers," Quinn pointed out from behind me.

"What he said," Gloria said, pointing down at Quinn with a careless, manicured hand. "So she's self-taught. She's probably had a *lot* of chance to practice."

"Especially trying to get time on her own," I mused. Everything Quinn had just told me only emphasized what lengths Ida might go to to get out from her mother's thumb. "Maybe looking for where Pluto's key would open. Oh, my goodness. What if she—do you think?"

Saki smiled wanly at me. "I think you are following Gloria's example and suspecting the person who acted last. You're forgetting the scream."

"Anybody can scream," Gloria countered.

"You're both right," Thorn broke in. "Ida could well be in danger. We have known kidnappers involved in this case. It has to be considered. But at the same time, Red's got a point. It's just possible that something—maybe her own magical strength—was a secret Ida was willing to do *anything* to keep. We have to consider her both a potential suspect *and* a potential victim."

"Why leave *now?*" Herc asked, looking up at Thorn.

The senior officer shook her head. "We won't know that until we find her. The trouble is, the main police force on the island is already looking for her."

"Poorly," Gloria remarked.

"What she said," Quinn added.

"I'm not saying that they'll find her," Thorn told them. "What I'm saying is, any one of us'd have a hard time convincing them to start looking *more* without going through a lot of explanations."

"I can recruit help," Officer Herc said unexpectedly. I looked at him, surprised, half expecting to see a younger, newer Officer Thorn standing in his place. She'd once used the very same lines on me. The familiarity was inescapable as he went on, "It's in the guidebook. They do a whole class on it at the Guild. Normally it's for smaller posts, like yours, Officer Thorn, but I can do it here too—can't I?"

"You can," she said, for a moment preening like a proud

mother hen. "Usually you'd need permission from a higher-ranking officer, but this is an emergency. You're well within the rules."

"We were going to look anyway," Gloria sighed.

"Yes, but now we can do it methodically and with full authorization," Thorn said, gaining steam. "Herc, you'll need to release your prisoner. With him, we have three teams of two. Arrest him again after we find Ida, if you want."

"Thanks," Quinn said dryly.

"He won't try to escape," Thorn added, eyeing him with full force despite the fact that she was wearing a white polo and flowered capris rather than her uniform. Quinn, much to my amusement—and slight suspicion—nodded meekly. Thorn went on, "I'll watch him myself. We'll head to the Botanical Garden—I'm the only one who's unknown there, and Quinn will be able to get access anywhere we need. Right?"

"It is rather neat," he admitted.

"Good," Thorn said, and continued briskly, "Gloria, you go with Herc. Herc, you'll have to keep a calm head on your shoulders. Go back to our villa and see if you can get anything from the scene. From there, go up to the mountain trail. It's where we found her last time, and chances are good she might go back. It's the biggest natural area outside the Garden itself."

Herc was looking at Thorn like a puppy told to *stay* while its friends went round the corner and had a treat, but I could tell what she was doing, and I thought that this, too, was "rather neat." Officer Herakles was not going to learn a thing sticking in Thorn's shadow. He clearly knew his handbook, and maybe having to argue with Gloria would help him step up a little more. And for her part, Gloria was the most accomplished hiker of any of us. She was already studying the mountain over our heads.

"That leaves you two," Thorn went on, looking down at Saki and me. "Red, you know what to do. Look after her. Don't let her do anything else extravagant. When she's ready, walk over to Town Hall. It's been the center of too many loose ends. Have some tea, keep an eye out for anything unusual, not just Ida herself."

I was feeling a little less amused to note that Thorn was giving me the same assignment she'd given Herc, but harder. "Looking after" Sakura when the mood to investigate came over her was no mean feat. And having tea while everyone else was busy felt like a consolation prize.

"Somebody ought to check Pluto," Saki muttered, only proving my concerns to be true.

"Somebody ought to," Quinn agreed abruptly, standing. "As it happens, I was just telling Red that I have, in my apartment, a means of communication with him. Given my conversation with him this morning, I am confident that if someone were to ring that bell, he would come. I do not suggest it as a means of getting myself away or warning him," he added, anticipating Thorn and Herc's protests. "In point of fact, I would suggest Red and Sakura be the ones to do it. My lodging is not far from here."

And so saying, he slipped one hand from the manacles on his wrists, reached into his trouser pocket, and tossed something at me. I caught it just in time: a plain set of two keys.

"Head back to Main and go two blocks west, to the building with the red door. One is for the outer door, one for the inner," he told me. "It's the second floor, door on the right. Mind the tripwire just inside the doorknob. I don't go in for wards, but I do have the odd mechanical security measure."

"That," said Gloria, "sounds exactly like a trap."

"Surely shadow witches don't get caught in those," Quinn said innocently. "Not to mention keen-eyed alchemists."

"One more word about that apple and I will put salt in all your ongoing experiments," I informed him, standing too. I was perfectly confident that Quinn *would* be the type to have ongoing experiments strewn about his house. And I'd made my decision: we'd do it. I knew without asking that Saki was game.

"You can't think it's a good idea," Gloria said, turning to Thorn this time.

"It's not," Thorn agreed. But her voice was more thoughtful.

"I should also mention that Ida knows me perfectly well, and knows where to find me should she want something done," Quinn added. "I like to think it's more than hubris on my part to suggest that she might, assuming she is free, show up at my lodging of her own accord, looking for a problem to be solved."

Saki lifted her head, though she didn't yet stand. "That does actually make sense."

"If it's a risk you're willing to take, do it," Thorn said, her gaze settling on me. "You know enough to know what you're getting yourself into. Everyone, plan to meet back here at sunset, if not sooner. Any further questions? Herc, do we have your approval?"

"Yes!" Officer Herc snapped upright, into a stiff and official posture, even saluting. When Thorn gave him a salute in return, he swelled up with such pride I thought he was in danger of floating away.

"Then let's go," Gloria decided. She marched off toward our villa, Herc matching her pace with enthusiasm.

Thorn watched them go for a moment, then grinned. She turned to look at Quinn. "Not too worried about manacles, eh? Rest assured I'll be keeping a tighter watch than circles of iron."

"I have no doubt," Quinn said, sweeping into a low bow. He left the iron bracelets lying on the stair behind him as he strode off behind Officer Thorn.

Saki sighed heavily. I turned to look down at her. "Are you sure about this?"

"I'm positive," she assured me. "But I'm really regretting that banishing spell about now."

26

Looking for Trouble

I had forgotten all about that. As Saki wobbled to her feet—and I helped her—I asked, "Does your spell mean he won't be able to show up when we ring the bell? I assume he's going to appear magically somehow?"

"Most likely, but my spell will only affect me," Saki said, distinctly glum. "You'll be able to see him just fine. Especially if I stay in the hall—just to make sure he can appear with no problem. Once he's just standing there, it'll be normal, aside from the fact that I won't be able to see him and, more importantly, give him a *very* large piece of my mind."

"Well, just let me know what you'd like me to say," I offered, smiling. "You okay walking? I have to admit, I thought Officer Thorn's idea about tea sounded a bit lame, but it *would* be a good idea to get a drink and some lunch on our way."

"You're probably right," Saki admitted. "But let's get it to go. I want to keep moving. When I sit still too long, everything starts to feel like lead."

"I can only imagine. Here." I rifled through my pouch for a moment and produced a small vial, which twinkled in the sunlight as we emerged from the shade. The liquid inside was a vibrant green. "I made this more for walking-too-much-and-seeing-sights fatigue, but it'll probably help with the physical side effects of magic fatigue, right? Just down it in one go."

Sakura did as I suggested, smiling gratefully at me. "Better already. Promise!"

I didn't *entirely* believe her, but at least she was more steady on her feet as we set off down the road. When we got to Main Street, we paused at the corner and I got us some strawberry iced teas and sandwich wraps packaged up in paper, as well as an enormous cookie shaped like a fish. Though it felt strange to be buying sweets while everyone else was searching for a victim-slash-suspect, I figured the sugar might give Saki a further boost. And while I didn't want her doing any more magic, I did want her to be as alert as possible: often, her wit and insight were even more helpful than anything magical she could do.

And besides, I was worried about her, purely as a friend. She'd admitted to her frustration and her fatigue, but something else seemed to be worrying her: her mouth was perpetually pulled down at the corner, almost as though she was sad.

Nevertheless, she nibbled on the fish's tail as we made our way down the street. Lunchtime was in full swing, and tourists sprawled out of every storefront that sold anything resembling food and drink. Tables and chairs, umbrellas, and playing children and pets created constant obstacles. Shop owners leaned out of antique stores, hawking everything from furniture to cursed vases. Music from street artists floated in the air. We walked slowly, clutching our drinks. I found myself very grateful that Quinn had elected to live so near the police station.

His directions, predictably, had been exactly adequate. Two blocks down the street, a building with a red door loomed on the corner. It was in all other respects exactly like every other building nearby, plastered white with a tile roof, rising three stories above the road. I glanced back at Saki, and she nodded tensely. I tried the first key, then the second, which let us inside.

The door opened to deposit us on a small landing, with a staircase immediately to the right. I held the door for Saki and shut it carefully, making sure it locked again behind us. Once the noise from the road was muffled, the building fell eerily quiet.

But it's not eerie, I reminded myself. *It's just a normal residential building whose residents are all outside, enjoying the sun.*

Saki nodded again, and I led the way up the stairs. We were met with another door, just as Quinn had described, though the staircase opened up onto a square landing with a few other doors waiting. I focused and used the inside key. It turned easily, noiselessly, but I nudged the door only barely open before activating the fingertips on my gloves and sliding the key out of the lock and past the doorknob, between the door and the frame. Sure enough, there was a small wire waiting there. I lifted it harmlessly and pushed the door open all the way.

The room before us was both entirely expected, and very odd. It was clearly a sitting room, furnished with the sort of stodgy armchairs and heavy rugs that might have been more welcome in a city like Brass than a hot climate like Helenia. There was even a fireplace on the far wall. Every single inch of the wallpaper was covered, though most of the coverings seemed to be papers with scrawled notes and mechanical drawings rather than actual pictures. A bookcase beside the fireplace was so full it was in danger of falling over. The windows along the outer wall were heavily curtained, and half-full tea cups had been abandoned on a nearby sidetable.

"I don't sense anything," Saki whispered. "No magic protections, like he said. I think he's generally truthful. Sort of."

"Says you," I replied lightly. "Alright, here we go."

We stepped inside, which had absolutely no effect whatsoever. Saki made her way gingerly to the back of the nearest armchair while I closed the door and turned to examine the tripwire. It settled into place, hooked into a loop on the inside of the door. The other end of the wire ran up along the door frame to a device set into the wall above my head.

"Simple and very effective," I commented. "I wonder what it would do if the wire was pulled?"

"Don't find out," Saki said, her voice tight.

"Don't worry." I fished my goggles out of my pouch and pulled them over my eyes. Through the lenses, I didn't find any more secrets. I hadn't really expected to. As soon as we stepped inside, the room had felt familiar—probably because it smelled exactly like my lab at home, an earthy, just slightly acrid smell of craft and endeavor. I found it was hard not to feel *too* comfortable, actually. Particularly when I turned and noticed that there was a long desk set against the wall behind me, which was—as I'd suspected—covered in all kinds of tinkering tools and potion bottles. Not to mention open books, a discarded straw hat, and a half-eaten scone.

"Red," Saki warned. "We're not here to steal his latest

invention."

"No," I agreed. *But it might serve him right!* I turned to the fireplace. "Let's see, he told me there was a bell on his mantle, I think. This has to be it," I added, walking carefully over the rug—and a pair of slippers, and a few more books. "Goodness, this is like visiting Luca."

At that, Saki smiled briefly. "Consider it a preview of what your apartment is going to look like when you get home."

I laughed. "Fortunately, we haven't figured out how to keep *more* books there yet. Okay. I just ring it, I guess?" I took up a post by the mantle, examining an aged brass bell with a wooden handle. "Where do you want to be when I give it a try?"

"It's one of the only things in here that looks magical," Saki said, worry creeping back into her voice. "And maybe that makes perfect sense, and all it does is exactly what he said. But—I can't tell for sure. Without spellwork—"

"Don't," I warned her. "No more today."

"I know, I know." She nodded absently and looked around the room. In the corner across from the door to the hall, there was another door, partly open and draped in what appeared to be a voluminous cloak. "I'll stand over there. I don't want to interfere with him getting here to see you, but I don't want to be too far."

"You could stand in the hall," I offered, eyeing the dubious darkness beyond the interior door. It might not be booby-trapped, but given the general mess, it seemed likely that the room beyond was a tripping hazard if nothing else.

"Okay." Saki nodded again, and again her absent mood struck me. *Might be fatigue?* I thought as I watched her carefully undo the trap on the main door. Either way, I was glad she wouldn't be directly in the action.

. . . Whatever that action would look like. As soon as Saki was out of eyeshot, I picked up the bell and rang it firmly.

And nothing happened.

I tried again—and then once more for good measure. My ears were ringing with the bell's tones, but they were just that—normal bell tones. Nothing else in the apartment seemed affected, and there was certainly no indication of someone teleporting onto the rug.

I reached out to tug one of the curtains open, as if that might help. It threw some light on the faded floral pattern of the armchairs, but nothing else. Out of ideas, I went to see Saki.

She was on the landing right outside the door, leaning her back against the wall. She was shifting one foot after the other, trying to give her legs a rest, her head tipped back as she studied the ceiling. Her white hair was mussed from being pressed too hard into the wall. The expression on her face was nothing short of miserable.

For a moment it shocked me. I'd never actually seen Saki look so uncomfortable before. Though she had no problem facing or talking about the less pleasant sides of life, she herself rarely seemed to be upset. Until this trip.

Then there was a small noise, perhaps just a sigh or a breeze beyond the front door. I glanced down the staircase. And who was standing there on the welcome mat but Pluto himself?

I startled back, colliding with the door frame and earning the attention of both the hallway's occupants. "What are you doing?" I asked Pluto, frowning.

"I was waiting," Saki said, surprised, from my right.

"She banished me," Pluto reminded me, sounding about as miserable as Saki looked.

"Why are you down there instead of in the room?" I asked him, unsympathetic.

"Who are you talking to?" With an effort, Saki pushed herself off the wall, putting the pieces together. Confusion creased her brows. "He came in the front door? I didn't hear anything."

"I use a back door in this hall when the bell rings," Pluto said. He sounded like he was describing a funeral, not visiting a friend. Or partner in crime. "I don't like to just *appear* in places."

Finding him staring at my friend hadn't started us off on a good foot. But I bit back my disbelieving reply. *He did do basically the same thing with the storeroom,* I reminded myself.

"What is he saying?" Sakura demanded. "He *is* there, I suppose?"

"He is," I answered slowly. "Saki, I thought you only wouldn't be able to *see* him?"

She looked worried. "I just assumed that because of the words I used when enacting the spell. But these things can— get a little out of control sometimes. It's the nature of shadow witchery."

"It is a very strong magic," Pluto said.

When I relayed this, Saki said, "Ask him to see how close he can come to me."

I glanced at Pluto. He nodded. He could hear her, but he didn't look especially happy about it. He started climbing the stairs, moving at about the speed of—well—*death*. He got to a stair just a few below the top, and stopped, perhaps two arm lengths away.

"Interesting," I murmured. "Saki, he's about two yards from you."

"About the distance we were on the patio," she mused, the distracted note in her voice again.

"Yeah. But much closer than the distance you were from Ida this morning," I observed. To Pluto, I added, "So. Do you know anything about Ida disappearing—again?"

27

Star-Crossed

Pluto acted as though he hadn't heard me speak. His dark gaze was fixed on Saki. "Why is she so tired?"

"Magic fatigue," I said shortly.

He glanced at me, then at her again. For a moment it seemed like he was leaning forward, but he didn't move from his stair. "Not merely from banishing me. It has been too long since then. What has happened?"

"Would you please answer *my* question first?" I reminded him.

He looked, actually, a little surprised. I had to remind him once more what my question had been. When I did, he shook his head. "I haven't seen Idunn since last night."

He also didn't seem too worried that when he'd last seen her, she'd been trapped in *his* spell. But at my side, Saki was quivering with impatience. "Well? Did she try to get to him?"

"N—no." I hesitated, giving Pluto a look as if to say, *stay right there, I'll be right back*—not that he seemed inclined to go anywhere at all. This conversation on two fronts was trying my nerves. Looking at Saki, I added, "I thought you thought she was abducted. But you say that like you think she meant him harm."

"It crossed my mind," Saki admitted, standing free of the wall and focused on me. There was still half a fish clasped in her hand, its pink frosting crumbling against the folds of her dress. "He's seen how much magic she can do, and she knows now that he knows she's got his card, and knows about the storeroom you found. After last night, she'll have realized that we wouldn't be able to keep tabs on him for her, and—"

Saki broke off. I understood where she was going, but her reasoning struck me as a little convoluted, perhaps. *Is this what she's been ruminating over? She thinks she put him in danger with her spell?* That made a lot of sense, but I hesitated to ask her directly while Pluto was still standing right there.

"You see now why I wanted her to keep out of it," the man in question said.

I turned back to him. "Excuse me?"

"You have access to Quinn's apartment," he said, looking up at me. "So he must have spoken to you. Clearly his idea of imprisoning her has not worked. I did not especially think it was going to. Even if he convinced the police to bring her in, why should she stay at the station when she is perfectly capable of getting out?"

He paused and I was silent, baffled. *I thought he meant Saki, but does he mean Ida?*

"Furthermore," said Pluto, gaining momentum, "in full knowledge that you can hear me and she can not, I will tell you that I believe *she* is in the greatest danger. You have arrived at the conclusion I have, that Idunn retained my card for her own purposes, including some secret which she is willing to kill for. However, I believe her reasoning to be in error. Idunn saw clearly last night that I have no interest in the matter. It is *she* who insisted upon investigating the isle. And she has the ability—a truly prodigious ability—to know what Idunn might do. Therefore *she* is the greatest obstacle, and must be removed as far from the situation as possible."

My head was spinning. "By *she* you mean Saki, right?"

"Of course." Pluto was watching her again, as if expecting her to pull out a deerstalker cap and a magnifying glass at any moment.

Saki herself stamped one foot. "I *hate* being talked about right in front of me. What is he saying?"

"More than I've ever heard him say, that's for sure," I mused, trying to put it all together. I addressed Pluto again. "By 'removed from the situation,' you mean—?"

"Safe," he said, his gaze snapping back to me. "Get her off the island. Take her home. Anywhere beyond Idunn's reach."

"And by 'island,' this time you mean Helenia." I sighed, shaking my head. "This would be a whole lot easier if the two of you would refer to each other by name once in a while. Also, though I see your point, you're forgetting that Saki and Ida were together all morning, and nothing happened. Until Ida disappeared. That was addressed to Pluto, by the way." I glanced at Saki. "Hold on a moment."

When I turned back to him, Pluto was watching me impatiently. "I put a containment spell on Idunn's magic last night. You saw me do so. But it was only temporary. I knew it would wear off overnight. I returned at that time, only to find the house empty."

"You returned too late," I told him, and explained what had happened.

He frowned slightly. "I did not think you would leave her

alone with Idunn. I had hoped Quinn would remove her by then. It was not my intention to be present myself, but when I did not hear from him, I had to see."

He left a lull in the conversation there, letting his disapproval become evident in the silence. I pondered. Ida's emotion had seemed genuine to me the night before, and I still wasn't sure I bought this idea of her as a magical criminal mastermind. The handkerchief she'd given back to me had certainly been soaked with real tears. But—I had indeed seen her in the grips of a spell, and it was true I had not seen her do any magic afterward. That part of the story made sense. But there were still a lot of loose ends—too many. "By the way," I said finally, "we thought you meant that spell for Saki."

Pluto was startled out of his stern air of criticism. "Why would I do that?"

"Because you didn't want her to see your storeroom," I reminded him.

"But the reason she should not go to the Garden is Idunn," Pluto replied, clearly confused.

"Then why didn't you just say that? What magic were you about to do?"

"I was going to repel whatever she was doing, to the best of my ability. Why would I say something directly, and make her an even more obvious target?"

"Red," Saki interrupted, "I'm dying here."

Pluto's eyes snapped to her in alarm. The look sparked recognition in me. It was a look I had seen that morning in Luca and William's faces. At last, I began to understand.

"Just an expression," I told him, suddenly finding all the sympathy I hadn't been able to muster earlier. *If* my suspicion was correct. I took a deep breath and turned to Sakura. "Okay, so, here's the deal. You think Pluto is in danger, he thinks *you* are in danger. You both think Ida is behind everything, which I'm not so sure about, just for the record. Basically, you both have seen all the same clues and have come up with the solution that the other one needs to be protected. He wants you off the island, by the way."

"To be safe," Pluto added fiercely.

"To be safe," I dutifully repeated. "Also, he says he did not mean that containment spell for you. He did it on Ida on purpose, because he thought it would give us time to get *you* to safety."

Sakura's blue eyes were wide as saucers, her mouth agape. I'd never seen her look so surprised. "Oh."

"'Oh'?" I grinned at her, teasing. If that was all she had to say, it meant a moment of respite for me. "While you think it over, let me propose something. To both of you. Pluto, I know Saki, and I really don't think she's going to agree to leave. Especially not when she paid for two more nights at the villa. Saki, from what I'm seeing of Pluto, it's also very clear that he's not going to give up. So let's work together. I have to believe that *together,* the two of you combined are more powerful than Ida is. Let's go back to the station, wait for the others, and make a plan to find her. Thanks to Pluto, I've remembered something that I think might help."

"Me?" Pluto glanced briefly in my direction.

It was *so* obvious now that I'd finally seen it. I grinned again and reached into my pocket, pulling out a folded white cloth. "I have here a handkerchief which was recently in Ida's possession, and covered in Ida's tears."

"Oh," Saki said again, a light coming back into her eyes. "I could trace—"

"Do not let her," Pluto growled at the same time.

"Actually," I told them both, "I was thinking something different. Pluto, how good is Flora's sense of smell?"

* * *

The plan forming in my mind was perfect—aside from the fact that, apparently, Flora was rooted to her spot in front of Pluto's door. Literally—or whatever the stone equivalent might be. Pluto explained this a little ruefully, but nonetheless he and Saki both agreed to come back to the station with me and cooperate.

As I locked up Quinn's apartment and headed down the stairs, I reflected that the other flaw in my plan was how awkward it was. Bad enough being a third wheel—but to be one caught between two people who couldn't come within two yards of each other made me feel like I was stuck in a bubble. It seemed like Pluto must be walking slow in front of me on purpose. But whenever I slowed down to give him space, Saki was practically breathing down my neck.

"Red," she said, as we reached the landing, Pluto standing at the door. "Could you tell him I'm really sorry?"

I glanced wryly at Pluto's face. "He can hear you."

"I know, but—it feels silly saying it when I can't see him," she explained, lingering on the last step.

I could understand that, but I also felt very silly repeating her words when Pluto wasn't looking at me anyway. "Well?" I asked him. "What do you want to say back?"

He looked at the floor. "I don't have anything to say," he said very quietly.

"Really?" I pressed, one hand on my hip. Truth be told,

now that his reticence and single-mindedness had a possible explanation, I found it a little endearing. I never would have guessed that a god could be *shy*, though.

"She believed I would act against her. She was right to protect herself," he said, sounding more melancholy than ever. "I'm the one who's sorry."

"Maybe bear that in mind next time you find yourself not telling us the whole story," I couldn't help but suggest. To Saki, I went on, "He's just sorry himself that he let it seem like he might do the containment spell on *you*."

Pluto didn't protest this summary, and Sakura looked speculative, biting her lip. "I'm not sure what to do about the banishing spell," she admitted. "Normal witchery is fairly straightforward to dispel if you do it properly. But shadow magic can be—squirrely. Normally I never do anything like this without really thinking it through. But I was so worked up I didn't think. That's my fault. My emotion at the time made it stronger, but that doesn't mean that it will go away now just because I know better. It's not that neat, unfortunately."

"It's fine," I assured her. "Especially since you should take a break from magic right now anyway. We can figure it out later."

Pluto's cool gaze was on me now. "You have a notebook?"

"I look like that kind of nerd, huh?" Since I did still have my goggles on my forehead and my gloves activated, the idea didn't bother me in the least. I smiled at him as I reached into my pouch and pulled out what was, indeed, a small lined travel journal. I hadn't had much chance to use it yet. "There's a pen attached to the side."

With gravity, Pluto took the little book from me. He removed one page and spent a moment writing, bracing the page on top of the notebook in one hand. Somewhere else in the building, a door opened and closed, and I was surprised to remember that there was a world beyond this bubble. Neither Pluto nor Saki took any notice.

Then, still with all the solemnity of a child protecting the oaths of a secret club, Pluto folded the paper and handed it to me. Feeling like I was in school passing notes, I dutifully handed the paper to Sakura—without looking. Something told me he'd probably perish on the spot of embarrassment if I did.

Saki, however, unfolded the page and read it with interest. She looked up—trying to meet his gaze, I realized. With a little *tut* of frustration she turned to me. Her blue eyes were bright. "Tell him I think it might work. It's worth trying, at least."

I rolled my eyes at her. "I'm glad you're excited, but again, he can hear you just fine." I turned to Pluto, expecting to have to prod him into an answer. But in the brief pause, footsteps were audible in the hall.

He'll never *talk while someone else is going by,* I thought. I looked up at Saki. The three of us looked normal enough to the outside eye, I supposed, aside from the fact that we were loitering by the door. *After this person leaves, we probably should too,* I thought. It wasn't sunset yet, but at the rate Saki and Pluto moved, it would take us some time to get back to the station.

I had just a second or two to think all this, and to note that the person approaching us was rather larger than expected. Then there was a cloud of smoke and I felt myself crumple— and then I knew nothing at all.

28

A Land Without Daylight

I woke with a start. My worries about the time and meeting our friends came flooding back to me. But I couldn't for the life of me tell what time it *was*. The light around me was hazy, dim, a dreamlike blue.

Sitting bolt upright, I was able to get a clearer picture—and appreciate what a *massive* headache I had. As I put my hand to my forehead, wincing, my arm brushed by leaves and flowers. In fact, I was sitting in a field of grass as high as my elbow, many of the stalks topped in delicate blue daisy-like blooms which seemed to faintly glow.

I wasn't alone, either. To my right was Pluto—bending over a prone figure obscured by the grass. *Sakura.*

"What happened?" I asked him, shifting closer. My voice sounded distant to my ears, as though coming from underwater. But, I realized, I could see Pluto with perfect clarity. Nothing about him was different than I'd come to expect— his skin the same dark gray, his black hair pulled back, his clothes demure and dark. But his face was almost startlingly expressive. His eyes met mine, brimming with desperation, worry, and despair.

"I know this place," he said, his voice low and strained, and rushed. "We are on the isle. But it doesn't matter. She hasn't woken. A magic suppressant was used on us, and it is still present, in the air. What if it has harmed her? She was already so drained."

"Hold on, let me see if I still have my things." I sat back on my heels, going through my pockets, feeling for my belt. Strangely, everything was present and accounted for. It was reminiscent of Gloria's and my experience with the apple. *Who abducts someone but doesn't try to take any tools from them that they could use to escape?*

Someone with absolute faith in their containment, that's who. The answer was unsettlingly obvious. But I set that aside for a moment to focus on Sakura.

"I've got two bottles left for headache, and one for fatigue," I said, dumping my pouch contents over my palm and sorting out the little vials. "I gave her one earlier and it seemed to help. Can you hold her upright?"

Pluto hesitated. "She banished me."

"You're sitting right next to her," I observed, raising one eyebrow.

"The spell is suppressed," he agreed. "But . . ."

I sighed. Obviously, our newest best friend Pluto had some serious scruples. "Okay, fine. In that case, though, move back. I'll prop her up myself." I scooted behind Saki, pulling her head and shoulders up over my knees as I knelt. From there, I could administer the vial of potion, knowing she'd at least be stable and unlikely to choke.

As I sat there, leaning over her head, Saki's eyelids fluttered. She frowned and squinted at me, most likely trying to make sense of the strange light, just like I had. Then her gaze fell sideways and stopped.

"Marcus Antoine Pluto," she announced, a bit hoarsely, "I'm going to banish you all over again for being so ridiculous. You had this lovely garden, and you *abandoned* it?"

"They wanted a proper Botanical Garden, above ground. They told me it would be better," he said, leaning toward her. The relief in his voice, even in the lines on his face was so evident it made my heart skip. "Can you move? Are you well?"

"I'm well enough." Saki pushed herself up so she was sitting cross-legged, shaking her head slowly. "Though I have a horrible headache. Red?"

"Me too," I agreed. "Here, I have two vials, we can each have one. Unless—Pluto?"

"I do not need one," he said.

Nonetheless, when Saki drank half of hers and then held it out, glaring at him, he accepted it meekly and drank.

"Catch me up," I said, offering Saki the last sip from mine. Given all she'd been through in the past day, she needed it more. She nodded her thanks as I went on, "You two obviously recognize this place? But it's not where Gloria and I were."

"Correct," Pluto said, still considering his empty vial in the half light. "You and your friend were in the storeroom above this place. That was, once, directly below my house, and this place . . . this is the heart of the island."

"Like a cave?" I frowned.

Saki handed her empty vial back to me. "Just look at it, Red."

With my head a little clearer, I did as she suggested. The light, which at first had seemed ghostly and omnipresent, I now saw was arching above us—like a sky with the sun stretched out over the entire dome, as if someone had melted it down and spread it like butter. The light here was nothing like sunlight, but it was clearly sufficient for the flowers, which carpeted the floor as far as I could see. By gauging shadows, I got the sense that the space we were in did have limits, which curved around us. Rather than being in a natural cavern, it was more like we were at the bottom of a snow globe.

And we weren't the only things present. Strewn around us haphazardly was a series of what appeared to be mismatched *beds.*

"It's like myths of the Elysian Fields," Saki said, presumably for my benefit. "Except for the furniture."

"I kept a piece of it just for me," Pluto told her. "To come and think. But I did not leave these things here when I left the isle."

"Well," I said, setting aside the myth for a moment to focus on the practical, "we'd probably better take a look. I have a feeling I know what we might find. If you think it's safe?"

I glanced between Saki and Pluto, who looked at each other. Saki looked back at me. "There's definitely something in the air dampening magic—you didn't leave that here either?" Pluto shook his head when she looked back at him briefly to check. "So," she went on, "my guess is, it's meant to keep us here, but dampening spells aren't usually selective. I doubt a magical trap could exist here for very long."

"Sounds good." I got to my feet, a little unsteady but otherwise none the worse for wear. My goggles were still on my forehead—I pulled them down over my eyes. "I'm going to go see."

As I made my way to the nearest bed, a four-poster with a pink canopy, Saki got up to follow me. Pluto got up to follow her. Which meant that there was a palpable domino effect of surprise as we each reached the foot of the bed and realized, in succession, that a *person* was in it. A person with pale skin, long dark hair, and a smiling, serene expression, as if in the middle of a very nice dream.

"Oh, my goodness," Saki murmured.

"I bet you we're looking at one of our missing persons," I said softly, having had a moment longer to collect my thoughts. "Quinn's sister, maybe?"

I glanced at Pluto, who shook his head. "I never met her, so I do not know. But I would suggest not touching her or the bed."

"Seconded," Saki agreed. "Red, can you see anything from here?"

"Well—I think she's fine," I said, focusing carefully on the scene through my goggles, zooming in on her chest, which rose and fell steadily under a blanket of purple velvet. "Her face is very peaceful. Everything about it would look entirely normal in a bedroom."

"But why would a sleeping spell work here, despite the dampening?" Saki asked, turning to Pluto with a crease between her brows. From his expression, Pluto was as confused as we were, but he smiled faintly at her, as though happy just to be asked.

I turned back to contemplating the furniture, feeling more like a third wheel than ever. Carvings had been etched into the post—carvings which injured the veneer, rather than having been purposefully preserved by it. From that detail, I knew that they'd been added later. "I have an idea. I think it's the beds themselves. Like how the magic inherent in my potions still worked for us—maybe objects can get around the spell?"

"Actually, yes, I think that would do it," Saki said slowly. "If they imbued the beds with magic before bringing them down here . . ." she turned, looking around the circle of antique furnishings. "I hate to be what Officer Thorn would call *morbid,* but have you noticed that there are more beds than known kidnapping victims here?"

Pluto looked too. "Three more."

"For us, then." I tugged my hand through my ponytail, unsettled. "Yikes. Okay. Maybe it's meant to happen naturally, in a way. They send somebody down here with magic—don't even bother taking their stuff or anything—the person is stuck here, decides *why not, I might as well sleep,* and . . ."

"And they don't wake," Saki agreed. "We can try with this one to make sure. Just definitely don't touch her or the bed."

Several solid minutes of yelling, tickling with flowers, and even a tiny explosion created by a leftover "snapper" firework in my pouch had no effect whatsoever on the sleeping person. We went round to check the others, and I found myself struggling to recall Pandora's list. *Wharton, the town hall secretary; Tangerine, the janitor* . . . I hadn't met any of them before, and hadn't seen pictures, but the array of people we discovered sleeping soundly here seemed to fit the bill.

"I'd say we certainly found them," I remarked as Saki, Pluto and I regrouped in the center of the room—far away from the three empty beds. "But we still don't know who put them here for sure, or why."

"Or how to get in land out." Sakura looked up at Pluto.

"I always teleported." Pluto looked thoughtfully up at the ceiling. "I did not think anyone else might think to look for it. To seal it away would have meant erasing it."

"But that also means that whoever found it again was

familiar enough with *you* to guess that it was here," Saki said, chewing on a fingernail as she thought.

"Or with the myth," I suggested. "Right? That's what you were saying earlier."

Saki glanced up at me, her eyes wide with a dawning realization. I hadn't thought I'd said anything so extraordinary.

But in the next breath, a new voice filled the space. "Oh, look at you. Putting the pieces together, are we?"

29

Lost Souls

The three of us turned as one. A familiar figure was walking towards us, though there was no indication of where she might have come from. I was almost distracted from looking, struck by how *odd* it felt to see her here. The white apron and jaunty, poofy hat, in particular, made no sense in such ethereal surroundings.

There really could be no question as to why she was here, but it was so utterly preposterous that my thoughts stalled. Saki asked the necessary question for us, her arms crossed over her chest. "What are *you* doing here?"

"Checking on you," Rhea said, with the same wide smile that was plastered on the side of every bakery cart in Helenia. In this setting, though, the curled horns that framed her face seemed more menacing, her deep brown eyes more calculating than friendly. "You came along so nicely, but you've been so bothersome, haven't you? I thought to myself, I'd better check on them after work to see how they're getting along. And lo and behold, not only are you resisting sleep, you're *plotting!*"

"No closer," Pluto broke in firmly. Rhea stopped short

several yards from us, near one of the beds. She didn't seem to have anything, no weapon or device, and if Saki had been correct, she wouldn't be able to wield magic. But this lack of obvious threat wasn't enough for Pluto, who stepped up so that he was obscuring Sakura's view.

I, on the other hand, was apparently on my own to face this scheming baker. "Isn't it hypocritical of you to accuse *us* of plotting?" I asked her.

"That, my dear, is precisely why I've had you followed," she informed me. "You're too *involved* by half. Your little showdown at Town Hall yesterday proved as much."

I startled, and then in a flash, remembered. "The bakery cart in the alley."

"I do like to keep an eye on things," Rhea said. "You learn these things in business. I'm told you two both have your own little shops back in Belville. And you—all I can say is, you should have known better," she told Pluto. Though he stood to my right, I couldn't make out his reaction. Rhea apparently didn't much care, because she went on, toying with her necklace. "It's always best to keep an eye on things."

"A linked scrying spell," Saki said. She remained behind Pluto and I, but must have been thinking through this new development keenly. "That's why you're always playing with your necklace. You can see what is going on down here—and I'll bet that's how you get in and out, too."

"Aren't you the little clever one," Rhea said. "You're a bit of a dark horse, dearie. I'd been far more worried about your feathered friend, based on the antics I saw yesterday. Didn't even want to risk sending the two of you here directly—I'd hoped the antechamber might be enough to cool your heels."

"Storeroom," I corrected, needled. "You did that? The apple

and everything?"

"Why so surprised? You saw as much in my show, didn't you?" Rhea grinned toothily at me. "Or, your friends did. Don't you talk?"

My stomach dropped. "Your performance was supposedly some kind of courtesy . . . that's what Pandora had said."

"That's what they all say," she said lightly. "What I paid them to say. Didn't I tell you that in business, you must pay attention? But I must say, it is so *refreshing* to be able to take credit for my hard work. And don't think I'm telling you out of goodness or ego, either, my dears. Oh no—there is a very practical purpose in all of this."

Somehow, that made this conversation even *more* worrisome. "Wait a moment," I said. "That you've noticed us investigating, I believe. That you followed us after town hall and lured us away with an apple you've just admitted. But at Quinn's? There was no apple there."

"Even you, curious as you are, couldn't fall for the same trick twice," Rhea agreed. "And I had my own second thoughts, let me tell you. I had these extra beds enchanted as a precaution, but the fourth was taking too long, and it occurred to me that you were simply too *active*. After the way you and your friend so handily escaped the antechamber, it struck me that a much better plan would be to get you evicted from the isle altogether. Should you make it to the surface, you'll find the police very uninterested in your stories, by the way," she told us with a complacent smile. "It's so *nice*, what money can do. They'll pack you off on the first flight home. *You* might as well go with them," she added carelessly to Pluto. "You've been of enough use here already.

"But to get to the point, dear," she said to me, "you ought to know by now that Idunn is my *dear* partner's child. And your friend Quinn, my partner's employee. It's only natural that I've been watching his apartment since Ida's disappearance. He should have known more," Rhea reflected, a frown crossing her face for just an instant. "But who should show up but the two of you! Clearly you were evading the police. The risk had become too great. Fortunately, the building has a back door, and a smoke alarm spell that's easily fooled. In the confusion of a false fire, it was easy enough to stuff the three of you into the bakery van."

She turned to look at Pluto again, thoughtfully. "I hadn't realized *you* were involved. I can't help but feel a debt to you, you know. It was very foolish of you to leave all this here for anyone to claim. Do you like what I've done with the place?"

"Release Sakura and Red," Pluto said quietly. "Though you are able to suppress magic, you can do nothing against a divine curse."

"I'm not afraid of you. The only true god of the underworld is Hades," Rhea snapped. For a moment, in anger, her shoulders rose and her hands clenched, and she really did look fearsome. But in the next instant, she let out a breath and wiped her hair away from her face, her composure back in place. "But it's perfectly true that I don't want you here. I came down here to offer the three of you a deal."

I set my hand on my hip—near the pouch on my belt. "A deal is only useful if both parties can trust the other."

"And that, dear, is why you aren't as successful in business as *I* am," she said, smug and satisfied once more. She went on, "All you have to do is follow my reasoning. I'm certain you'll make the right choice. You had an opportunity for sleep—that's still on the table, should you like to take it. It's Hypnos's own spell, and cost me no small fortune. I hear the dreams are very pleasant. But if you will not take it—

"Then I will lay out your other option." Her voice became cold, almost harsh. "Accompany me to the surface, where my guard will take charge of you. You'll be brought to the police station and formally charged with disturbing the peace in Helenia, and all duly exiled. It will not be a pleasant mark on your record, perhaps, but you will be free to continue your life elsewhere."

"And if we did choose sleep?" Saki asked pointedly. "What kind of 'continuation of life' is that?"

"The safest kind, aside from exile," Rhea assured her easily. "The sleepers you see here will all wake and be discovered amongst the island's ruins once my plans are finished. You could be among their number if you want to extend your vacation."

"And will your plans *ever* be finished?" Saki pressed, her voice arch.

"Of course they will, dear," Rhea said with a laugh. "I don't have time for impractical matters. I'm very near now to the ultimate success."

I shifted, moving my hand over my pouch. I didn't like the sound of something so vague and so clearly power-hungry.

"You would like it too, little alchemist," Rhea assured me. "All those nasty tariffs. They already gave you a hard time at the air station, didn't they? Wouldn't it be so much nicer to have *completely* free trade? Aside from the cost of goods, of course!"

Rhea cackled this time—truly cackled, tipping her head up to the hazy blue above us. Her horns and shoulders shook. I risked a glance back at Saki. Her eyes were hard, but she nodded at me.

I took that as encouragement to take over the question-asking. And I knew just how to start. "All the people you abducted have been associated with town hall," I observed. "So—you're hoping to influence the government's decision, then?"

"*Abducted* is too strong a word," Rhea said, rather than answer. "I haven't touched anyone. You know yourself how persuasive a bit of gold can be."

"You lured them away," I offered, holding to my point. "Because you have plans to infiltrate town hall somehow?"

"Before the month is out, I will be the official business advisor," Rhea confirmed. "There's no one else for the role—and no one to say I paid off key officials for it, either. They really are so *touchy* about that kind of thing in Helenia. Is it the same where you are from?"

"Let me guess," I said dryly, ignoring her question in a tit-for-tat moment. "Another helpful person you paid off will suggest that advisors be life-time roles."

"Aren't you funny? That's precisely why little Wharton had to be removed. He didn't have the stomach to go through with the proposal, and I had to find someone else. Fortunately, Hestia found that her desire for funding for a 'native investigations unit' outweighed her worries."

Yikes. I ran my free hand through my hair. "What about Eurie? She knew you'd lured away Wharton?"

Rhea shrugged. "She must have."

"What do you mean, 'she must have'?" Saki broke her silence, stepping forward. Pluto immediately shifted in front of her again, so they were both crowding my space.

And since Rhea had nothing else to say on the matter, I tried a different angle. "What about the pattern of disappearance?"

Rhea shrugged again. "It was a useful coincidence at the beginning, but if you want to be successful with your little store, you'll learn to cut your losses when it's time. The way it created fodder for the paper and the public was useful, of course—anxious voters do like advisors, I've found. But if it's outlived its usefulness, then so be it."

"Wait, so—you didn't plan that?" I frowned, thinking this through.

"It's only natural that as my plan got closer to fruition, more people would notice—or hope to profit by telling their little reporter friends," Rhea said. "I have a great many people on my payroll. You have to spend money to make it, as they say."

Tangerine and Pandora. I winced. Rhea did *not* go in for common sympathy, that much was clear. But she was very forthcoming, and that was showing me some flaws in the case. "People saw the pattern that had been created by accident, and you began using it to your advantage," I guessed. "But you're not beholden to it. Which means that Eurie's and Ida's encounter, even though it fit into the pattern, was—what? Accident?"

"Oh, it was hardly an accident, dear," Rhea said. "But it wasn't part of my plan."

"Are you really saying you had nothing to do with it?" Sakura couldn't have sounded more disbelieving, and Pluto shifted uncomfortably at the note of challenge in her words.

Rhea toyed with her necklace. "Do you see either of them here? No? Then I don't see why we are having this discussion. Decide whether you will take my deal or not. Now."

"Or what?" Pluto asked calmly.

"Or I leave, and make your choice for you," Rhea replied. "I really am very busy. You've already taken up too much of my time. How's this—I'll give you a count. Five . . . four . . ."

30

Divine Intervention

"Three . . . two . . ."

I was braced with my hand on my tools, but unfortunately, I didn't have much more than weak acid and a small travel journal left. Saki had her hand on my arm and Pluto had both hands raised, as though he thought he might fight off Rhea's leaving.

But she never made it down to *one*.

Instead the very ground beneath us seemed to speak, interrupting her count. The world rumbled, like we were indeed in a snow globe and it had been rolled down a set of stairs. But instead of moving down, we—and the field of flowers, the beds, and even Rhea—lurched *up*. Saki and I braced each other, looking at Pluto with wide-eyed astonishment. But amid the confusion, he shook his head. It wasn't his doing.

The hazy blue light flickered out around us. Then the world went dark—dark and *leafy*.

My hands went up to my face automatically, and I was fighting off branches and twigs, choking on bits of leaf. A hand on my shoulder tugged me forward—Saki. I focused

237

on her face as the world settled back into place. Beyond her, there was shadow, and the pastel shades of twilight as fresh air flooded over the flowers.

The blue flowers of Pluto's garden, which still shivered around our knees. But now, there were the hedge walls, too. I'd just been inside one. Looking around, I realized that the heart of the island was now *on* the island—

—and *in* the maze.

"We've been brought straight up," Saki said, thinking along the same lines. "Rhea must still be here, just around a corner. And everyone she kidnapped, too. We just have to find them. The suppression spell is lifting—"

"*No!*" Pluto's voice, but he was farther away than he'd been before. Fortunately, against the faintly glowing flowers, he stood out—or *sat* out? He was on his back, as though he'd been batted away from us, farther down a corridor in the maze. His gaze was fixed on me. "Don't let her do it. I will."

There was only one reason he'd be talking to me and not to her. I glanced at my friend, who was still taking in the maze around us, making her plans. "Saki. Your banishment spell. It's back?"

She looked startled, scanning the hedges and flowers as though she'd lost something. "It is, you're right. Is he okay?"

"He's fine," I said. "He says let him go after Rhea instead of you. You've still done enough magic for the day, remember?"

"Okay. He'll do it?" Sakura's eyes were intent and worried on mine.

I glanced at Pluto, feeling a bit like a mirror, reflecting these looks around. He'd made it to his feet. "I will catch her. It is my fault she was able to carry out this plan. This is my responsibility."

I relayed this to Sakura, and she nodded. "Okay. Yes. Wait!" Pluto, who had already been striding off into the maze, stopped in place.

"Make sure he knows," Saki said, holding my sleeve now—gripping it like it would bear witness, "not to do anything reckless. All he has to do is catch her, for the police. The police must be coming—somebody must be here already, to have done this. He doesn't have to be some kind of hero. Make him promise to be responsible for his own safety, too."

Pluto's shimmery mask was back, but even so, I could watch his expression shift from impassive to soft as Saki spoke, until at the end he was smiling gently back at us. "I will come back to her. I promise."

I sighed as he left. Saki poked me irritably, and it made me laugh. "He said you both ought to learn each other's names if you're going to be so besotted."

"That is *not* what he said!" Saki protested, her free hand rising to cover her cheek—but not before her blush became obvious, even in the twilight.

"Alright, fine. He said he promises to come back. Hopefully he meant that figuratively, not literally, because I don't think it's a good idea for us to stay here." I looked around the maze again, my goggles scanning in the dark. I could hear, distantly, applause or a crowd roaring—the Garden was probably hosting some kind of evening show. But other than that, there was nothing. No villains yelling, *we're going to get you!*

But even so, my feet itched to get out of this maze.

"We have no idea where we are," Saki said, hesitant. "I agree with you that it's not a good idea to stay here, trapped, but is it a *better* idea to move around? Especially when we don't know the key to the maze."

Privately, I thought there was no way I wanted to let myself be cowed by a maze I *knew* Quinn had created. I'd already been bested by a golden apple—an insufferable inventor-turned-detective was too much to take. I began searching through my pockets again. The glass bottles were clear, of course, and the notebook was boringly paper-colored, but . . .

"Here," I said triumphantly, holding up my vial of emergency acid, meant for cleaning or un-sticking things. This particular acid was very weak, technically speaking, but it was also a vibrant red. "I still don't know how color helps solve the maze, if it does, but let's find out. If you're up for it?"

Saki squinted at the vial, then finally nodded. "It's better than a rose, I guess. And if we get *really* lost I can levitate."

"Sure, and put me immediately in Pluto's bad graces," I retorted. "Come on. It won't be that bad. Like you said, there's probably somebody else here already . . ."

Whether they were friend or foe, though, neither of us could say.

We started out cautiously, creeping to the end of the corridor we were in. At its end, the maze stretched out to the left and to the right. No one—and no beds—were visible in either direction, but the vial in my hand seemed to tug, very slightly. The liquid sloshed and pooled on the left side.

"Huh," I said, following the suggestion and walking down the path on the left. "I think it *might* work."

"Can you hear anything?" Saki was scanning the sky above us.

We passed by a spur on the right without a twitch from the vial. I kept us moving. "No, earlier I thought I could hear some applause, maybe. Does the Garden do night time events?"

"Don't you remember?" Sakura sounded surprised. "Oh—that's right. You hadn't joined us yet. Medu was telling Gloria and me that they have a whole series of concerts. He said a lot of the artists who perform are friends of the Garden. He even gave me a schedule."

Though the vial now seemed to be faintly pulling my hand forward, I paused mid-step. "Saki. Is that how you knew Raffael was a musician?"

"Is it?" Again, she seemed surprised, leaning on my elbow. "I might have seen his name there and put it together without thinking, I suppose. 'Orpheus' was definitely on the schedule, I remember that, because of the myth. But then I figured it'd be faster to find him by going directly to musicians and asking around. Why? Does it matter?"

"I'm not sure," I admitted.

"Let's keep going," Saki said, pressing against my arm now. "I'm worried that we can't hear Rhea or Pluto. She can't have ended up so far. What if we went left again up here?"

"I thought we were following the key," I protested, but not very strongly. I, too, was curious.

We started moving again. The vial still pulled forward, stronger than ever—maybe now that I was better at paying attention, I noticed it more. But now I was distracted, too. Saki had made a very good point. A left turn was coming up, and I was tempted to take it no matter what the vial said.

In the end, though, neither Saki nor I—nor even the vial—made the choice. Around a corner ahead of us, several shadows appeared. Before we reached our turn, they were upon us, yelling.

"Red! Saki!"

"*There* you are!"

"What's happened?"

In order, I recognized Gloria, Ida, and Herc.

And then I found myself being hugged by Ida, who was, perhaps unsurprisingly, in tears. Gloria was standing to the side and had taken over supporting Saki, who was smiling despite the worry in her eyes. And Herc, standing in front of us, was still talking. Reporting, in fact.

"When you didn't show up at sunset, Officer Thorn said we needed to look for *you* now," he was saying, his hat in his hands. "Look! We found Ida! She was on the mountain, just like Officer Thorn said. And she helped us find these flowers and you in the maze!"

"Oh my gods, Red, I'm so sorry," Ida was bawling into my shoulder. "I thought I was going away to make things *easier* for you, and I made them worse!"

It was so familiar, yet in such an eerie setting, that it made me laugh. "We can talk everything through as soon as we're out of here. Officer Herc, you should know that it's not just flowers. Saki and I, and Pluto too, were in a sort of hollow in the island where Rhea was keeping the kidnapping victims. All of us were in there, and we've all been lifted up."

"Rhea?" Gloria's brow creased. "Isn't that the baker?"

Herc was similarly confused. "You found the kidnapping victims?"

"We got kidnapped," Saki said.

"Like I said, lots of details for later," I added, gently pressing Ida back on to her own feet. "If you all are okay, we'd better focus on finding the victims. They were in a series of beds, but they're probably all over the maze now. Ida?"

"I always thought there was something weird about the maze," she answered, uncertainly. In the darkness, her pale, tear-stained face was ghostly. "Mom never wanted me to do anything about it. It was her place to be alone, she said. I never really thought about how it is really the center of the Garden. But when Gloria said maybe you were in the store room again—I thought maybe—if there *had* been a house here—?"

"You didn't find the store room, but you did better," I told her. "How much more can you do? Can you find people in the maze?"

Ida shook her head. "I was only able to feel it because of the flowers, I think. I have no idea who's in here. But it feels—alive. More than it should."

"That's because Pluto's still in the maze, looking for Rhea," Saki said grimly. "He's probably using his connection with the space to help him."

"And we're okay with that?" Gloria asked.

"Don't get her started," I replied for Saki. "Basically, yes. Okay. So are you all lost in here too? I have something red if we need it."

"I know how to navigate it," Ida said. "We make sure all the staff, even temporary ones, know."

"I'm glad we found you," Herc broke in, "but if it's true—and there's other victims in here—"

"It's true," I assured him. "At least, we think so. How about you take Ida, and try to mark out their locations? You could draw a map in your notebook, right? Just watch out—they've all been under a sleeping spell, which was attached to the beds they're in. So, maybe don't touch them yet until you can get a Witch or someone in."

Officer Herc nodded firmly. "That's a good idea. That's what we'll do. If you'll come with me, Ida?"

"Of course, I can draw the map for you as we go," Ida said, reaching out for his notebook. To me, she added, "We'll go deeper in, then, and you'll go out?"

"That sounds like the plan," I agreed. "We'll wait in the conservatory, if it's open."

"It is," Gloria said. "We'll probably find Thorn and Quinn around there. After you two disappeared, we figured we'd all better stick a little closer together. And it didn't seem like you could have gone anywhere else, honestly."

"Tell Officer Thorn what we're doing," Herc said, as he and Ida took the lefthand turn to go toward the maze's center. I waved them both off reassuringly, amused. *Does he want her to know because she can help coordinate, or so he can earn points?*

Their footsteps quickly receded, and in one turn they were obscured from view. Another dim roar echoed from somewhere else in the garden—a happy crowd, I reminded myself. Gloria cleared her throat. "So, obviously, you two have some explaining to do."

"Let's walk and talk," I suggested. As night fell, the maze was starting to get chilly, and now that Herc was in charge of the victims, I saw no reason to stay. "Saki?"

"Fine," she said, drawing out the syllable like an angsty teen.

I led the way with my little red vial, continuing down the corridor. Behind me, Gloria and Saki walked in step—Gloria taking very *small* steps, for her, still supporting a very drained Sakura. Despite her long day, Saki's voice became more and more animated as she recounted our misadventure for Gloria's benefit. To her credit, she even admitted the inconvenience her banishing spell had caused—though she very delicately skirted around the awkward emotional situation she'd found herself in.

We'd taken a right and a quick left, and I was just considering teasing Saki about all the things she was leaving out, when a scream pierced the air.

"HELP! HELP! IN THE MAZE!"

As though struck by lightning, the three of us pulled up.

"That was Rhea," Saki said. "Pluto—we have to find them—"

"It was deeper in the maze," Gloria observed.

"I didn't think he was going to hurt her," I said, more slowly. "Just catch her. Maybe she's trying to act innocent? Or—"

Before I could say the words, somebody darted down a side corridor and ran right into my side.

31

A Lullaby

I f there was one complaint I could make about my time in Helenia—aside from the crime, of course—it was that I was getting *really* tired of people running into me.

But I didn't say that, because there were already words on the tip of my tongue.

Maybe she's trying to act innocent . . . or maybe she's calling out to her conspirators.

Because really, would someone with as much money as Rhea work alone?

The person who had run into my side wasn't in any shape to answer questions at first. We both toppled to the ground. My vial slipped from my fingers, falling amongst the flowers. And as I struggled to sit up, disentangling myself from my accidental assailant, it was by the glow of those flowers that I recognized the newcomer.

"Raffael?" I stayed on the ground for a moment as I processed this. "Why are you here?"

"I—I—I'm here to play the concert, but I heard Rh—I heard somebody cry for help," he said, sitting up. He ran a hand

246

through his gorgeous wavy locks before looking at the three of us. "Uh—who are you again? Do you—work here?"

"Nice try," Gloria said, her voice flinty. "We literally met you in the street yesterday. And *you* were the one to suggest the gondola ride."

"Not to mention you were at the bakery cart on the corner we passed this afternoon," Saki added.

"Was that you?" I considered him again. "Why would you be working for Rhea?"

Raffael glanced around us, scooting back through the flowers. "I work a lot of odd jobs. Sorry I don't remember you, okay? I—I was just trying to help whoever screamed."

"Your employer," I reminded him.

"Just—sometimes," he said, scooting back again.

You have to spend money to make it. Rhea had just said that earlier . . . and so had Raffael, days ago.

It was nothing, really, as far as clues went. Anybody could use a mercenary saying like that. But combined with the way he was acting—and the way Rhea had acted. *She acted like she really didn't know much about Eurie,* I recalled. It had bothered me at the time. Now the answer was on its butt in front of us. *She didn't need to, if it was* someone else *who had dealt with Eurie . . .*

. . . Someone who was supposed to be her partner. My heart twisted in my chest, but I had to try it. I sat up, focusing on him. "Sometimes, like when she asks you to commit murder?"

Raffael rocked farther back, hitting the hedge behind him. His eyes were wide. "Rhea never said that. She wouldn't."

"Are you so sure?" Saki asked sweetly. I could be certain that she had my back.

"She's pretty preoccupied at the moment," Gloria added, not

to be outdone.

"She wouldn't have," Raffael repeated.

"Really?" I pressed. "Because things are unraveling, Raffael. You must know that. You can see the flowers all around us. The secret lair, the kidnapping scheme—it's all uncovered. Literally. Now's the time for all the secrets to come out."

"What—I don't even know what you *mean,*" he protested plaintively. "The flowers? So what? What about them?"

If this was an act, he deserved to be in the theater, not behind his guitar. I cocked my head to the side. "You really don't know?"

"Gods above," he went on, almost as though he hadn't heard me. "*Flowers.* Always flowers. No, I don't know anything about them! Why should I? They don't actually matter. Flowers can't keep secrets, and if you ask me, people who like them can't keep secrets either!"

I was watching him every minute, ready to jump on him if he tried to escape. But for one more time—the last time—it wasn't him I was seeing, but Eurie, back at the bar. *People don't realize.* So earnest. The final pieces fell into place—not like puzzle pieces—like petals. Soft, but undeniable. "You *don't* know," I realized aloud. "Because you're exactly what you look like, aren't you, Raffael? Nothing less—and nothing more. A musician working too hard in a rough business. Business is a lot easier with a patron, right?

"Maybe it started innocently," I went on. He was watching me with wide eyes, like he'd been hypnotized, so I kept playing it out. "Rhea likes to support a lot of things, likes to get her name out there. Theater. Music. You got lucky, I bet. But it must have been a while ago . . . long enough ago that you began to notice that things at town hall had a way of working out in Rhea's favor. Long enough that your loyalty to Rhea outweighed your new relationship. Even if it was with someone *beautiful.*"

At this point, he looked downright scared. I felt Saki's weight against my back as she stepped up behind me, leaning into me in a show of support. "Maybe," she suggested, making no effort to hide her disdain, "it was more a matter of loyalty to *yourself.*"

"Because if Rhea was revealed, you would suffer too, right?" I saw the flicker of anger and knew we were on the right track. "As one of her pet acts, you'd be mixed up in the scandal. And more than that—you'd lose your gig. You told us yourself how easy it is to be forgotten on the music scene. You'd carved out a place for yourself—but it was precarious. And revealing Rhea was exactly what Eurie planned to do, wasn't it?

"Did she tell you?" I needed to know how he'd realized it. But unexpected tears rose in a lump in my throat, and I had to pause. "Did she tell you—because she wanted support? Or was she hoping to *warn* you?"

Raffael stirred, finally. "She didn't tell me nothing."

"She knew better, then," Gloria snapped.

"But someone else didn't," I reasoned. "Your alibi for that night—you were playing a boat party. Everyone thought it suspicious that Pluto was there, but he wasn't the only one, not by a long shot. The word Herc used—'bigwigs.' The kind who might work at town hall? The kind who might mention to you, by way of making conversation, that they were supposed to meet with your girlfriend in the morning?"

"You knew Pluto was on that boat," Saki added. "You made a point of saying it. And more than that, *you knew that Pluto had met Ida.* Something Herc would never have mentioned.

Something you would have found out later, from the card in her pocket."

Raffael pressed himself further into the hedge wall. "How do you know all this?"

"Because you weren't very smart," Gloria retorted with a snort. "It's not hard to guess."

"Not once you realize that all this was done in desperation," I agreed. "You weren't planning to meet Ida and Eurie. They were waiting for someone else. Maybe Ida was even waiting for Quinn, hoping he'd show up and might help them. But at that point, you'd already heard the news, and you guessed why Eurie might meet with someone at town hall. You were terrified. You had to stop her. You must have seen how she'd reacted when Wharton went missing . . ."

At that, Raffael broke. "Wharton was *nothing*," he insisted, leaning forward, anger flicking through his eyes again. "Just a little secretary. She acted like it was a tragedy! Kept saying she was supposed to be making a *difference*. She never saw that someone *else* was making a difference—for all of us!"

"I doubt Rhea cares about making a difference for *you*," Gloria commented.

"You think you're so smart!" Raffael glowered up at her. "I know what you are saying. And it's true! I know it! Rhea doesn't care about me—why should she? It's enough that I rise in her wake. But all that would mean nothing—all that work, for *nothing*—Rhea doesn't have to care, but *I* do!"

"You acted completely alone," I concluded. "You got out of your show early—left your bandmates to play alone, I'll bet. By such a late point in the party, who would notice, anyway? You told us yourself how you used to train by swimming. You made it to shore, and you knew how to find Eurie—at her favorite bar."

"The only real question is, why involve Pluto?" Saki put in. "Why leave Ida with him?"

Raffael ran his hands through his hair again.

"You think he doesn't have his own ways of finding out?" Saki pressed. "You think he *appreciates* being drawn into this?"

At that, Raffael shuddered. "I knew it was a mistake," he groaned. "I knew it was a mistake as soon as I found the card. I had to knock them both out, that was easy enough, just find a rock. They were practically joined at the hip. I had to take care of Ida if I was going to do anything about Eurie. I figured I'd go through her pockets—make it look like a robbery—then I find *that*. He'd kill me! I didn't want to get on the wrong side of those people. The last thing I needed was him to come after me looking for revenge. I thought if I left her there . . . No harm done . . ."

"How'd you find the house?" Saki asked.

"I went there once when I was starting out," Raffael said miserably. "When Rhea first paid me. I had real money for the first time. I wanted to buy a guitar, a really good one . . ."

"A charmed one," Saki corrected, adding smugly, "I bet he didn't sell you one."

Raffael shrugged. "Took me almost until dawn, but I found it again. Carrying her all that way was no joke. If I didn't work out I couldn't have done it, but I did. I had to. Left her there with the card. Hoped that'd be enough."

He seemed to truly believe Pluto was at the head of some sort of shadowy gang who might come looking for him, because he'd done harm to Ida. He could hardly have been more wrong, but I decided not to correct him on that front.

"Eurie," I pressed instead. "Before you left with Ida, you

killed Eurie. To keep her from sharing whatever she'd learned with Theseus."

Raffael's gaze returned to mine, and it was empty. "Yeah. That's about it."

That's about it? That's all he could say? Rage burned through me. Before I could say anything, though, he smiled.

"The good thing," he said, sitting up again, "is that none of you are *from* here. It's just your word against mine. Rhea can fix that."

"Why should she bother?" Gloria challenged him.

"She knows what I've done for her," Raffael said. He began standing, and likewise, I scrambled up as he continued, "I had to tell her. She knows all about it. She won't let it come out. But *you*—"

He lunged. Saki and I, nearest to him, were ready—but for the second time, he tumbled to the ground at our feet. This time he was even harmlessly rolled up in a contraption of rope.

"Do you know, I must agree with him," said Quinn. He emerged from the darkness to our right, Officer Thorn at his shoulder. And in his free hand, he held the modified flare gun that had shot the rope net. "We foreigners must be *so* annoying."

32

On the Other Side

Early the next morning, I sat in a meeting room in the police station, distracted.

"These just arrived," Thorn announced, carrying a basket full of pastries and a tray of drinks into the cozy room. It was a far cry from the empty lobby and dark interview rooms of yesterday—now, we were in the official conference room, surrounded by white-paneled walls and windows that looked out onto the officers' desks. Thorn deposited breakfast onto the oak table that took up most of the space. "*Not* from Minotaur Bakeries."

"I wonder what will happen to it?" Sakura leaned over me to snag a muffin and an iced coffee. She'd been bouncing in her chair ever since we arrived to put together the pieces of the night before. I attributed her nervous energy to the fact that we hadn't yet seen Pluto.

"Thinking of expanding the Pomegranate Café?" Gloria asked from my right. She was the only one of us who seemed entirely unruffled by catching a murderer *and* a kidnapper as well as finding six sleeping victims. There was already a bagel and a puff pastry piped with chocolate piled on the plate in front of her.

Saki stuck out her tongue. "Ew. No, thank you."

Thorn, taking a seat at the end of the table near Gloria, chuckled. She, too, had loaded up—no fewer than three croissants were balanced on the lid of her coffee cup. "Give it time. It takes patience to see how these things work out. What's your problem, Red?"

"I tried calling Luca before we got here, but he didn't pick up," I admitted. With a sigh, I reached for a bagel of my own, and one of the iced chais. "It's probably nothing . . ."

As if on cue, Officer Herc appeared in the doorway. He actually had to fit one shoulder through at a time. But what was truly surprising was that his grin fit through the door, too. "Guess what?" he announced. "Chief said I might get a *commendation!*"

"Well-deserved," said Officer Thorn, clapping. The rest of us dutifully followed suit, scattering crumbs and sugar across the table.

"And he also said I can handle debriefing you all by myself," Herc said, still beaming as he took the chair across from Gloria and me. I caught Thorn's eye briefly, grinning, one eyebrow raised. *Maybe the elusive Chief just doesn't want to have to face a fellow officer and admit he was behind the ball the whole time.* The glint in Thorn's eye told me she agreed.

But even so, it was fitting—truly, sweet—for Herc to be the one to wrap up the case. He laid a fresh, uncrumpled notebook on the table and, with a shy glance at Officer Thorn, grabbed the other iced chai for himself. Then he glanced around at all of us, the alert look of a hunting dog eager for the chase settling over his wide face. "We've got Raffael and Rhea in custody, officially," he began without preamble. "Raffael made a full confession. Rhea's not telling us as much, but Raffael pretty much gave her away, and there's strong evidence tying her to the hidden garden." He nodded at Saki as he said it, and I recalled Rhea's snow globe necklace, which Saki had guessed was a scrying device tied to the "hidden garden," as Herc called it. I could well imagine how conclusive that evidence might be.

"Raffael doesn't have the magic required to carry out the kidnappings," Saki confirmed, sipping her coffee while keeping one eye on the window. As if waiting for someone else to arrive.

"Right," Herc said. "We sent officers out to the theater to get some of their props and statements, by the way. So we should be able to put together a pretty clear picture of how Rhea was actually doing it. And why, especially as the victims wake up."

He glanced at Thorn this time, and she took her cue, nodding gravely. "You've got them all looked after?"

"They're in the medical center next door," Herc told her proudly. "I found them all last night, Ida and I did, and we were able to map it out so the magic team could come in and get them. You were right," he added to me. "They said the beds were so magicked that they would have put any of us to sleep if we touched them."

"That wasn't just me," I said, glancing at Saki again. She was fully watching the window now.

"They're waking up now," Herc continued. "Actually they all woke up earlier, as soon as the Witches moved them out of the beds. But we wanted to keep them here to get their statements and make sure they're okay. It's pretty confusing for some of them, especially the ones who were gone a long time. So far they all said the same thing, about the apple, that you said," Herc told me again. "They never actually saw Rhea themselves, but it always happened right after they'd realized she was paying off lawmakers. One, Harley, saw a transaction happen at the back of the records room," Herc said, ticking it off on his fingers. "Then Rhea tried to get smarter, doing it at night, but that one, the janitor Tangerine broke in on. Then Rhea probably started moving the cash transfers off site, but both Winter and Pokey said they heard people whispering about it in the hall, and Pokey wouldn't take a bribe to rearrange security. All stuff like that."

"You mentioned Ida earlier," Gloria said. "What happened to her?"

"She went home last night," Herc said, shifting back. "It was . . . uncomfortable. Chief said he got a lot of calls."

Thorn's gaze from the end of the table sharpened. "Anything serious?"

"Just a lot of questions and needing confirmation," Herc answered. "I guess she didn't really take Ida's word for things—Edda, I mean. I mean—I don't know if you all knew this, but—she *was* dating Rhea."

"We heard that," Gloria confirmed. "So is she saying she never knew anything about it? Really? It was in *her* garden. Under her *maze.*"

"Ida did mention that Edda thought of the maze as her own place—and so did Quinn, in a way," I added thoughtfully. "But that might just have been, I don't know, a bit of selfishness."

Gloria snorted, but didn't disagree.

"They're both supposed to come in in a little bit," Herc said. "Ida and Edda, I mean. And the other members of Orpheus, the band. I thought we could get some final answers about the alibi," he added, looking at Thorn. "I should've talked to them sooner, I guess. I just . . ."

"Didn't assume he and the others might be leaving something out when they said the band played the party?" I suggested kindly.

"It's always good to be thorough," Officer Thorn added, the maternal note back in her voice. "You'd have got there eventually, but it's good you're doing it now. Let this be a lesson for next time."

"Yeah." Herc nodded, clearly relieved, then looked back at his notes. "We got a full statement from Quinn last night, when he helped bring in Raffael. He retracted everything about—um." Herc glanced at Sakura, then at his notes again. "We still haven't, uh, got hold of Mister Pluto."

Saki sat up. "You must have seen him last night?"

"We found Rhea at the center of the maze alone," Herc said, shaking his head ponderously. "She was, uh, she was sort of trapped in a big bubble. You couldn't hear her or anything. She wasn't hurt, but she was pretty mad. It, um, took a while to get her out. A couple of the Witches had to do it this morning."

I glanced at Saki again—from the smug smile on her face, I guessed she knew how that might have happened. I had to admit, it was a little bit of unorthodox divine justice that made me want to chuckle, too. "That must have happened right after we heard her cry out, then," I concluded. "No wonder she didn't keep yelling."

"Yeah, that's what I thought too," Herc said eagerly. He glanced at Sakura with more hesitation. "I don't know if you all know how to get hold of him, though . . . ? It'd be good if he could explain the flowers. And the—haunted store room you mentioned in your other report?" Herc squinted at his notes, then at Gloria and me.

"I can tell you right now that that was harmless," Saki said.

Gloria glanced at her across me. "Didn't seem that way as we were walking out."

"That's because he wanted it to seem like a bad place to go," said Saki, rolling her eyes. "It was all just magical phantoms. I knew *that* much when you first told us about it. It'd take way too much power to actually imprison any creature down there and then *leave* it there for years afterward. For an empty room? Not worth it. Even Rhea didn't bother."

"The laughter, then?" Gloria challenged.

I remembered the noise of the crowd the night before, drifting through the maze, and blushed slightly. "Maybe we should check the Garden's schedule and see if they were doing some kind of theater at the time."

"Still, we do kind of need to talk to him," Herc insisted.

"Didn't you ask Quinn?" Saki returned.

"He was nice about Raffael, but he wasn't too pleased about, um, everything else," Herc admitted.

This time I *did* chuckle to myself. Next to me, Gloria hid her sly smile behind her iced tea.

In the pause, we could hear voices outside the meeting room. Saki stood at once, looking toward the door—and sat again when it was Ida who popped her head in.

"Oh, there you are!" she said. Then, with a quick glance behind her, she stepped through the door and pulled it shut. "You have no idea how glad I am to see you. Everything these past few days has *happened*, right? Only, I've been back and forth so much with my mom about it all night that I don't even know any more!"

She collapsed into a chair beside Thorn, who passed her the

basket of pastries with a sympathetic look. Gloria caught my eye again, and winked.

"Hey, Ida," I said. "We were just going over everything, actually. I've been wondering about a couple things. Weren't you and Eurie waiting for someone, that night at the bar? Someone you didn't want us involved with?"

"Yes! I'll tell you everything, *finally*," Ida said through a mouthful of hazelnut croissant. "I'm so sick of half truths and lies, and I'm not even worried any more, anyway. So, that day, we went into town, right? Eurie was getting an award. But she didn't want to go alone. She'd been acting kind of weird for a while, and I thought it was about Wharton, you know, like she was just sad he'd gone missing. But then when we were there, getting the award, she kind of pulled Hestia aside and talked to her, I guess to put a meeting on the schedule to see Theseus? He wasn't there for the award ceremony, something about getting ready for a party or something, but he was supposed to come back later in the day and Hestia promised to tell him then.

"So that was when I knew it was something important, whatever Eurie was thinking. But she said she didn't want to tell me too much, and that it didn't have to do with painting. Still I figured it was something really big, and that's why I didn't want to tell you either! But it was obvious she needed *someone* to help, and I thought, Quinn was supposed to be good at solving things. But Eurie didn't want to just go to his house. I think she thought she was being followed maybe? Like I said, she got pretty paranoid. But I knew Mom had asked him to follow me around when we went into town, so I thought, why not stay out late? He'd be bound to say something or try to make us go home—that's what I thought, anyway. Only, it ended up being *so* late when he finally *did* show up, and Eurie just wasn't having it—it had been all my idea anyway—and then we were both drunk, and she just got nervous. She did that, sometimes, you know, that's why I would go with her for the murals. She never really needed my help," Ida said. Her voice trailed off, a mixture of deep affection and sadness coloring her expression.

"You did help her," Thorn said gently. "You found Wharton, and everyone else."

"Oh my gods." Ida dropped the rest of her croissant on the table, her blue eyes wide. Though her face was lined and shadowed from a sleepless night, in that moment, it was as though the stress melted off her. "Oh my gods. Do you really think so? She would—she would love that. But it wasn't just me. I wouldn't have ever looked if it wasn't for all of you, and—seriously." She glanced around the table. "I know I've been, like, the *worst* house guest. You all have been so kind. I should've known you would come looking for me—I'm really sorry about that. It was just, after that magical explosion, and Saki still looking so weak the next morning—" Ida glanced across the table at her, truly looking sorry. "I felt so guilty, I just had to leave. I couldn't think what else to do."

"Saying something would be a good choice, next time," Saki said a little stiffly.

"You're right, I know." Ida dipped her head. "You know— it was meeting Pluto that morning that made me not want to go back. Because he was just so . . . not dramatic about it all, you know? Just *nice*. It hadn't really occurred to me that people could be that way. I mean, Eurie was obviously, but I just hadn't *seen* it properly before. And then, with all of you . . ." She sighed, glancing over her shoulder toward the door. "I should get back out there. Who *knows* what they are saying. But I can't run away again. I—I just wanted to say, it was meeting him that made me think things can be different, and—it's been meeting you all that made me think I can *make* things different. You know?"

"We're honored," I told her warmly, on behalf of my friends. Though Saki's reserve was justified, after all the trouble she'd been through, I couldn't help but feel encouraged by Ida's words. After all, Ida's worries about "being a hassle" had, in some way, echoed my own worries about breaking my promise to Luca and my friends. And here she was, on the other side, sounding positive. "You can always write to Red's Alchemy and Potions in Belville, if you want. But—really quickly, before you go—that first morning, after the night in the bar, I woke up early. I realized later maybe it was because there was someone outside. Was it you?"

"Oh!" Ida's eyes widened again. "I bet it was! I didn't know it was your house at the time. But it's right on a trail that goes up the mountain—that's how I left the other day. Just a little trail—only someone who knows the mountain would know it. Or flowers."

"I thought so," I said, satisfied.

"Wouldn't *that* have been nice to know," Gloria muttered beside me.

I laughed. Before I could reply, though, more shapes appeared at the windows. I glanced up expecting Edda, and perhaps even the heretofore-unseen Chief, but got the shock of the morning when instead I saw Quinn and Pluto—with Luca and William beside them.

33

Myths to Live By

"Obviously," said William, "we weren't just going to leave that last call at *that*."

"We were worried," Luca agreed. "We didn't want to crash your party, but, well—"

"It didn't sound like much of a *party* to me," William interrupted, with a suspicious canine glare at Pluto's back.

I laughed. The meeting room hadn't been big enough to contain all our surprise and catching up, so my friends and I had spilled out onto the police station's front steps. Officer Herc and Thorn remained talking near the door, while Pluto and Quinn stood with Gloria some distance away. Saki was *near* William, Luca, and me, but I knew she was thinking about something else. "Well, either way, I'm really glad to see you. I think it's fine that you showed up. I don't think Saki minds, do you?"

Sakura glanced down from her higher step, and smiled at me for a moment. "The main thing was just to give you a chance to get some perspective on your upcoming wedding. Funny, isn't it?"

"I definitely had some serious thoughts about life's ups and downs," I admitted, thinking of the way Eurie's passion had made me worry. But especially after having spoken to Ida one last time, I felt more comfortable now realizing that even if those passions didn't make us invincible, they made life worthwhile.

"At least you know for sure we'll be there with you, through them," Luca said, a little abashed.

I smiled at him. "You were never far from my mind, trust me. I wonder," I added, glancing up at Saki again, "if we can return the favor."

Sakura turned beet red. Luca and William, however, looked interested. "Do either of you know how we might undo a banishing spell?" I asked them.

"Pluto did have an idea," Saki said—whispered really. "But . . ."

William panted. "Are you that sure you want to be able to see him again?"

Saki nodded.

"In that case, even if it's shadow magic, you should be able to break through it," Luca mused. "Based on everything I've read, anyway. I looked up some more sources on mediating banishing spells after our talk yesterday. If you have someone magical—like William, say—who is able to make sure that the banishing spell doesn't rebound—and of course you'll need someone neutral to facilitate whatever you need to do, and who can explain to Pluto what is going on—"

"Go and try it," I told the three of them, laughing. "Whatever it is, I'll watch safely from here."

They trooped off, Saki a little hesitantly, Luca looking positively delighted to put his magical research to use. As they circled Pluto, Quinn broke away and came over to me.

"So," he said, smirking from under his hat, "I take it the ragamuffins Marcus and I found on the road outside your villa are friends of yours?"

"Yes, and we won't bother asking why you and Pluto were there," I returned.

He shifted so that he could watch the goings-on at the other end of the stairs. Gloria had retreated to the safety of Thorn and Herc. "Why else? I think Marcus was hoping something at the scene of the crime might help undo the spell."

"Our veranda is hardly a crime scene," I protested. But this question of motivation made me think. I looked at Quinn more seriously. "You've got your sister back now. I never did ask *why* you took on the maze job. Didn't you worry, knowing the old story?"

He shrugged, his gaze faraway. "I was too full of myself, to tell the truth. I thought it wouldn't matter—that it couldn't happen to me. I'd be too smart." Before I could say something sympathetic, like *we never know for sure how these stories will go anyway,* he glanced over at me and added, "I've learned a lot from my time in Helenia. When Harley recovers, I think it might be time to try somewhere new. Not Belville, don't worry! But I find I like the idea of going back to Argen."

I'd visited the city myself, years before, and could see why someone might like to live there. But I was more interested in what he'd learned. "Does that 'learning' include ancient experiments from Pluto's collection?"

"Naturally." Quinn grinned. "I never did tell you: congratulations on solving the maze!"

"You never did explain it," I retorted. "Was it some kind of color magic? How did it work with the vial? I didn't even remember until this morning—Medu had told us it only worked with red *flowers!*"

"Maybe it worked with your intention," Quinn replied. "Who said it was color magic?"

"Didn't *you?*"

"Maybe it was just a play on your chosen nickname," he suggested.

"You're never going to explain it, are you." I sighed, looking back at Luca and William, who had conjured up a small blue circle around Saki and Pluto.

"No, but I do explain *some* things." Quinn was watching them too, but he glanced at me and I saw his mouth quirk up. "Did you know, for example, that poor Marcus overheard part of our conversation in his garden? Only enough, though, to leave him thinking it was you and *Sakura* who were engaged."

"Really?" I laughed in surprise. "I figured he had listening spells or something, but that was when I was worried about illegal artifacts—not relationships. So you enlightened him, huh?"

"Yesterday morning," Quinn agreed. Now, if he was a bit smug, I could forgive him. "I may have suggested a particularly ancient remedy to baneful magic, too."

We watched as Saki, guided carefully by a glowing-blue Luca, leaned down from her stair and kissed Pluto's head. Even *I* could feel the magical reverberation as the banishing spell collapsed. When Saki lost her balance and toppled down onto Pluto's chest, for a moment his expression was completely readable. It was bliss.

"Okay," I admitted. "For giving them that idea, on that score, you win."

* * *

After that, Quinn said his farewells and went to the medical center to look after his sister. Pluto, unsurprisingly, didn't look like he was going anywhere. Instead, he suggested an out-of-the-way beach where we might all relax for the day—at last. Each and every one of us could get on board with that plan. We said another farewell, this one to Officer Herakles, and took off for picnic supplies and bathing suits.

It was heavenly. We had a slice of white sand and crystal blue water all to ourselves. Thorn and Gloria soon had a two-person game of volleyball going on. Saki and Pluto sat shyly on the rocks bordering one side of the beach, in charge of the drinks and snacks. Luca and I raced each other into the waves, egged on by William's amused laughter. Diving into the water was a true relief.

"We'll still definitely have to come back some time," Luca said, bobbing beside me as he looked back at Helenia with awe on his face.

"I'll show you all the sights," I agreed. "*Aside* from the police station."

Luca laughed. "I told you! It always happens when you travel."

"You did." Thinking of what Saki had said at the beginning of the trip, I paused for a moment and watched our friends on the beach. "I know we've talked about it before, the way things are drawn to me, but . . . I just have to check. Do you mind it?"

"I couldn't," Luca replied. "Because you found me that way. And I know how much it means to you."

He just couldn't have been any more endearing. I leaned

through the water and kissed him, before a wave caught us both. We came up laughing again.

"Just make sure," he said, spitting out water, "next time you bring me along on purpose!"

"It's a promise," I called back as we were swept closer to shore.

A promise I knew I would keep.

Epilogue

A letter from Pandora

To Red at Red's Alchemy & Potions, Belville:

My main purpose in writing is to ask you for an introduction to Leo, of *Belville & Beyond.* Her mining series was a huge inspiration to me and I would be forever grateful if you could tell her to look out for a letter from me! I'm sure she gets too much mail to personally read it all.

But you might also like an update from Helenia. I've just finished interviewing Quinn Doyle—he was the one who told me you knew Leo. After you put in a good word for me with Officer Herakles—thank you for that—I've gotten first access to everyone involved, and my paper is running a special edition on the case. I'll send you a copy once it's printed.

My plan is to include a full-page spread on each victim along with the story of the case, the trial, and its aftermath. You'll be glad to hear that all six victims are doing well: Harley turned down the offer of her old job in the records department, and is planning to travel with her brother, Quinn, but everyone else is making an effort to resume their lives here in town. Pokey is back in charge of security, and wanted me to tell you that he was very impressed by what he heard of Officer Thorn. Winter has gone back to school with allowances for the time he missed, and my own friend, Tangerine, is adding Defense and Awareness classes to his fitness coaching business. Town hall unanimously agreed on support and therapy for each victim, in light of what happened and why. In a direct quote, Theseus called them all "modern heroes" for making stands against corruption.

Wharton is working on a memorial for Eurydice, with fellow former-victim Vesta and Ida's help. Edda remains in charge of the Botanical Garden. They got Pluto's help to return the maze to normal, and to officially seal off any remaining structures related to his time there. Rumors still abound, of course.

In what might be an ironic twist, Theseus has announced that he does plan to approve a proposal to appoint government advisor roles. However, he clearly stated that the roles will have term limits and no official powers: they're just meant to help inform decision-making on things like trade, security, and natural resources. Despite being a "newcomer" to the island, Ida is rumored to be the favorite for environmental advisor. Inside sources say her mother declined the role.

Meanwhile, Rhea's trial concluded yesterday. Raffael's trial was simple and quick, as he admitted guilt and chose to take an oath of service at one of Helenia's remote monasteries. Rhea, on the other hand, caused a big stir. In the end she was sentenced to serve her oath in exile—which was a big deal, since she had been a local hero. She's also been ordered to give up any profits from her business dealings during the past year, as well as renouncing her leadership in the businesses themselves. No one's sure yet who will be taking over those businesses; there's still a lot of paperwork to be done. However, investigators did compile a list of everyone at town hall who accepted money from her, and have used that to start corruption trials.

You mentioned that you and your friends often get pulled into cases like this. I can't imagine encountering such impactful and deep-rooted scandals everywhere you go! I'm sure it'd make a great story. If you want to give an interview, or maybe do some kind of collaboration with Leo too, keep me in mind.

That's it for now—

Tilia

AKA *Pandora*

P.S. When I interviewed Pluto, he didn't tell me very much aside from how you all (especially your friend Sakura? I didn't meet her, myself) would have solved it faster if it wasn't for him. He seemed kind of sad about it? It's probably a natural reaction for someone involved in a case like this, but I thought I might tell you, in case you wanted to check on him. It doesn't seem like he gets out much.

Recipes

The recipes included here have been submitted by the residents of Belville (and friends), collected (and at times translated) by the author. Mistakes might have been made at any part of the process, but with any luck, these will bring a bit of fun and inspiration to you, our readers! Always feel free to experiment with the recipes included. And if you do, reach out to info@ellehartford.com to let us know how it went!

That said, without further ado . . .

Red's Favorite Salad

Best prepared while not *trying to interview a witness or discuss a criminal enterprise.*

Makes 4-6 servings

Ingredients:
 1 medium red onion, thinly sliced
 4 medium tomatoes, sliced into wedges
 1 cucumber, sliced
 1 handful pitted olives
 1 1/2 tsp oregano (dried)
 Salt, to taste

1/4 C extra virgin olive oil

1 Tbsp red wine vinegar

7 ounces feta cheese, cut or crumbled into bite-size chunks

Instructions:

1. If you'd like to mellow the onion's taste, fill a small bowl with ice water. Add 1 tsp of red wine vinegar to the water, then add the sliced onion. Set aside to soak for 10 minutes or so.
2. Place the tomato, cucumber, bell pepper, and olives in a large serving dish. Remove the onions from the water and add to the dish as well.
3. Sprinkle the vegetables with 3/4 teaspoon of oregano and a pinch of kosher salt. Add the oil and vinegar, then mix gently.
4. Top the salad with the feta and remaining oregano. Enjoy!

* * *

Sakura's Salted Caramel Pancakes

Perfect for sharing with friends . . . or eating all by yourself! Making your own caramel sauce requires a little bit of multitasking, but if you prefer to take your mornings slowly, consider preparing the sauce ahead of time and heating it up on the stove while the pancakes cook.

Makes 4 servings (or fewer)

Ingredients:

Salted Caramel Sauce:
  1 C sugar
  1/2 C water
  1/4 C butter (unsalted)
  1/2 C heavy whipping cream
  1/2 Tbsp vanilla
  1/2 tsp salt, or more to taste

Pancakes:
  1 1/2 C flour
  2 tsp baking powder
  1/2 tsp salt
  2 Tbsp sugar
  1 C milk
  1 egg
  3 Tbsp melted butter (unsalted)
  1 tsp vanilla
  Sea salt flakes to garnish

Instructions:

1. Beginning with the caramel sauce: In a medium sauce pan, combine the sugar and water. Cook over medium-low heat until the sugar is completely dissolved, about 3 to 5 minutes. Add the butter and let it melt.

2. Over medium heat, bring the mixture to a boil. Allow to boil until the mixture turns a deep gold, about 10-15

minutes. Keep an eye on it, but do not stir. If needed, simply tip the pan from side to side to help the sauce cook evenly.

3. Meanwhile, in a large mixing bowl, whisk together the all-purpose flour, baking powder, salt, and sugar for the pancakes.

4. In a separate bowl, whisk together the milk, egg, melted butter, and vanilla until smooth.

5. Pour the wet ingredients into the dry ingredients and stir gently. A few lumps in the batter are perfectly fine.

6. Heat a non-stick skillet or griddle over medium heat. Lightly grease with a little butter to prevent sticking.

7. Pour 1/4 cup of batter onto the skillet for each pancake. Cook until bubbles form on the surface, about 2-3 minutes.

8. Carefully flip the pancake and cook for an additional 1-2 minutes, or until golden brown.

9. Returning to the sauce: when you notice it is a nice deep gold color, remove the pan from the heat and add in the heavy whipping cream in a slow, steady stream, whisking as you do so. The caramel will bubble up, so be careful! Whisk until well combined.

10. To finish off the sauce, add the vanilla extract and half a teaspoon of salt and whisk to combine. Add additional salt to your desired saltiness.

11. Serve the pancakes hot, generously drizzled with salted caramel sauce and sprinkled with sea salt flakes. Yum!

* * *

Pluto's Tips for Making Custom Drinks

We don't all have fancy glasses, magicked stirring sticks, or rare ingredients, but we can still delight our friends and charm investigators with these thoughtful tips.

1. Do your research. Check out specialty drinks at restaurants and/or read books on the subject to find inspiration for clever combinations, delivery, taste profiles, and more.

2. It's okay to start slowly. Don't feel like you need to jump in to creating a drink with half a dozen ingredients and sparkles—in fact, it's best to start out by tasting individual ingredients yourself, and adding them in simple combinations one or two at a time.

3. Begin with a base in mind. This could be a distilled spirit (if you and your fellow drinker are of age, of course!), or it could be sparkling water, black tea, lemonade, or whatever your mind can conjure.

4. Decide which flavor profile you want to build. Something herby or floral, for someone who likes to "taste the leaves" (like a certain alchemist, or possibly a certain author's husband)? Something dark and smoky for an enigmatic ally? Or something deliciously sweet for your new crush?

5. Think about balance. Even if you're going for a sweet drink, there *is* such a thing as "too sweet." Most drinks balance sweetness and acidity to some degree.

6. And think outside the box. For example, not everyone would think to put tarragon in a drink, but to the right recipient, it's amazing. Don't be afraid to experiment—

only with edible ingredients, of course, and don't forget to taste some of the concoction yourself before foisting it on someone else.

7. Presentation is important. To the best of your ability, match your drink creation to the glass you choose—and to all the accompaniments: ice cubes? *Shaped* ice cubes? A single huge "statement" ice cube? Flavored ice? Straw? Twirly straw? Spoon that says "I love you" on the side? You get the idea. Be creative! While also being mindful of the impression you want your drink to make.

8. When in doubt: simplicity is often best!

***

William's Recipe for Embracing the Heroic: Hercules

"Way back when," says everybody's favorite magical stargazing dog, "in *Cold As Snow*, we talked about the winter constellation Orion. But there's more than one ancient hero in the sky. Are you surprised? You shouldn't be.

"The actual constellation is a bit . . . boxy. Not unlike Helenia's current, *official* Herakles. If you're in the Northern Hemisphere, your best chance of finding it is on a clear night between March and September. Technically, your *very* best chance is midnight in June, when it will be directly overhead. Look for the lopsided box first—it'll be near the small but very bright Lyra, which we talked about in *A Thousand and One Alibis*. You *are* taking notes on all these, aren't you?"

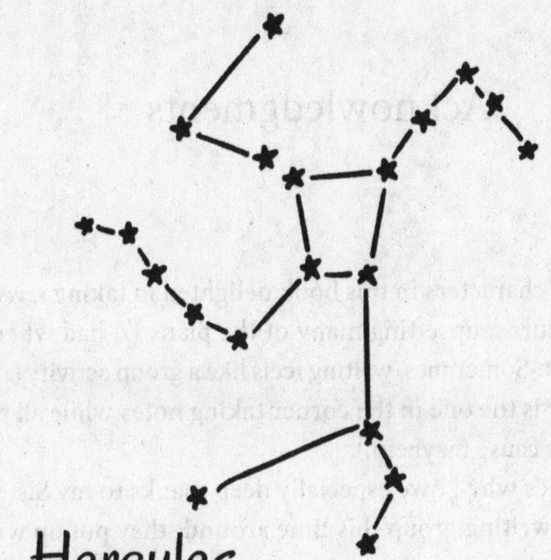

Hercules
the summer hero

Acknowledgments

Well! The characters in this book delighted in taking *several* hard left turns, upsetting many of the plans I'd had when I started out. Sometimes, writing feels like a group activity (and the writer is the one in the corner taking notes while all the characters cause mayhem!).

And that's why I owe especially deep thanks to my Sisters in Crime writing group this time around: they put up with a great deal of confusion on my part, and were unfailingly encouraging! As were many of my author friends and the folks in my newsletter community, who heard a great deal about this book-in-progress and responded with empathy and enthusiasm. Seriously, thank you!

Of course, as always, I am also eternally grateful to Sisters in Crime and Mystery Writers of America, to the welcoming cozy fantasy community, the wonderful book lovers on Instagram, and last but never, ever least, my excellent ARC readers!

On top of that, I'm thankful to *you*, for coming along on this journey with me. If you've enjoyed the stories in these pages, I hope you'll take a moment to tell someone or write a review online!

About the Author

Elle adores cozy mysteries, fairy tales, and above all, learning new things. As a historian and educator, she believes in the value of stories as a mirror for complicated realities. She currently lives in New Jersey with a grumpy tortoise and a three-legged cat.

Find more stories of Red and her friends at **ellehart-ford.com**. And while you're there, sign up for Elle's newsletter to get bonus material, behind-the-scenes sneak peeks, and terrible jokes!

Also by Elle Hartford

The Alchemical Tales, a cozy mystery-meets-cozy fantasy series, includes:

Beauty and the Alchemist (book one)
Cold as Snow (book two)
Mermaid for Danger (book three)
Cry Big Bad Wolf (book four)
Cinders to Dust (book five)
Death Pulls the Strings (book six)
A Thousand and One Alibis (book seven)
Tangled Up in Murder (book eight)

A spin-off series of cozy fantasy romance, Pomegranate Cafe Romance, includes:

Worthy in Love (book one)
A Tale of Rowan and Daisy (extra novella)
Strong in Love (book two)
Steady in Love (book three)
Sweet in Love (book four)

A cozy fantasy spin-off series, Marine Magic, includes:
How to Care for Cursed Fish (book one)
How to Treat Talking Beasts (book two)

And a noir-meets-cozy spin-off series with reporter Leo begins:
The Silver Deck (book one)